Tenzin Dickie is a writer and literary translator in New York City. Her writings and translations have appeared in *Tibetan Review*, *Indian Literature*, *Cultural Anthropology*, *The Washington Post* online, *Himal SouthAsian*, *Words Without Borders, and Modern Poetry in Translation*. She is editor of *The Treasury of Lives*, a biographical encyclopedia of Tibet, Inner Asia and the Himalayan Region. A 2014–15 fellow of the American Literary Translators' Association, she holds an MFA from Columbia and a BA in English literature from Harvard.

OLD DEMONS NEW DEITIES

CONTEMPORARY STORIES FROM TIBET

edited by
TENZIN DICKIE

navayana

Old Demons New Deities: Contemporary Stories from Tibet
Edited by Tenzin Dickie

First published in 2017. Reprinted 2020
Navayana Publishing Pvt Ltd
155, 2nd Floor, Shahpur Jat, New Delhi 110049
with permission from OR Books, New York
navayana.org

ISBN 9788189059828

"Wink" by Pema Bhum first appeared in *Words Without Borders*, reprinted by permission of the publisher. "The Silence" by Jamyang Norbu first appeared in *The Tibet Journal*, reprinted by permission of the author. "The Agate and the Singer" by Kyabchen Dedrol first appeared in *Words Without Borders*, reprinted by permission of the publisher. "Nyima Tsering's Tears" by Woeser first appeared in *Manoa Journal*, reprinted by permission of the author. "Hunter's Moon" by Jamyang Norbu first appeared in *The Hindustan Times Weekly*, reprinted by permission of the author. "Letter for Love" by Tsering Wangmo Dhompa first appeared in *Caravan Magazine*, reprinted by permission of the author. "Light" by Tsering Lama first appeared in *Lalit Magazine*, reprinted by permission of the author. "The Dream of a Wandering Minstrel" by Pema Tseden first appeared in *Words Without Borders*, reprinted by permission of the publisher. "Winter in Patlikuhl" by Tenzin Dickie first appeared in *Himal SouthAsian*, reprinted by permission of the author.

Printed by Sanjiv Palliwal in New Delhi

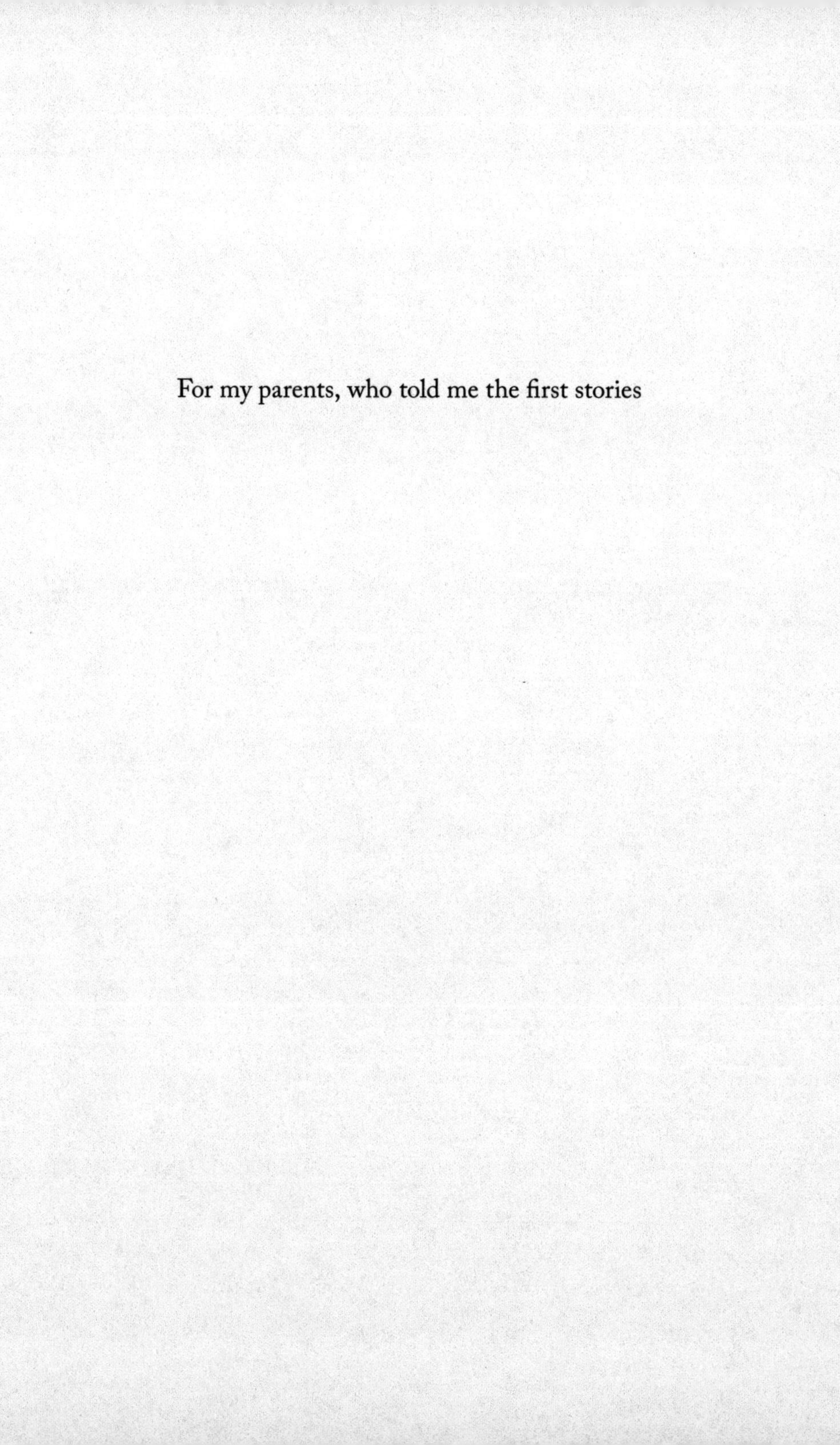

For my parents, who told me the first stories

CONTENTS

INTRODUCTION
TENZIN DICKIE

In October 2014, I wrote to a small group of Tibetan writers I knew and admired. I told them that I was hoping to put together a collection of modern Tibetan short stories and asked if they would contribute to it. The book would be in English but the writers would be from all over, from both Tibet and exile, writing originally in English, Tibetan and Chinese. I hoped, I wrote, that the anthology would be a contribution to contemporary Tibetan literature. Every single writer I asked said yes. I planned to finish the book in a year, which was evidently too optimistic. Collecting the stories alone took me a year, and the translating and editing took another. The business of living also takes its time. In the meantime, I kept adding stories and authors to the collection. In the event, it would be three years before the book was finished. But it is the collection I had wished for, with writers from Tibet, China, India, Nepal, Canada and the US, including the best Tibetan writers at work today.

I had read any number of mainstream Penguin and Norton anthologies of literature from elsewhere, but there was no such anthology of Tibetan literature. There were academic books. The journal *Mānoa* from the University of Hawaii had done an issue of Tibetan literature with poetry, stories and essays. The Library of Tibetan Works and Archives in India had published a booklet of four stories translated by Riika Virtanen. Duke University Press had published Lauran Hartley and Patricia Schiaffini-Vedani's *Modern Tibetan Studies* and *Social Change*, scholarly writings on modern Tibetan literature. And Lexington Books had recently come out with Lama Jabb's examination of *Tibetan literature titled Oral and Literary Continuities in Modern Tibetan Literature*. But there was no anthology of modern Tibetan fiction for the reading public, no curated or comprehensive collection of modern Tibetan fiction, the kind that I would have loved to read when I was growing up, the kind of book that might have made me want to become a writer sooner. But then, I grew up in a very particular space, in an artistic vacuum.

I was around twelve when I saw my first Tibetan film. I had no idea what I was seeing.

This was at my Tibetan boarding school in Dharamsala, the capital of exile Tibet. One night our usual evening study session was canceled. Instead, the school monitors herded us into the main hall. A white sheet hung as a screen onstage and we watched the images projected onto it. A Tibetan man wearing army fatigues gets off a bus. With his crew cut and military physique, he is clearly a soldier in the Tibetan unit of the Indian army, a soldier retired and returning home to his Tibetan settlement in the Indian South.

Carrying an oversized duffel bag and with a stereo loudly blaring Bollywood music on his shoulder, he saunters into the alleys of the settlement as kids watch him admiringly. He learns English from a Tibetan woman in a scene that causes the hall to ring with delighted laughter, as my classmates and I see mirrored on the screen our own struggles with foreign languages, Hindi and English. She tells him he's an idiot and he annoys her by saying things like, "If P-U-T is 'poot', then why isn't C-U-T 'coot'?" At the end of half an hour, the man and the woman run into the fields and chase each other around a tree in the leitmotif of all Hindi filmy prem kahaniya.

I watched the whole thing, entranced and bewildered. It was only at the very end of the half hour, when the couple circled the tree in the recurring Indian cinematic trope of romantic love, that I finally realized with a jolt what I was watching: this was a Tibetan film, a Tibetan romantic comedy. I had never seen a Tibetan film before. There were none. There were no Tibetan films, no Tibetan short stories, no Tibetan novels. Junot Diaz says, "You know how vampires have no reflections in the mirror? If you want to make a human being a monster, deny them, at the cultural level, any reflection of themselves." We grew up, those of us who grew up in exile but also those of us who grew up in Tibet, all of us, without reflections.

Why was that? Why did we grow up as, to use Edwidge Danticat's phrase, "literary orphans"?

Tibetan literature has a millennia-long storied history. The Tibetan writing system was developed in the seventh century by grammarian and savant Tonmi Sambhota, sent by his King Songtsen Gampo to study in India for expressly this purpose. Since then, the Tibetan literary canon has grown into one of the largest in the world. In fact the epic of King Gesar, a living epic that is still sung today by bards across the Tibetan plateau as it was a thousand years ago, is considered by scholars to be the longest literary work in the world.

However, the great oral epic of Gesar aside, the extreme majority of Tibet's literary canon contained Buddhist works, tracts on ethics, metaphysics, medicine, epistemology and the like. Beginning with the establishment of the first monastery of

Samye in the eighth century, the Tibetan centers of learning were all religious institutions. Tibet's great universities were monastic universities. Tibet's great figures were Buddhist masters. The Tibetan literary arts as such were only one sub-branch of knowledge taught in monastic institutions by monks to other monks.

And the Buddhist ideal had always been the elimination of desire. The ultimate Buddhist hero was the enlightened one, beyond desire. Desire, or attachment, was one of the three poisons that obscured the ultimate nature of reality. Fiction, of course, begins with desire. Fiction begins with a character wanting something. It is this desire that animates character, incites plot and seeks resolution. So did the Tibetan national fascination with Buddhism, and the attendant demonization of desire, delay the organic evolution of Tibetan fiction? After all, the great disenchantment with religion and the rise of secularism in the West correlates with the gradual rise of the novel.

But perhaps even more important than any potential philosophical or ideological constraints imposed by Buddhist culture on Tibetan literary arts was a very material one. Tibetan printing was done in the form of traditional woodblock printing, a very laborious and expensive process that needed the resources of a major monastery or estate. Each page of a manuscript had to be hand-carved on a piece of wood, which was not easily available in many parts of Tibet. Even Shol Parkhang, the Printing House of the Potala Palace, could not get enough wood at one point and needed it to be supplied from the Kingdom of Bhutan.

Professor Tsering Shakya, the premier historian of modern Tibet, notes that the Thirteenth Dalai Lama would certainly have known of the printing press from his travels in Russia and India in the early years of the twentieth century, so why didn't he adopt the innovation for Shol Printing House? Because of the strictures of received Buddhist prejudice from India. Metal-working was considered a contamination and metal-workers were pollutants. It was unthinkable that the *Kangyur* and *Tengyur*, the canonical collection of the Buddha's Teachings and the Commentaries, should be contaminated by metal type. So Tibetans held fast to woodblock printing and publishing remained a luxury, reserved only for the most meritorious of books—these were of course the ones that explored the path to nirvana, never the ones that searched for meaning in samsara—and only with the resources of a major monastery or the wealthiest landed estates.

In this historical context, it is not surprising that the evolution of modern Tibetan literature was rather uneven and delayed. Nor is it unexpected that the first Tibetan novel should come from Dokhar Tsering Wangyal, inheritor of one of Tibet's greatest estates and a minister of the cabinet, whose colleague facilitated the printing of at least one of his books from Shol Printing House at the foot of the Potala Palace. Polymath and politician, Dokhar was not just the first novelist—he also wrote the first political biography and the first secular autobiography. Finished in the 1720s, *Zhonnu Damed kyi Tamgyud* or *The Tale of the Incomparable Prince*, is based on the life of the Buddha, and draws from the usual corpus of Bodhisattva biographies, the Jataka Tales, and the *Ramayana* as well as the Gesar epic. A rather heroic pastiche, it's more properly called Tibet's first pre-modern novel.

The arrival of modern Tibetan literature as we know it would take another two hundred and fifty years and crystalize in the towering, tragic figure of Dhondup Gyal in the 1980s. But before Dhondup Gyal, there was Gendun Chopel, Tibet's first great modernist and early twentieth century poet, writer, artist and historian. A one-time monk scholar who left the monastery behind for a secular life, he traveled widely both on the Tibetan plateau and in the Indian subcontinent, and bridged the gaps between nineteenth and twentieth century Tibet, between Tibet and the outside world. His friend and contemporary was Babu Tharchin, a Christian of Tibetan descent from the Kinnaur region of northern India, and publisher of the first-ever Tibetan language newspaper, *The Mirror of the World*. Tharchin operated out of Kalimpong in India, the cosmopolitan hill station known as the Paris of the East and a hub for the international Tibetan elite of the time, and sent his newspapers into Tibet on yakback. Around this time, formal schools for lay students were established for the first time in Lhasa and elsewhere in Tibet. The stage was finally set for an organic evolution of Tibetan literary arts.

But it was not to be. Instead of continuity and evolution, there was rupture—first a backlash by the conservative and monastic elements of Tibetan society, leading to a closing of the modern schools, followed by foreign invasion. Mao sent his army into Tibet in 1949. By 1959, the brutal Chinese military takeover was complete and Tibetan society was upended. The young Dalai Lama escaped into exile in India, followed by tens of thousands of Tibetans.

From 1966 till 1976, the Chinese Cultural Revolution swept through Tibet. Monasteries were destroyed, books were burned and Tibetan identity suppressed. Except in pockets here and there, the teaching of Tibetan language stopped entirely. It was only with Mao's death and the end of the Cultural Revolution that Tibetan language was allowed to revive again by the Communist state. Dhondup Gyal, poet, writer and historian, was the great figure of this revival. As he began publishing in the late 1970s, his writings electrified the Tibetan world. In 1980 and 1981, the first Tibetan language literary journals, *Tibetan Art and Literature* and *Light Rain*, began publishing. In January 1981, Dhondup Gyal published *The Dawn of Clear and Simple Writing*, a selection of sixteen of his best poems, essays and short stories published over the previous years. Brilliant and troubled, Dhondup Gyal committed suicide three years later at the age of thirty-two. His legacy endured. Modern Tibetan literature had finally arrived.

My family on both sides left Tibet when the Chinese came and followed the Dalai Lama into exile. I was born and raised in one of the Tibetan refugee settlements of north India. As a function of growing up in Tibet-in-India, a young society, an exile community trying to re-root itself in foreign soil, we were cut off from our historical past, from our historical literature and culture. Of course, for Tibetans growing up on the other side of the mountains, this break from the past was imposed by the Chinese state. This separation from our literary past was compounded by the fact that modern Tibetan literature was still in its infancy. Thus on both sides of the Himalayas, we grew up orphaned from our literature. We were missing the point of departure, the runway from which to lift off.

For the young reader in me, this meant a peculiar kind of abandonment and isolation—the lack of one's reflection in the surfaces, and the depths, around oneself—an insular isolation that only makes itself known when something finally pierces it. For me, that moment was when I read Tenzin Tsundue's poem "When It Rains in Dharamsala". I read it, electrified, and began to write a poem. It was not just that I knew the rain in Dharamsala, it was that I knew Tsundue and he was like me. I had always been a reader, but that was the first time I thought maybe I could be a writer as well.

Pema Bhum, Woeser, Jamyang Norbu, Tsering Dondrup, Tsering Wangmo Dhompa, Pema Tseden, Kyabchen Dedrol, Takbum Gyal, Pema Tsewang Shastri, Tenzin Tsundue, Bhuchung D Sonam—these are our writers now. Their works fill our shelves and their words echo our lives. Every now and then, I can catch a glimpse of myself, or someone who looks very like me, in the looking glass. It's not a small thing that these writers—and filmmakers and artists and musicians—have given us. It's only when art gives us entry into the lives of people like ourselves, with our loves and losses, our joys and sorrows, our hope and our despair, that we can begin to make sense of our own lives—to understand, to cherish, and to glory in our own humanity—to find divinity in it.

These writers come from Tibet, China, India, Nepal, US and Canada, and they write in multiple languages. Pema Bhum, Tsering Dondrup, Pema Tsewang Shastri, Kyabchen Dedrol, Pema Tseden, Takbum Gyal and Dhondup Tashi Rekjong write in Tibetan. Jamyang Norbu, Tsering Wangmo Dhompa, Tenzin Tsundue, Bhuchung D Sonam, Tsering Lama, Tenzin Dorjee and Tsering Namgyal Khortsa write in English. Woeser writes in Chinese. They work in multiple genres. They write memoirs, novels, essays, poems but whatever else they do, they also write short stories. Short stories have become one of the primary modern Tibetan art forms.

But the non-Tibetan world is completely unaware that Tibetans even write short stories. So I like to think of this book as the coming-out of the Tibetan short story. And coming-outs are moments fraught with danger, power and possibility. Through these sometimes absurd, sometimes strange, and always moving stories, the writers give the English-reading audience a more authentic look at the lives of ordinary Tibetans navigating the space between tradition and modernity, occupation and exile, the national and the personal. For Tibetans, they do something a great deal more. They examine and explain our heartbreak—the heartbreak of our occupation, our exile, our diaspora—and in doing so, they give us comfort, clarity, and a measure of belonging.

Born and raised in the Kullu-Manali valley and Dharamsala, I am in some ways a Himachali, like a few of the other Tibetan writers in this book—namely Dhompa, Tsundue, Dorjee, Sonam. Tsundue's young parents and my grandparents, nearing retirement, worked on road building projects in Pandoh, Kullu, Manali; they helped to develop the Indian north. My parents were born in Tibet, schooled in India and made a life there, living and working in Tibetan refugee schools. Tibetans lived in settlements across India, clustering in Himachal Pradesh in the north and Karnataka in the south. These settlements were a parallel world, existing alongside the Indian world. This was Prime Minister Nehru's penance; his disastrous China policy had offered no help to the Tibetans as they were invaded but he now took personal responsibility for the fate of the Tibetans in exile. The responsibility for Tibetan refugee affairs was lodged with the Ministry of External Affairs, Nehru's own portfolio, rather than the Home Ministry. Nehru agreed with the young Dalai Lama that the Tibetan settlements should be intentionally enclosed settlements, self-sustaining communities that were meant not just to ensure the survival of the people but to secure the survival of their language, culture and institutions.

Therefore this measure of belonging that our writers give us is no mean measure. Occupation, exile and diaspora—as amorphous and overarching as these terms are, they define very specific and concrete conditions. For instance, I did not grow up in my family home, a large two storied house that my grandfather built in Kyirong the year before the Chinese came. For instance, the humble Tsuklakhang temple that I know in Dharamsala, where I go for prayer and solace, where I have prayed any number of times to do well in any number of exams, is not the original Tsuklakhang in Lhasa but its shadow institution. The original

Tsuklakhang, the Jokhang, housing Tibet's holiest image of the Buddha, the Jowo Shakyamuni, comprises multiple chapels in its wings and exhibits a historic slab of stone which, it is said, if you listen to very carefully, still sounds the waves of that ancient sea from which rose the city of Lhasa. (When I finally made it back to Tibet in 2006, I pressed my ear against the rock and listened very hard for the sound of the sea but my senses were not keen enough.)

Tsuklakhang, Norbulingka, Mentseekhang, Namgyal Monastery, Gyuto Monastery etc—their originals stand in Tibet. Our institutions are shadow institutions, founded this side of 1959, by refugee Tibetans who sought to rebuild in India, in exile, their traditional institutions of ritual, scholasticism and yes, refuge. And what does that mean for us as a measure of loss, that all our institutions are shadow institutions, duplicates and derivatives lacking not just the majesty but the history of their originals? What does it mean that home always means elsewhere and not where we are? What does it mean that for us return is not an individual decision but a national project? What does it mean that we are not in control of our destiny?

These are questions that the writers tackle obliquely in this book, coming at these questions sideways, slantingly, heeding Emily Dickinson's invocation to, "Tell all the truth but tell it slant." Apart from two stories that seemingly take place out of time, Pema Tseden's story of the wandering minstrel in search of a dream and Jamyang Norbu's tale of a mute musician, the others all take place after Tibet was forcibly incorporated into the People's Republic of China and proffer deeply sympathetic portrayals of Tibetans' lives since 1959. Pema Bhum's "Wink" shows us the absurdism of life during the Cultural Revolution. Tenpa and Lhamo's escape from their hometown is a light hearted story that nevertheless underscores the brutality of the Cultural Revolution as experienced by scores of Tibetans. In "The Valley of the Black Foxes", Tsering Dondrup captures the fraught resettlement of a Tibetan family from their nomadic pasturelands into an artificial township. Their old way of life now lost to them, they struggle to adapt to the vicissitudes of life in town, which includes a good measure of bureaucratic indifference, incompetence and inhumanity, and find the game is rigged against them.

"The New Road Controversy" by Takbum Gyal tells of a Tibetan village in transition; a modern road is to be constructed and its people, who have no use for a road, are in revolt. The road is built nonetheless and now "the people of the village are elated with happiness." The last line, resonant with irony, completes the farce. Elsewhere, in Dhondup Tashi Rekjong's "Dolma", a young boy in Amdo in northeastern Tibet discovers first love; in Tsering Wangmo Dhompa's "Letter for Love", a middle-aged woman in Kathmandu comes to terms with the end of promise as her daughter begins to taste the beginning of it; in "The Connection" by Bhuchung D. Sonam, a young man comes face to face with the limits of his character and his circumstances; and in "Nyima Tsering's Tears" by Woeser, a monk and government official on tour duty in Norway faces the most significant moment of his life and decides he must return to Tibet. "If we all leave, to whom will Tibet be left?" he asks.

From the kora of the holy Mount Machen Pomra in Tibet to the seedy brothels of New York's Chinatown, from the seedy brothels of Tibetan trading towns to the Buddhist retreat centers of upstate New York, we see Tibetan men and women, young and old—loving, plotting, desiring, failing, enduring, and living, simply living. Breathing in and out, and claiming space, and a measure of your attention. These are our Tibetan lives now. This is how we live now.

WINK

PEMA BHUM TRANSLATED BY TENZIN DICKIE

1.

It seemed that even the birds nestling atop the rafters of Tenpa's house were tiring of the rain. They sat perched in a line along a wooden beam and watched the rain drizzling down. Cocking their heads this way and that, the birds crooned softly. A steady drip of water fell gently and steadily from the eaves of the house, and the sound carried throughout the courtyard.

Tenpa entered the gate carrying Darmar in the folds of his *chupa*. The birds resting atop the gate fled into the courtyard, flapping their wings. Tenpa was wearing trousers that he had folded up to his knees. He was barefoot. Raising first one leg and then the other, he washed the mud off his feet under the water dropping from his roof.

"Did the doctor look at the child?" said Lhamo, who was picking out stones from a spill of grains on the balcony.

"Oh, oh. Darmar is throwing up." Without answering Lhamo's question, Tenpa hurried out into the courtyard as fast as he could. He had a limp.

Lhamo understood that Tenpa had no good answer. She picked up Darmar from out of Tenpa's robes, cleaned up the bits of vomit from Darmar's mouth and chin with the end of her *kera*, and then propped him up on the floor among the folds of some sheepskin *chupas*. Lhamo gave Darmar a kiss on the blue veins of his forehead and said, "Poor darling, Aba and Ama will take you to see the doctor very soon. And the doctor will give you a sweet candy pill."

Tenpa took out a needle from his right collar and, using it to pull out a thorn embedded in the heel of his right foot, said, "When I said Darmar's name, the doctor almost took a look at him but when he heard my name he withdrew his hands."

When Darmar gave a small cry, Lhamo placed in front of him *Quotations of Chairman Mao Tse-tung* and a button with Chairman Mao's face on it, both of which he had been playing with earlier. But Darmar continued to cry and raise his hands to her, so Lhamo opened the book and showed him the picture of Chairman Mao, whereupon Darmar instantly stopped crying. Darmar grabbed the book with his hand and brought it to his drooling mouth.

Lhamo said, "If we sell these goatskins, it might be enough to buy his medicine. That old cleft-lipped Chinese buyer doesn't come here anymore. Can't we take them somewhere else to sell them?"

Heeding the proverb that a chewed up thorn will not prick one again, Tenpa chewed at the thorn he had pulled out of his foot as he said, "Who knows where in China they sell these goatskins? And here I am, from one of the four bad elements, without the freedom to even go to the lower valley—" He broke off as someone opened their door. It was Gonpo, the leader of the work brigade.

"Today he has an important message to relay," Tenpa thought to himself. During holidays and special occasions, as well as on days when work had to be halted because of rain or snow, it was the duty of the people that belonged to the four bad elements to relay messages between the production team and the people. But this was the first time that the leader of the work brigade himself had come to Tenpa's house.

Leader Gonpo was wearing a greenish raincoat and a pair of shining black rain boots. He entered the balcony and unbuttoned his raincoat as he said, "Looks like the skies have been torn apart. If we get two more days of rain like this, there is danger of the harvest going to rot. The sheaves of grain are already starting to heat up." He took off his raincoat and put it on the balcony wall.

It seemed impossible that the leader of the work brigade should be at the home of a bad element like Tenpa, but Gonpo was not only in their home, he was speaking so kindly to Tenpa and Lhamo that they couldn't believe it was happening. They just looked at each other, without the faintest idea of how to respond to him. In fact, it didn't even occur to them to offer him their welcome and greetings.

"Are your walls alright? Because of the rain, Aku Namgyal's back wall has collapsed in one corner," Leader Gonpo of the work brigade said, trying once again to strike up a conversation.

Aku Namgyal was Lhamo's father. To ensure that Tenpa's own status of being a bad element wouldn't harm Lhamo's family, Tenpa never visited Aku Namgyal's house. Tenpa stuttered, trying to reply, "Oh. Oh. That's . . . that's fine then."

Then he said to his wife, "Won't you offer even a cup of tea to Leader Gonpo?" He pulled out a rug and insisted that Leader Gonpo sit on the rug.

"The weather may be very bad but I have some very good news to give you," said Leader Gonpo as he lit up a cigarette. "From today onward, you are a comrade of our revolutionary ranks. We have decided to take off your black hat of the four bad elements." He patted the floor next to him in a signal for Tenpa to sit down.

Tenpa had never even imagined that the taint of his crime—using torn pages from *Quotations from Chairman Mao Tse-tung* as kindling for fire—might dissolve like this within a few short years. Uneasy as he sat down, now shoulder to shoulder with Leader Gonpo, he kept only half his butt on the rug. There was a pause but he could not even think of what to say in order to thank Leader Gonpo.

Leader Gonpo did not wait for Tenpa's response. He continued, "The political re-education work team came here and for six months we examined your behavior and your thoughts."

Leader Gonpo coughed up a piece of phlegm, which he spat out into the courtyard before continuing. "When we first heard that your son's name was Darmar, Red Flag, we felt that you were atoning for your crime—"

Tenpa felt that now was a chance to ask for some medicine for Darmar. "My son has been sick for some days now." He didn't even realize that he had interrupted Leader Gonpo as he said in a trembling voice, "We couldn't take him to the doctor because we don't have the money. But maybe now I can request some medicine for my son?"

But Leader Gonpo, it seemed, just wanted to finish what he had to say. Without answering Tenpa's question, he said, "But just your son's name alone wasn't enough to take off this black hat of yours, that I don't even have to tell you. As you well know, your ancestors' crime of exploiting the poor masses was no small crime. We struggled with you and re-educated you, as you will remember well." He fixed his gaze on a scar on the right side of Tenpa's head. This was a scar from when he was wounded during a struggle session.

Tenpa felt his scar beginning to itch. He found nothing to say in response to Leader Gonpo. The rain still fell steadily in the courtyard and rainwater drained continually from the roof.

"Comrade Tenpa," thus Leader Gonpo addressed Tenpa. "Don't sit there with that long face. Tomorrow we'll announce the good news at the village assembly."

Tenpa thought again about his son needing a doctor and said, "Mr. Leader . . . uh . . . uh . . . My son has been sick for three days . . ."

"I see, I see. Your son needs medicine . . ." Leader Gonpo started to say. But then another thought struck him. "Oh, no, when we take off your bad hat of the four black elements, then you will be just like anyone else. You won't need to pay for medicine when you go to the hospital, will you?" he said, looking at the sky. The rain had stopped and the sky was just clearing.

Lhamo came out of the kitchen to pour some tea for Leader Gonpo and her husband. She had Darmar strapped on her back and she carried a thermos in her right hand and two cups in her left. From the kitchen, she must have heard what Leader Gonpo said. Her eyes were red at the edges. Darmar held a wet piece of paper in his hand, which he put into his mouth. He gurgled.

Lhamo bent down to pour some black tea for the leader of the work brigade. In a low voice, she said, "We don't have any cows or *dris*," apologizing for the lack of butter for the tea, but Leader Gonpo interrupted her before she had finished. "Not at all, not at all. The black tea is a good match for this black weather," he said.

As Lhamo was pouring tea into Tenpa's cup, the wet piece of paper in Darmar's hand dropped in front of Leader Gonpo and Tenpa. It was the picture of Chairman Mao torn from the pages of *Quotations from Chairman Mao Tse-tung*. The picture was not only sodden with Darmar's drool but on the right side it was torn from the eye to the shoulder. The remaining part of the eye stared out at Leader Gonpo and Tenpa.

From his perch behind Lhamo's back, Darmar waved two small hands at Leader Gonpo and Tenpa and gurgled at them. He didn't look sick now at all. Leader Gonpo started to smile but then suddenly his smile vanished. He stubbed out his cigarette, paused for an instant, then stood up and left. When he reached the courtyard he came back to the balcony, grabbed his raincoat, and without saying a word or looking at them once, he slammed the main door behind him and left. A thin blue smoke rose from the cigarette stub that he put out on the ground. "I took *Quotations of Chairman Mao Tse-tung* away from the child. It never even occurred to me that Darmar might have torn Mao's picture out and still had it in his hands," said Lhamo with tears in her eyes as she threw out the leftover tea from Leader Gonpo's teacup in the courtyard. Tenpa didn't say anything. He just stared into the courtyard. The drip of water draining from the roof had stopped and it was silent now. Here and there a bubble burst in the puddles collecting on the ground.

2.

Tenpa was awake but remained in bed. He lit his pipe, inhaled and asked, "What time is it?" The dim lamp hanging from the pillar by the hearth flickered. Beneath the lamplight, Lhamo was wrapping three porcelain bowls in a dishrag.

"It's hard to say," she said. "I can't see the stars because of the clouds. But the cocks have yet to crow."

Putting the bowls in a shoulder bag, she said, "Do we really have to leave in this way? There are so many copies now of *Quotations from Chairman Mao Tse-tung* that lots of families don't know what to do with them. They throw them in the trash."

"Do you think it is okay for people to do the same things now with *Quotations from Chairman Mao Tse-tung* that they did before the Line Education Movement?" Tenpa asked, but then answered the question himself in a loud voice, "No, it's not okay!" He woke Darmar who was sleeping next to him. The child gave a low cry and Tenpa stopped talking and put his hand on Darmar. Moving his lips a little, Darmar fell back asleep.

Tenpa continued speaking, but in a very low voice: "That's why that shit Leader Gonpo left so suddenly yesterday, because it's not okay. Didn't you see yesterday how furious he was when he left? Didn't you hear how furious he was when he slammed our door?" Tenpa's voice rose again as he was speaking.

Lhamo knew that when Tenpa felt as if she was challenging him, his words not only became harsher but he could even raise a hand to her. Usually when Tenpa became very angry, Lhamo kept quiet, but this time she could see that the end result of their leaving might well be that they'd have nowhere to go and no home to which they could return. Instead of backing down as Tenpa got angrier, Lhamo tried to put off their escape.

"Of course I would go if I can get to Ogya County and get that Chinese doctor to look at the child, but who knows if we can get him to her? Who knows if she's even there," said Lhamo as she pinned the Chairman Mao button on her undershirt in the hope that it might help to keep Darmar quiet on the way.

"The child! After I have been arrested, will you still stand there asking when can we get the child to a doctor?" he said and sucked at his pipe.

Lhamo began to cry. Darmar woke up and began to cry as well. As they both cried, Tenpa found it difficult to stay angry. He gave a small cough and said, "Before they catch me, I must try and get Darmar to a doctor or . . ." He choked up and could not finish his sentence. Just then, from a distance, came the faint crowing of a cock: "Cock-a-doodle-doo!" Then, from another direction, came a clearer and stronger crowing. Then their next-door-neighbor's cock also began to crow.

Tenpa put his pipe away in his tobacco pouch. He put on the fur-lined coat he was wearing as a blanket. As he got up from bed, he said to himself, "May the lamas save us and keep us from meeting anyone on our way!"

"May the lamas save us, may the lamas save us! In the last few days, that's all you have been saying, 'May the lamas save us!'" said Lhamo as she unhooked the lamp from the pillar and brought it near Tenpa. She held the lamp aloft and they both looked at Darmar's face for a moment. She continued, "Didn't you use to say that Ogya County is so advanced and that in Ogya County no one says 'May the lamas save us'? They only say, 'May Chairman Mao save us!'"

Darmar's eyelids fluttered and then closed in sleep again. A soft snore came from him. His lips were dry and a little cracked and a couple of thin blue veins stood out on his forehead just below a tuft of hair. A small wooden parrot with a broken beak lay to the right of his pillow. This parrot was Darmar's only toy, one that Tenpa had carved by hand from a piece of wood. Although Darmar used to play with this toy constantly, ever since he had become sick, he only cried whenever he saw the toy.

"His fever hasn't gone up but I wonder, what if it rises at night?" said Tenpa as he briefly touched Darmar's forehead with the back of his hand. He roused Darmar from his sleep and bundled him into the front fold of Lhamo's *chupa* where her dress made a deep pocket at the waist. He took the lamp from her hand. Darmar began to cry again but Lhamo, rocking and shushing him with her body, put a breast in his mouth and he quieted down.

By the time Tenpa dipped his fingers two or three times into the *tsampa* bowl and finished the breakfast that Lhamo had prepared for him, the cocks had crowed again. "Let's go, let's go. The cocks have crowed a second time," said Tenpa. He slung the bag on his shoulder and went to the door.

But Lhamo, instead of going for the door, made her way toward the shelves on the wall. She picked up two porcelain bowls and a wooden one and placed them on the hearth. Coming toward Tenpa, she took out the bundle of butter from his bag and put a dollop into each bowl. Then she poured tea that was still hot from a kettle into the bowls, one by one.

"Come now," Tenpa said. He stood in the doorway waiting for her. Lhamo watched the butter melt slowly in the bowls. Lhamo wanted to say something but she didn't know what. She felt her throat close as she teared up. She picked up some soot from the chimney with her fingertip and marked Darmar between the eyes with this soot to protect him from harm and evil spirits. Then she blew out the lamp and followed Tenpa out the door.

They walked out their main gate. They heard a dog bark in the village and then a dog appeared suddenly in front of them. Inside Lhamo's robes, Darmar started to cry but stopped right away as Lhamo suckled him. The stray dog approached them. As it neared them it stopped barking and whined instead, rubbing against Tenpa and then against Lhamo with its head. It licked them. Then other stray dogs appeared and did the same, rubbing against them with their heads and licking them. Lhamo said to herself, "Poor dogs. They must know that we are going far, far away."

3.

"Oh, we are here," yelled Tenpa as he realized that the crowd of houses clustering in the center of the green plain that stretched out in front of them was the seat of Ogya County. Perhaps Lhamo didn't hear her husband because she gave him no answer. At one end of the back of the tractor, Lhamo had covered Darmar's head with the end of her *kera* belt to keep the dust out of his face and she held Darmar tightly against her body so that he wouldn't be jarred too much by the tractor's rattling. It wasn't necessary to answer him anyway. In a moment, the tractor that was carrying them came to a stop and then went quiet. When Tenpa got up to check, they had arrived at the town. He saw two soldiers from the People's Army with rifles in front of the tractor but then a storm of dust rose and obscured everything around them. When the dust settled, he saw that the soldiers were speaking to their driver.

"But how did they know that we were in this tractor?" said Tenpa to himself, assuming that the soldiers knew they had run away and were there to seize them. Lhamo, in answer, held Darmar to her mouth. In her arms, Darmar's eyes were wide open as he stared up at the sky. The soot that Lhamo had pressed between his eyes that morning was no longer a line between his eyebrows and was now smeared all over his forehead and his eyebrows. Lhamo put some spit on Darmar's forehead and tried to wipe the soot off with the end of her *kera*.

One of the armed soldiers came to the rear of the tractor and said to Tenpa and Lhamo, "Get off. Get off. Go that way," he said, pointing. Tenpa began walking in the direction the soldier pointed, with Lhamo following him. The soldier walked behind Lhamo, still carrying his rifle across his shoulder. They had no idea where the soldier was taking them.

Tenpa looked back. The tractor still idled by the side of the road. The driver and the other soldier still stood there by the car. Darmar was crying now in Lhamo's arms, giving out a low wail every now and then.

The street where they stood was the town's only street. The street ran very wide and very straight. All the administrative buildings of the town were built on either side of this street. From the loudspeakers mounted on electric poles along the sidewalks came music that neither Tenpa nor Lhamo had ever heard before. The people who were on the road walked silently without speaking to each other. They all had black armbands tied around their upper arms and a white flower made of cloth pinned to their chests. Rows of armed soldiers were posted at intervals along the street.

The soldier led Tenpa and Lhamo, who were trying to make sense of all these things, into a yard. The yard was basically a grassy meadow with three houses in the center. Perhaps it was because the soldiers kept animals out of this meadow that the grass grew long and yellow compared to the other pastures. There were ten or so people loitering by the houses. They seemed to be strangers to each other. A man sat next to a grazing yak smoking his pipe. When Tenpa saw him, he felt the itch to smoke too and he touched his pipe.

"Wait here for a moment," said the soldier to Tenpa and Lhamo, leaving them at the door of the first house. The soldier was just about to knock on the door when the door opened. Out walked a man who seemed very drunk. He kept his eyes carefully on his feet and swayed as he walked. Another armed soldier took this man by the sleeve and led him toward the group of people on the right.

Inside the house, Tenpa and Lhamo could no longer hear the loud music of the street. But they could hear another sound now, the banging and hissing of a metal stove. Tenpa was reminded of the day many years ago when he came to town as a stable hand for some Chinese horse traders. After herding the horses that the Chinese traders had brought down from the mountains, they had gone into someone's house and Tenpa had heard the same banging and hissing of a metal stove.

Darmar began to fuss and cry into Lhamo's *chupa*. Lhamo tried to suckle him again to make him stop. Though Darmar suckled at the breast in his mouth, he still sobbed through his nose. He closed one hand on the button of Chairman Mao pinned to Lhamo's chest. When Lhamo tried to loosen Darmar's hand from the button, Darmar let the breast slip from his mouth and gave a loud wail.

A man sat at a table facing them and smoking. The soldier who brought them into the house went toward him. This other man, obviously an officer or a superior, had the same black armband and the white flower on his breast. A small handgun in a leather holster hung from a belt on the wall behind him. Below the handgun was a marble bust of Chairman Mao on a stack of four books, all collections of Chairman Mao's speeches and writings. The bust seemed to be looking down at the Chief's table. The soldier said something in a low voice to the officer. The officer looked at Lhamo. When he blinked, the muscle of his cheek twitched in a tic. Lhamo wondered if Tenpa was mad that she had pinned the Chairman Mao button on her chest and hid it from him. But Tenpa didn't seem mad at all. Still looking at Lhamo, the officer slowly got up from his chair. The muscle of his cheek twitched faster and more prominently. His cheek now twitched twice in one blink of his eye.

Tenpa was going to confess that it was he who had pinned the Mao button to Lhamo's undershirt in order to keep Darmar quiet. The words "It was me" were on the very tip of his tongue. Tenpa had expected to hear the officer rage and thunder at them, so when the officer said in a low and sad voice, "Our peerless and wonderful leader Chairman Mao has passed away today," he wasn't sure he had him heard correctly. "Can Chairman Mao actually die, after all, like other people?" he thought.

The officer gave each of them a black armband and a white flower made of cloth. "This is to symbolize our mourning for Chairman Mao's death. If you are seen out on the street without wearing these, another soldier will bring you back here. If you come in here a second time, I can't allow you outside again. Then we'll put you with those other detainees that we are holding over there."

Tenpa let out a breath as he realized that their being brought to this house had nothing to do with their flight. He remembered the man next to the young yak who was smoking a pipe. Feeling the itch to smoke again, he raised his hands to touch the pipe in his *chupa*. Seeing the black armband and the white flower in his hands, he wondered, "But is a bad element allowed to mourn Chairman Mao's death?"

Just then Darmar gave a small cry. Tenpa, starting as if he had been woken from sleep, stared at Darmar. Darmar's eyes blinked open and closed. His lips also opened and closed. His lips were dry and Tenpa could see a little crack on his lips.

"Poor kid," the officer said. "See how his tiny hands grab at Mao's button. Even though he can't even speak yet, he knows in his heart that something terrible has happened." He patted Darmar on the head and said, "When did he begin doing this?"

The picture of Chairman Mao from yesterday, torn and soaked in Darmar's drool, flashed in front of Tenpa's eyes. He said, "Early this morning."

"See," said the officer. "Even though Chairman Mao passed away last night, the sad news was not circulated until this afternoon. It seems your son knew something had happened even before the announcement was made." His cheek twitched again.

Tenpa and Lhamo went outside the house. The loudspeakers were still broadcasting. But instead of the same loud music from before, now the speakers were loudly broadcasting something in Tibetan. "The Central Committee of the Communist Party of China, the Central Military Commission of the Communist Party of China, the State Council of the People's Republic of

China . . ." The names of the governmental bodies were being read out loud very slowly and clearly.

The soldier who brought them into the compound brought them back to the gate, pointed to the left side of the street, and said, "Look up there. Go and join those people up there." Tenpa knew that that was where the town hall was. He had been in that town all those years ago to herd horses for the Chinese traders. He had gone there often to watch movies. But he could not even begin to guess why they were supposed to go there now and why people were gathering there. However, he also knew that the county hospital was just beyond the town hall.

In fact, there was only a wall between them. Tenpa remembered the gray-haired Chinese doctor who only cared about people and not at all about their class status. Wearing her glasses on her nose, she had pressed the stethoscope to his chest and his back and listened carefully. This was all those years ago, during the time Tenpa worked for the Chinese horse traders, but he remembered it as if it had happened yesterday.

Tenpa had brought his family to Ogya County because of this hospital and this doctor. Now that they were here, why did they have to go inside the town hall? How long would it take inside? Was the gray-haired Chinese doctor still at this hospital? He wanted to ask the Chinese soldier but now he was nowhere to be seen. Instead, a horse carrying an antelope on its back trotted into his view. He could see a scattering of dried blood on the horse's shoulder. A soldier wearing two long rifles on his back led this horse. In front of them, but behind the horse, walked a strong-looking fellow in a new sheepskin *chupa* and a pair of black sunglasses. The man's hands were tied behind his back with a rope, the end of which the soldier held in his hands, leading both man and horse.

"How pathetic of Chairman Keldo," said one of two women

walking next to Tenpa and Lhamo. She looked around and then said to her friend, her voice dropping lower as she spoke, "He must have wanted some delicious antelope *momos* tonight. How could he have guessed, even in his wildest dreams, that Chairman Mao had passed away?" She looked again at the horse carrying the antelope. The other girl said, "Aku Tseten too, not knowing that Chairman Mao had kicked the bucket"—she immediately stuck her tongue out, looked around and continued—"not knowing that Chairman Mao had passed away, he was drinking up by the Sho river when they arrested him."

Tenpa remembered the drunken man that he and Lhamo saw earlier in the compound, the one who could only stare at his feet. Just then Lhamo gave a low cry and Tenpa turned around to look at her. She held Darmar closely to her breast, watching him as she walked. The veins in his forehead were bluer and his cheeks were redder than before. As Darmar blinked his eyes, weakly opening and closing his eyelids, Tenpa noticed that his eyes looked paler and whiter than before.

They heard a voice saying, "Step in, step in. Don't block the way." Tenpa assumed that they were now where the soldier had said they should go. Two lines of soldiers from the People's Army stood watch as two long lines of people weaved between them, one line going indoors and another coming outdoors. Tenpa and Lhamo were in the line going indoors. They found themselves pushed into the hall. As they entered, the loud music they had heard earlier from the loudspeakers filled their ears again. Then Tenpa saw the huge portrait of Chairman Mao hanging on one of the walls. It was a black and white portrait, not color, and it had a black border drawn all around it. Heaps of white cloth flowers were scattered in front of the portrait, making a round rosary as tall as a man. Two soldiers stood at attention, stiff and unmoving, on each side of the portrait, rifles on their shoulders and their eyes fixed in front of them.

The line moved, sweeping Tenpa and Lhamo toward the portrait of Chairman Mao. Even though the hall was huge, the music being blasted from the speakers was so loud that it almost felt as if the hall couldn't contain it. No one in line spoke or said anything, but the sounds of sniffles and sobbing came both from in front of them and from behind. At times, someone would wail in a loud voice. Tenpa felt a little uneasy that neither he nor Lhamo felt like crying.

He watched carefully to see what he should do when he got in front of Chairman Mao's portrait. The majority of the people stood there for a moment then bowed three times before leaving. A woman who looked Chinese bowed three times very quickly as soon as she came in front of the portrait, then pressed her hand to her mouth, probably to stop herself from crying, and left. An old woman, supported by a young man, cried out in a loud cry as she stood in front of Chairman Mao's portrait, "Oh, Red Sun!" She bowed in front of Chairman Mao's portrait and then instead of straightening like other people, she stayed there bowed at the waist. "Oh, this fate of ours," she said as she began to cry and wail. "Oh, Red Sun of our hearts, how could you go and leave us behind?" She gave a terrible scream. Just then Tenpa felt Lhamo tugging at his clothes. Darmar's mouth was open wider than before and his eyes looked even whiter and paler than before. When Tenpa held his ear to Darmar's nose, he heard a thin, wheezing breath. Tenpa pulled Lhamo out of the line. The old woman, now supported by two young men, was also pulled out of line and came near Tenpa and Lhamo. *"Kema! Kema kehu!"* she was shouting and her cries were even louder than before. "Oh Chairman Mao, you . . ." she could not get the words out.

"Mother, Mother," said one of the young men helping her

as they led her toward the gate. Tenpa and Lhamo followed them. Lhamo, holding Darmar closely to her breast, sobbed as she walked behind Tenpa. As they reached the exit, the lines moving in and out the door stalled as people made way for them to pass, staring at Tenpa and Lhamo as they let them through. When they made it outside of the hall, a man wearing a camera around his neck ran up to them and said, "The hospital is this way!" Then running in front of them, he began to take picture after picture.

When the doctor took Darmar from Lhamo's arms, Darmar's tiny right hand was still clasping the button of Chairman Mao at Lhamo's breast. They pulled his fingers open one by one to loosen the button. This time he didn't cry. The photographer wove in and out, moving this way and that way, taking endless pictures of them. The flash of photography lit up Lhamo's chest again and again. As soon as Darmar's mouth let go of Lhamo's breast, she unrolled her undershirt to cover herself.

4.

"*Ama, Ama!* Look at his face!" Lhamo gave a cry of wonder. Whenever Lhamo was happy, she easily cried out in wonderment over such small matters. It had been two days since Darmar began to eat *tsampa*. In those two days, Lhamo had given many cries of delight and wonder. Darmar now sat with a small porcelain bowl full of *tsampa* porridge in front of him, with *tsampa* smeared all over his hands and his mouth. It was this sight that caused Lhamo to burst out in delight.

"All right, this is it," said Tenpa, looking out the window.

"What is it?" asked Lhamo. She went to the window to look out, too.

Outside, the nurse who checked Darmar's temperature was

speaking with an official from the Public Security Bureau and also another man. She was pointing out their room, the sick room where Darmar was kept, to the men.

"They can go ahead and arrest me," said Tenpa, looking out the window. "The child's getting better now. But how will you two get back to our village?"

"How will we go back home without you?" Lhamo cried, interrupting him.

"Pa, pa, pa . . . da, da, da . . ." Darmar's babbling stopped Lhamo's tears. His face and his right hand were smeared with *tsampa* again. He continued making his nonsensical sounds.

A man entered their room, calling out "Comrade Tenpa" as he did so. It was the man Tenpa had seen from his window, the man with the Public Security Bureau official.

The PSB man entered the room after him. The official had a smile on his face but he stayed silent and didn't say anything.

The other man said, "I heard that your child had taken ill. But I wasn't able to come and visit before, because the last few days I have been so busy arranging the mourning ceremonies following the departure of the Red Sun."

The PSB official, noticing that Tenpa and Lhamo looked completely bewildered, explained, "This is Chairman Keldo of the Revolutionary Committee of Ogya County." He looked at Chairman Keldo and then said, "It was the chairman who ordered that your son should be looked after." He looked toward Chairman Keldo again.

"Yes," Chairman Keldo said, "when I heard that such a small child was so inconsolable at the death of Chairman Mao, I felt such concern and sorrow for him." He looked around at the hospital room and said, "How is the room? Is there anything that you are lacking?" Before Tenpa and Lhamo could answer, the PSB official said, "Oh yes, this is a special room that Chairman Keldo ordered for you. Otherwise that's where you would be staying right now." He pointed out the window at the hospital's yard.

The yard was full of cotton and felt tents. By the door of one tent, an old man picked lice from the sheepskin *chupa* spread out in front of him. Near him two naked children played.

Chairman Keldo sat down on Darmar's bed. He stretched out his hand to pat Darmar on the head but this frightened Darmar, who cried and held out his hands for Lhamo. As Lhamo prepared to pick him up, Chairman Keldo took out a plastic Chairman Mao button from his shirt pocket and showed it to Darmar. Darmar stopped crying as soon as he saw Chairman Mao's smiling face.

"I have pulled out the pin from the button," said Chairman Keldo, looking at the Mao button on Lhamo's chest and seeing Lhamo flex her hands. He looked at Darmar again and said, "When you grow up, I will buy you a Red Army uniform and a Red Army hat. Then, with a Chairman Mao button pinned to your lapel, you will look like a proper soldier indeed." Darmar looked back at Chairman Keldo and, raising the Mao badge in his hand, said, "Pa, pa, pa . . . da, da, da." It almost seemed as if he were saying something in response to Chairman Keldo.

"I read all the news. It is no ordinary thing when a child of such tender years is so grieved at the passing of Chairman Mao that he actually falls ill," Chairman Keldo said. He unfolded the newspaper tucked under his arm and showed it to Tenpa and Lhamo. Both Tenpa and Lhamo were astonished when they saw the photos in the newspaper. The first picture they saw was of the old woman in the hall. Her body was still bowed but she was lifting her face, her hair clumped together from her tears and her eyes closed. Her mouth was open, to mutter prayers, and they could see clearly where her teeth had fallen out. To the right of this photo was a photo of Darmar, with his mouth still fastened to Lhamo's breast, holding on tightly with one hand to the

Mao button on Lhamo's *chupa*. When Lhamo saw her breast in the picture, she couldn't help pulling up the collar of her *chupa*. There was a lot of writing beneath the two photographs. Tenpa slowly read the large caption: "A one-year-old . . . infant . . . to . . . a seventy-year-old . . . mourn . . ."

"It appears that on September 9, Darmar held on to Chairman Mao's button and began to cry for two whole days and nights, is that right?" Chairman Keldo asked them.

Lhamo, who had no idea how to answer this question, looked at Tenpa. Tenpa was also flustered. "Yes, yes. But he is now getting better. He even ate some *tsampa* porridge yesterday."

Although Tenpa's response didn't quite answer Chairman Keldo's question, he just said, "How would such a small child have so much devotion to Chairman Mao without the good influence of his parents? If our county had a family such as yours, the family would be the jewel of the county." Tenpa and Lhamo were completely astonished. Lhamo just looked at Tenpa. Tenpa wanted to say something in response but the words were stuck in his throat.

When Chairman Keldo saw how dumbfounded the couple was, he said, "We were hoping that we can get your family to stay in our county. We went ahead and assigned you to the production team here. From the Revolutionary Committee, we got a tent and some milking and pack animals for you." He looked at the PSB official.

The PSB official took out some documents from his shoulder bag and said to Tenpa, "Please stamp your fingerprint here." Tenpa, confused and bewildered, just stood there in shock.

Chairman Keldo said, "The production team isn't far from the center of town. A journalist will come to see you the day after tomorrow." He opened the hospital room door and left.

The PSB official took Tenpa's finger, pressed it into the

inkpad, then pressed it on the document and said, "Tomorrow evening I'll come to take you to the production team." He closed the door behind himself.

Tenpa was still in shock. The door opened again and the PSB official stuck his head inside the door and said to them, "There's no need to tell anyone that you are not a native of this village. No need to tell the journalist, either." And again he closed the door behind him.

The tip of Tenpa's finger, which had been dipped in the ink pad, felt cold. He looked at the red pad of his finger—underneath the red ink, to his great surprise, he could still see in his fingertip the image of a white conch that coiled to the right. At least once a day Tenpa looked at his fingertips when he was eating *tsampa* porridge. He wondered why he had never noticed this white conch on his fingertip before.

Just then, Tenpa caught a whiff of a distinctive odor. And he heard Lhamo utter another one of her joyful exclamations of wonder, "Look at this little demon child!" When Tenpa looked at Darmar, he saw that this time Lhamo's joyful exclamation celebrated no small thing. Darmar had produced a soft pile of stool on the bed as round as a coin. He drooled as he dragged the Chairman Mao button through this soft stool babbling the same nonsensical sounds, "Pa, pa, pa . . . da, da, da."

This was the first time in a great many days that Darmar had passed stool. At the sight of this, Tenpa felt a smile appear on his face, his first smile in a great many days. Then the smile disappeared swiftly. Tenpa quickly locked the door from the inside. Lhamo hurriedly took the button from Darmar's hands and, taking a large sip from the leftover tea in the teacup, spit the tea out all over the badge. Most of the tea missed the button. Where a drop of tea did fall on the badge, it cleared up one smiling eye of the Chairman. Now Chairman Mao appeared to have one eye open and one eye closed in a wink, and it seemed to Tenpa and Lhamo as if the Chairman were sharing with them a playful and secret sign.

THE SILENCE

JAMYANG NORBU

The last rays of the setting sun struck the massive sides of the snow-clad range and bounced off in sparkles of orange and crimson. The tallest of the peaks, rising high over the others like an upright flaming sword, stabbed the darkening sky—a last attempt to fight back the night. This towering peak, single and majestic, was known to the people of the surrounding country as the residence of the great spirit Tengri Lhachen: one of the oldest earth guardians of Tibet and the true son of the great Argali spirit Nyenchen Thangla, ruler of the Trans-Himalayan range.

On a low ridge, overlooking the peak, a flock of sheep grazed contentedly on the scanty tufts of grass that grew there. The shepherd, who had been sitting on a boulder and viewing the glowing peaks, got up and whistled for his dog. Feeling the first chill of the evening, he shivered and pulled up his sheepskin robe over his shoulders. The dog came bounding out of a patch of rocks. The man signaled to it with his stick, and the animal obeyed, running off to round up the scattered flock. The dog cleverly managed to get the sheep moving down a rough track—snapping and barking all the while at the more recalcitrant members of the flock. The shepherd picked up his rough goatskin bag that had contained his mid-day meal, now eaten, and slung it on his shoulder. With his stick in one hand and his *piwang*, his two-stringed fiddle, in his other hand, he followed his sheep down the track.

He was a young man around twenty-five and he was very handsome. His big eyes were dark and deep-set, giving him the appearance of constantly squinting under the shade of his heavy brow. His long hair hung in black untidy locks over his broad shoulders and his body, well-proportioned, was of an exceptional height. He looked rugged and hardy and his bronze weather-beaten face revealed a man who had not had an easy life.

After an hour, the track broadened into a dusty path and below him he could see the village, though it was rather indistinct in the fast receding light. A few dots of light showed up in the windows where butter-lamps were burning in the huts. He turned around and looked at the distant peaks which were now darkly outlined in the dim gray sky. He lowered his head and offered a silent prayer to the Guardian and, picking up a piece of flint, placed it on a nearby cairn as an offering.

The villagers were coming in from the fields with hoes and rakes over their shoulders. Some of them shouted greetings to the shepherd as he and his flock passed by. He raised his hand in return and smiled. It was dark when he passed the first houses of the village. His flock was held up by a train of donkeys carrying firewood. He paused to watch the patient beasts pass by, thc bells on their necks tinkling merrily amidst the bleating of the sheep and the babble of conversation of the men returning home. The donkeys plodded on; the shepherd's dog barked. The flock moved past. Through an open door he saw bright flames flickering in a hearth, lighting up the tired but contented face of a man resting with a bowl of hot tea raised to his parched lips. The shepherd hurried on.

He reached his home and after shutting his sheep securely in their pen he went into his dark room with his dog ambling behind him. Opening the door he went over to the low hearth on one side of the room. He bent over and blew on the few surviving embers until a little glow of fire sprang up. He fed the fire with a few dry twigs and soon the flames of a merry blaze flickered and jumped, casting strange sudden shadows on the walls. He poured himself a bowl of beer from an earthen jug. Sitting by the fire, he drank the brew slowly.

He had never known who his parents were. All he knew was that they were Drokpas, nomads of the Great Northern Plain and that they had been attacked by bandits while going on a pilgrimage. He had been a baby then and he was the only survivor. People from the village nearby had found him and looked after him. He had grown up into a strapping young lad who could easily outrun and outwrestle any boy in the village. They called him Nyima, since he had been found on a Sunday. He was liked by everyone, even the boys whom he constantly defeated in childish feats of strength, for the simple reason that he was such a jolly fellow, always smiling and ready to help anybody. When he was old enough he started to earn his living by looking after the flocks of the poorer villagers who could not, like the rich families, afford shepherds of their own.

While tending sheep he had learned to play the *piwang*, and in the course of time he had become an exceptionally good fiddler. He could play all the tunes of the district and had learned the airs of other counties and even a couple of the boisterous tunes played in the taverns of Lhasa from passing muleteers and traders. Marriage songs, love songs, harvest tunes, and the ancient riddle songs passed through the bow and the strings of his simple instrument with a sweetness and resonance that people in the village rarely heard. The village boasted of his prowess and declared to any traveler willing to listen that there never had been such a musician in all the land and that even the lords and ladies of Lhasa would be pleasantly surprised to hear the music of Nyima. They never referred to him as a shepherd, but always called him Nyima the Musician.

And yet there was another side of his life that was not as sweet and beautiful as his music. He lived his life in silence, because he could not speak. Some people might call him dumb. But there was nothing bestial about him: no grunts, whines, or croaks made with clumsy brutal effort. He was just silent. He could communicate well enough with his fellow men, using his eyes, a few economical gestures, a range of smiles and sometimes, but very rarely, a frown. A shepherd has not much need for the gift of speech. What use is the human voice when one has only sheep, flowers, the stars, and the mountains to speak to?

He finished his beer and put his empty bowl aside, feeding a few cakes of dry yak dung to the fire. There was a knock on the door and someone shouted from outside, "Nyima, let me in! It's me, Dorjee!"

He got up and opened the door for his friend, a lad of his own age. The boy came in and stamped his chilled feet on the floor.

"Come on, Nyima. Pick up that fiddle of yours and let's go."

Nyima gave him a questioning look.

"Oh! Didn't you know? There's going to be a banquet at grandfather Chodar's home tonight. His wife's got another baby. Buddha only knows how he ever manages it . . . at his age."

Nyima grinned with amusement.

"Come on, we must hurry. Pema is going to be there also and I guess she would be unhappy if you did not come."

Nyima's heart raced—she would be there. The fairest girl in the village. Nay, the fairest in the three worlds. She would be there, with her dark limpid eyes that talked to him as no one else's ever did; that told him, among other things, that he was a very special man—and that she was waiting for him.

They hurried into the night, through the narrow alleys, while the first snowflakes of the coming winter drifted silently over their heads. When they reached grandfather Chodar's house, the party had already commenced. As Nyima entered, the whole company shouted with pleasure and some younger folk rose from their seats and stamped their feet in their eagerness to dance.

"Ah! Now we shall have some music."

"Dance! Let us dance."

A more thoughtful soul said, "Let him have some beer before he plays."

Nyima smiled at them, but his eyes searched for her. She was there in the corner, beside old Mrs. Chodar. She looked at him and her eyes smiled. "I am glad you have come," they seemed to say.

Another girl came up to Nyima with a pot of beer. When he had drunk the three customary bowls, grandfather Chodar came over to him. Putting one hand on his shoulder, he raised his other hand to ask his guests for silence.

"Today is a very happy day," he began. "As I can now announce to you, my dear friends and neighbors, that even though I am an old man and unworthy of such a favor, I have yet been blessed with a son. And if I may proudly add, for the seventh time."

The guests laughed and shouted their congratulations.

The old man waited till they were silent again and continued, "Now I will ask my young friend, the best fiddler of our country and a gem among musicians, to play a special tune to honor my son. I have in my mind an old favorite, 'The Little Bird So Beautiful.'" Everyone shouted their approval. The old man raised his hands once again. "But no dancing now."

A few groans came from the younger lads but the old man ignored them.

"I do not like the stamping of feet as it disturbs the tune. But I will compromise. You may all sing and when the quicker half of the song is played, you may dance then. Now my young musician, play your fiddle so that the mellow notes may soothe my ancient ears."

Nyima pulled out his fiddle from the folds of his robe. He sat down and spent a minute or two tuning the instrument. And then he began to play. The guests sang softly to accompany the rich clear strains of the *piwang:*

The little bird so beautiful
The little bird so beautiful
Sings not everywhere
But when the gods and lamas
But when the gods and lamas
Come to the temple
Then he sings the sweetest.

The little bird so beautiful
The little bird so beautiful
Sings not everywhere
But when the son and father
But when the son and father
Go on a pilgrimage
Then he sings the sweetest.

Many songs were sung that night and feet tirelessly skipped and stamped out the many intricate steps. And Nyima danced too, relinquishing his instrument to another fiddler. He was a good dancer and the many bowls of beer he drank this night made him feel light and carefree. Before midnight he felt the need for some fresh air and he stepped out of the stuffy room into the small courtyard. The snow was by now falling thickly. He stretched out his hand from under the roof and caught a few flakes of the elusive white snow.

"Nyima?" A voice. Her voice.

He turned around and she came up to him and held his hands.

"It's cold."

He nodded and smiled at her.

"You played wonderfully this evening. You shouldn't stay in this village, Nyima. You should go to Lhasa and play for the lords and ladies. Your music is wasted here."

He shook his head in disagreement. Holding her hands tightly, he looked into her eyes.

"Me? Why think of me?" she said. "There are, I hear, much prettier girls in Lhasa. Anyhow . . ." she stopped.

Something in his mind flashed a warning. He looked into her eyes and searched for an answer. She turned her head away.

"Winter has come, Nyima, and . . . next spring . . . I am to be betrothed. My father has promised him."

His breath stopped and a coldness gripped his heart. A dull haze of confusion descended on him. Finally he looked at her.

"I can't help it, Nyima. I must . . . oh! I must obey my father."

She buried her head in his chest and wept. After a moment, he pulled her gently away and pointed his finger to the west, the direction of Lhasa. She shook her head.

"No, Nyima, I can't run away with you. My father's old and . . . I can't. I just can't. But I love you all the same, Nyima. I love you."

"Yes. You love me," he thought, "but how much? Your love is like a child's love for her puppy. I am a man and it's not enough."

"I am sorry, Nyima. My father likes you, honestly. It's only that . . . how can I marry a dumb man?"

The bluntness of her words struck him with agonizing clarity. He understood the finality of the moment. He turned away from her and, suddenly, ran out into the darkness.

He ran through the alleys to the main path of the village, his thick felt boots crunching the undisturbed drifts of snow. He ran like a man possessed, his mind a flaming darkness and his breath coming in hot painful gasps that metamorphized instantly into white transient puffs of vapor. He ran wildly and aimlessly, like a wounded animal, vainly trying to escape the cold grasp of a terrible sadness that stalked him—till at last through sheer exhaustion he stumbled and fell. Time passed. Eventually, he began to feel the cool caress of snow on his cheeks and he raised his head.

At that moment, the bright moon shone through a pocket in the clouds and Nyima found himself looking at the mountain. The peak glittered eerily in the cold unearthly light, reflected and magnified by the bright mirror of snow that covered the land.

"An omen," he thought. "A message from the Guardian." His fevered mind hammered out a chain of wild thoughts. "Yes. The Guardian. He has the power . . . He will heal my tongue . . . give me speech. And then she will be mine, only mine . . . .ah yes! The Guardian. To him I must go."

He scrambled to his feet and looked up at the mountain peak, but then the fickle clouds closed up again and the mountain vanished in the darkness. Nyima knew what he had to do. He walked forward in the night and something guided him as he marched on, as he slipped and stumbled in the snow. For many hours he plodded on, unheedful of his aching legs. Beads of sweat trickled down the ends of his coarse black hair and tumbled down his cheeks. His throat was almost closed with thirst, making every breath a struggle. And with each step his brains screamed out a single prayer. "Oh Great

Spirit, give me my voice . . . give me my voice . . . give me my voice!"

He crossed the ridge that divided the village from the range. He stumbled and fell many times as he descended. At last he stood at the base of the mountain, dead with exhaustion. Spasms of pain streaked through his tortured legs. He felt a dull numbness in his toes and he knew that they were finished with frostbite. Yet he did not pause to rest. He began to climb. He scrambled up, slipping and stumbling for a few hundred yards, then he felt a great weight on his body dragging him down. "Give me my voice . . . give me my voice . . . give me my voice." His knees buckled under him and he dropped heavily on the snow. His ravaged feet were dead . . . useless. He closed his mind to the pain and thought of her. "Pema, Pema." With his arms and his fingers painfully digging holds in the snow he dragged himself up a few more feet. Then his fingers froze into steely claws and his arms stiffened with the pain. He stopped. "Give me my voice." His mind raced on. He gritted his teeth with the pain and threw his head back—and again he saw the mountain.

Suddenly, an intense cold filled his heart and entered every corner of his body. A dull thundering sound filled his head. The mountain shone like polished jewels and flashes of color appeared before his blurred eyes. After a long, long time the cold reluctantly went away and the painful sounds diminished. He looked up again at the familiar darkness. Silence. Then he felt it—very slightly at first. Slowly it coursed up through the walls of his lungs and entered his windpipe, higher and higher. His throat swelled. And he knew! Up it went in his throat and remained, poised on the tip of his tongue. Then like a mighty cataract breaking over the rocks, his voice burst out, "Pema! Pema! Pema!" . . . and he was free.

Next spring, when the great snows had receded, they found his body. It had been buried under a great mass of snow. An avalanche—probably set off by some loud sound.

RALO

TSERING DONDRUP

TRANSLATED BY CHRISTOPHER PEACOCK

1.

I don't look forward to this blank page before me, where I must write down the story of Ralo. When I think of him, that thick yellow snot hanging from his nose starts to swing back and forth before my eyes.

His mother was the only family he'd ever known. When he learned how to talk, some cruel men from the village would have a laugh by asking him who his dad was. As far as Ralo was concerned, this was a question for his mother.

"Mom, who's my dad?"

"Don't ever mention that word again." His mother slapped him and then squeezed him tightly to her breast. Before long, however, a man began to appear at their house in the evenings. Later on, he started to visit during the day, too, and eventually he simply moved in with them. "Ralo, my darling, this is your dad," his mother lovingly informed him. But, unlike the other dads in the village, this man never gave his son a single sweet or a single kiss. On top of this, whenever Ralo came near him, he would recoil in disgust: "Hey! Look at that snot—get away from me." Ralo's snot was like running water: as soon as he wiped it away, it came flowing right back. "His brains are dripping out again," his mother always said.

Before Ralo knew it, he was fourteen years old, but the snot hanging from his nose was even thicker and longer than before.

By this time, all the other kids of his age could ride a horse and shoot a bow and arrow. He was the only one who still didn't dare to ride a tame horse on his own—he still had to ride in the saddle with his mother. "Ralo, you riding in your mom's lap again?" the others would tease him.

One morning the family was preparing to move to their winter camp. As Ralo clung to the guide rope of the yak that his stepfather was loading, the animal started bucking. "Hold on tight!" his stepfather said.

With a line of snot running from his nose into his mouth, Ralo grit his teeth, bit his lip, and clung on to the yak for dear life.

"It's always better to have a man than a dog," said his stepfather with satisfaction. "Hold on tight, hold—" but before he could finish, the yak reared again and Ralo was tossed to the ground face-first, losing his grip on the guide rope. The old yak bolted like a thing possessed, flinging its saddle down to its belly and scattering the family possessions, which were all trampled beyond salvation.

You're angry at the yak, but it's the horse that gets the whip, as the saying goes. The stepfather charged over in a fit of rage and screamed, "You useless snotty little goat! Can't even hold onto a yak properly!" With that he delivered two hard slaps to Ralo's face, causing the snot on the boy's chin to drip down to his chest. "Don't you dare hit my son!" called out his mother, running over to them. "If you lay a finger on my son again . . . you won't have a home here anymore!"

"Ha! The only reason I stayed here in the first place was because I felt sorry for the two of you. I'm leaving." And his stepfather did indeed set off on his way.

"Don't let dad leave . . ."

"Shut your dog mouth! What dad?" His mother slapped him and held him to her breast. Both mother and son burst into tears.

How many people there are in this world! But apart from his mother, Ralo did not have a single relative, just as his mother had no one apart from Ralo. And yet, the Lord of Death had not the slightest bit of compassion for the two of them. Like a wolf pouncing into a flock of sheep, he came to pluck Ralo's mother from the multitudes of the world and lead her into the next life. Though Ralo and his mother had no family but each other, when the villagers heard about his mother's death, there wasn't a single dry eye. No doubt, this was out of compassion for Ralo.

2.

In the summer of the year that Ralo's mother died, a few decent folks from the village got together and decided to send Ralo off to board at the district primary school. In reality, this was not so much in order for him to learn to read and write as it was to put a roof over his head.

As it happened, I started school that same year, so Ralo and I became classmates. But Ralo was five years older than me. In fact he was older than everyone else in the class.

At first, Ralo was a great student. He memorized the thirty letters of the alphabet before any of the other students in the class, causing the teacher to declare, "Everyone should learn from Ralo." However, a few days later when the teacher asked us to write each letter on the board, Ralo couldn't even write the first one, prompting the class to fall into hysterics. "No one should learn from Ralo," the teacher said.

"No one should learn from Ralo." This phrase spread throughout the school.

It turned out that we really shouldn't learn from Ralo. By the time we moved up to the next grade, Ralo still couldn't write the alphabet. He was terrible at his studies. His hygiene was terrible—snot constantly dripping from his nose—and he was always smoking. He was terrible at following the rules, too. So in the end, he was held back. But as far as Ralo was concerned, none of this was anything to be worried about because there was no one who would reproach him for it. The main things Ralo cared about were where he would stay for the summer holidays and how he was going to get cigarettes once all the teachers and students had gone home. He found a way: in the end, Ralo got all his cigarettes in exchange for cleaning the teachers' houses, washing clothes and getting food for the older students, and by subbing for his classmates when it was their turn to tidy up the classroom.

Students from nomad areas had a bad habit of not coming back for the start of term on time. At the end of the summer and winter holidays, there was often a delay of five or six days before classes could begin in earnest. Ralo, however, never once took leave to go back home, and moreover he always arrived at school before the new term even began. On this point, everyone really should have learned from Ralo.

A few fights are always going to break out in any school, and ours was no exception. Some of the troublemakers would deliberately shout "No one should learn from Ralo!" within his earshot. Ralo would chase them madly, but if one stopped to face him and looked like he was up for a fight, Ralo would say, "Teacher said I'm not allowed to fight," and like that his nerve would be gone. But as soon as the boy turned to leave, Ralo would pursue him once again demanding to know "Why shouldn't you learn from me?" and butting him with his shoulder. One day, a student seven years younger than Ralo shoved him to the ground and jumped on his back. "Look how fast my horse is!" the boy yelled, bouncing on Ralo and pretending to ride him. "Ah—Teacher . . ." cried Ralo, his flowing tears mixing with his snot, which in turn glued together with the dirt on his face. No matter how much he bucked, he couldn't shake the boy. From that point on, everyone knew that Ralo might be big physically but he didn't have an ounce of strength. And so the bullies multiplied.

When we moved up a grade for the second time, Ralo could just barely recognize the thirty letters of the alphabet but he still couldn't write any of them, so he was held back again. The third and fourth years were the same. But whenever the teachers needed a sheep slaughtered, Ralo was indispensable, so it seemed that there wasn't any harm in keeping him around.

At the end of the fifth year I finished primary school and moved to the County Nationalities' Middle School.

3.

One morning in the middle of winter, as a typical snowstorm of the northwest highlands was dancing in the sky, I was in my office stoking a fire in the stove.

Suddenly, a nomad charged in without even knocking. "Is this the People's Court?"

"Yes, can I help you with something?"

"Well, well! Aren't you Dondrup?"

"Yes, and you . . ."

"Don't act like you don't know me!" He dragged a stool over to the stove and sat himself down. "You become a cadre and you forget your old classmates, is that it?"

Wait, was this Ralo, my classmate from ten years ago? *Ah tsi,* he really had aged. His forehead was lined with wrinkles and a cluster of uneven whiskers sprouted around his mouth. What hadn't changed was the thick yellow snot coming from his nose.

"Ah, well of course I know you. Is something the matter?"

"Of course something's the matter!" Ralo said, sucking in his snot before continuing. "Someone stole my wife. He's called

Sonam Dargye. He's the most terrible man in the village. If you don't believe me, just go down to Drakmar village—ask anyone there, and they'll tell you the same thing. Last year the bastard stole Aku Rapgye's horse, and this year he sold Ani Tsokyi's old *dzo* to some Muslim! And then yesterday, he beats me up and steals my wife, like it's nothing. Doesn't your court have the power to punish him, or are you afraid of him? Is your People's Court going to help Ralo the proletarian, or aren't you? I want to know today!" As Ralo went on and on, the snot ran down his chin.

"Of course you'll get help, but this is the criminal court, you need to take your case to the civil court."

"I don't understand this criminal civil stuff."

Ralo was getting angry.

"If you're not afraid of Sonam Dargye, then go arrest him and get my wife back! Come to think of it, you can arrest her, too, while you're at it."

"Don't get all worked up," I said.

I passed Ralo a cigarette.

"Ralo, my old classmate. We haven't seen each other in years. How about we catch up first? What have you been up to all this time?"

"Okay. Alright then." Ralo gradually calmed down and we started to talk.

4.

Despite the fact that Ralo still couldn't write the alphabet, he had grown older than most of the teachers at the school and there was just no way he could stay on, so in the end he was expelled. The reason given for his expulsion was that he had knocked on a female teacher's door late one night. After being expelled, with no home and no family, what choice did Ralo have but to become a drifter?

At first, Ralo staved off the cold and hunger by stopping at any house he came across and volunteering to do manual work or put the cattle out to pasture. Once, an old man at one of these houses thought to himself, "Eh, it's about time for our daughter to get a husband. This drifter Ralo can't control his snot, but he's not a bad herder, and at least he doesn't have sticky fingers. If we get him as our son-in-law, we won't have to get any betrothal gifts, either. Not bad!"

For Ralo, this was most welcome indeed.

The strange thing was that Ralo, as if he'd been bewitched, gradually stopped doing any work at all, and wouldn't even go graze the cattle. "I'm your son-in-law, not your slave," he would say. This infuriated the old man. "Gah! The ingratitude of it! If I don't teach that snot-nosed bum one hell of a lesson, then I'm no man!" Ralo paid the old man no mind and carried on doing whatever he pleased. Though there was nothing he could do about the snot, his cracked lips seemed to be healing and his face began to emit a red glow. Every day he combed his short, fine marmot-tail braid, as he drew out his speech into a slow, aristocratic drawl: "Ah . . ." "Oh . . ." "Really . . ." "Strange . . ." "I've never heard that before . . ." "There's an old saying . . ." You'd never think that this was the same man who'd been a snot-nosed drifter only a few days before.

But how could Ralo know that "one hell of a lesson" awaited him?

For a few days, the family had been stockpiling beer, cigarettes, and sweets, making bread, and slaughtering sheep and cows, as if they were preparing for a grand celebration. When Ralo asked what was going on, they said that a great lama was coming to visit.

"Oh, what good fortune for us!" said Ralo, combing his braid.

Ralo had a habit of getting out of bed very late in the morning. That day being no exception, it was almost midday before he was up. Putting on his fur-lined coat and exiting the tent, he saw a great many horses tied up outside and heard the sounds of raucous laughter and singing. Thinking to himself that the lama had arrived, he immediately fastened his belt and rushed over, but on entering the other tent he found everyone staring at him curiously. Puzzled, Ralo looked about and discovered his wife, decked out in her finest splendor, kneeling next to another young man. "What's all this?" he demanded, even more puzzled now.

"Our family is getting a son-in-law," his wife's younger brother replied.

"Who are we getting a son-in-law for?"

"My sister, who else? He's not for me." Everyone burst out laughing.

"Is having two husbands allowed?"

"What? What two husbands?"

"Me, him."

"Hahaha! A snotty little bum like you who gets drunk without even drinking? You're the family's sheep herder, how could you be her husband?"

"This is impossible! You can't insult someone like this! If I don't die right here in front of you, then I'm no man!" Ralo brandished his fists and leapt forward as the crowd struggled to restrain him. You can't stop a mad dog, and you can't restrain a madman, as the saying goes, and Ralo worked himself up into an even greater frenzy. "Haha! Have you never heard of the royal genealogies of the Ralo family? My fathers were kings, and my mothers were queens! If I don't bathe this village in blood today then my name's not Ralo! I'm Ralo, you . . ." Ralo ranted on and on until the snot running into his mouth finally brought him to a halt.

The crowd, moved to hysterics by this absurd scene, let him go. Ralo didn't dare raise his fists to the brother, so he just butted him with his shoulder. "It's my sister's wedding day, so I'm not getting in a fight with a snotty little bum like you. Get a grip on yourself and piss off back to wherever you came from," said the younger brother. But Ralo simply wouldn't leave him alone and continued to butt him with his shoulder until the brother, his patience exhausted, grabbed Ralo's braid and tossed him to the floor, pulling the braid out at the roots as he did so.

"*Ah ho,* my braid! It's worth a whole yak . . ." Ralo rolled about on the floor in a fit. "If you don't repay me for my braid then I'm not going anywhere!"

"If you don't leave I'll cut your ear off." Unsheathing his knife, the brother stepped toward him. Ralo jumped to his feet and ran like the wind.

5.

Ralo wasn't worried at all about his wife getting married to someone else. What he was worried about was how he could face other people without his beautiful braid. But before long his stomach was empty, and he had no choice but to return to civilization once more.

Ralo passed through many different villages and stayed at many different houses. At first, he would volunteer to do manual work or put the cattle out to pasture at any house he came across. But as soon as his belly was full, he'd give up his herding duties and start talking with that slow drawl: "Ah . . ." "Oh . . ." "There's an old saying . . ." Some houses kicked him out with a "Get lost," while he left others of his own accord.

One day Ralo arrived at a monastery. As the monastery was in the process of being rebuilt, it just so happened that they were taking in monks.

"There was never any point in drifting through the mundane world anyway, and since that asshole cut off my precious braid, I've really got no way to face people. I might as well become a monk, that way I can at least chant some scriptures for my dear old mother." With these thoughts in mind, Ralo shed his lay clothing and adopted the robes of a monk, taking as his Dharma name "Choying Drakpa."

Choying Drakpa didn't miss a single assembly, and he memorized the Vows of Refuge and other elementary chants before any of the other monks. "This chanting scriptures business is much easier than what we did in school. This is my kind of studying!" he thought to himself. His continued devotion to his studies earned him the repeated praise of the disciplinarian, praise that almost reached the level of that phrase from his youth: "Everyone should learn from Ralo."

But gradually Choying Drakpa came to know of the "secret activities" and "open deeds" of certain lamas and monks. "If that's the way it is, then what's the point?" he thought. From then on, he was only at the monastery if there was something to eat and drink, or if there were families of the deceased offering donations to the monks. The rest of the time he spent in the nearby town watching movies, smoking cigarettes, and even drinking beer (which he called "fruit juice"), and so that other phrase from his youth once again reared its head: "No one should learn from Ralo."

Worse than that, one afternoon a rumor blew through the monastery that Choying Drakpa had been chasing after a girl down in the village. Soon this rumor also reached the ears of the disciplinarian and some of the old monks. "Choying Drakpa might be lazy," thought the disciplinarian, "but he has renounced worldly existence and turned his mind to the sacred Dharma, so there's no way he could get up to such shameless things. Perhaps it's nothing but lies and slander. I'll believe it when I see it with my own eyes!"

But there were two monks who did indeed see it with their own eyes. Choying Drakpa had gone down to the banks of the Tsechu to drink a "fruit juice." It was a summer afternoon and the rays of the midday sun were streaming over Tsezhung county. Amidst the soft green grass of the highlands great bouquets of globeflowers were blooming—from a distance it looked just like someone had laid out a green carpet dotted with yellow. Through this whole scene the Tsechu River flowed gently. If anyone with even a single artistic bone in their body were to come here, then the strains of "The Blue Danube" might naturally drift into their ears. No matter what angle you looked at it from, the Tsechu really was just as lovely as the beautiful Danube.

Just then a girl from the village over the river came to fetch water. She was just as beautiful as the river. As she drew water she cast a glance at Choying Drakpa from the corner of her eye, and he fell like an animal into a trap. "At the end of the day, the most beautiful thing in the world is a woman," he thought. Seized with a sudden impulse, he struck up a Malho love song:

Can the wild yak climb
On the misty mountain?
Can the little goldfish swim
In the emerald lake?
Can I have the company
Of the enchanting girl?

Without giving it much thought, the water-fetching girl responded with her own Ganlho love song:

> The black clouds with the yellow lining
> Are made up of frost and hail.
> The monk who's neither clergy nor layman
> Is the enemy of Buddhist teachings.

Because she sang quickly, Choying Drakpa didn't quite get the gist of the song, nor did he stop to give it much consideration. "Usually it's pretty rare for girls to sing to boys," he thought to himself, "but this one replied to me straight away. She must be into me!" Overcome with joy and completely forgetting both the disciplinarian and his vows, he plowed into the Tsechu without even taking his off his boots.

The girl had at first thought that the monk was just kidding around with her, so she wanted to kid around with him, but as soon as she saw Choying Drakpa rushing toward her, boots still on and snot running down to his chin, she thought to herself, "This monk must be crazy!" Throwing aside her water bucket, she fled in terror.

When they witnessed this farcical scene, the monks who had been studying by the river couldn't help but burst into laughter. At that moment, Choying Drakpa came to his senses and stood dazed in the middle of the river.

6.

The sun set, and the monastery became even more still and peaceful.

The greatest burden in the world isn't having work to do, but having nothing to do. It was indeed as if Choying Drakpa was suffering under the weight of having nothing to do. He got up late in the morning and couldn't get to sleep at night. The water-fetching girl's alluring features and that sidelong glance (which he took as flirtatious) refused to disappear from his mind. Heaving a sigh, he left his monk's quarters.

The curved sickle moon hung in the southwest sky like an old man leaning on his walking stick. The sound of dogs barking drifted over from the village on the other side of the Tsechu, and looking in that direction Choying Drakpa could see each of the homes clearly. One place had a fire going in the stove, and he could see it even more clearly than the others.

The face of the water-fetching girl appeared before Choying Drakpa's eyes like a film projected on the screen of his mind. He returned to his room, took off his monk's robes, and put on his old fur-lined coat.

It was just over two kilometers from the monastery to the village over the river, so Choying Drakpa arrived there in no time at all. He turned toward the home with the blazing lamplight, and tiptoeing up to the flap of the tent he peeked inside, but there was only one person in there. It was a woman, but sadly it wasn't the water-fetching girl. She was sitting by the stove with her head in her hands, as though something were weighing on her mind.

Choying Drakpa forgot about the water-fetching girl entirely and couldn't help but enter the tent. The woman jumped up in fright, an "*Ah ma!*" escaping her mouth. After a moment she calmed down, and asked who he was.

"I'm a passer-by," Choying Drakpa answered with a grin. "Can I stay the night here?"

The woman sized up Choying Drakpa in detail. He was tall and skinny with thick eyebrows and a purplish complexion.

"*Ah tsi*, of course you can." She got up, and with a smile poured Choying Drakpa a cup of tea. "Have a seat on the mat."

Choying Drakpa took a seat and examined his surroundings, and gradually his gaze came to rest on the woman. She was around thirty, with dark red cheeks and a high nose. She was plump and had a bulging chest. Choying Drakpa felt his skin tingle with desire. "Is it just you here?" he asked her, flushing.

"Eh . . ." she sighed, and a forlorn expression appeared on her face. "I had a good-for-nothing husband, but he left me and ran off to become a monk."

"Ah, how terrible! Most monks are shameless like that. I can't stand monks."

"Absolutely. There's no one in the world who loves to eat and hates to work more than a monk."

"Rubbish!"

"Huh?"

"Oh—I mean those monks love to talk rubbish, too."

"Do you smoke?" The woman asked.

"Of course not . . . oh . . . yes, I do, I do."

"Give me one, would you? This loneliness has made me take it up."

After expounding for a while on the joys and benefits of smoking, Choying Drakpa fished around in his pocket. "Oh—too bad! I didn't bring any today."

Choying Drakpa and the woman talked for some time, and now and then he would send some compliments her way. After a while their intentions began to align.

"Ah, you know what they say, 'There's no suffering in the recitation hall, but you have to sit 'til your butt's numb, and there's no happiness in samsara, but you can still dispel your troubles.'"

"What? You've been in a recitation hall?"

"I was before, it was pointless. What if the two of us could be together our whole lives, wouldn't that be great?"

"If that's what you want, then it's easily done."

"Of course that's what I want! But we can't stay here, because . . ." Choying Drakpa recounted all of his troubles to her. After hiding out at her place for a few days, he helped her gather up all of her necessities, and under the cover of the moonlight they headed for Choying Drakpa's home town.

7.

When Choying Drakpa was a monk, if someone called him "Ralo" instead of "Choying Drakpa" he would get angry and butt them with his shoulder. Now that he had returned home, people called him "Ralo" once again, and he let them.

Ralo's household registration was still here in his village, and his mother's nomad tent and her belongings were still there in the village storehouse. The Nomad Committee gave him a relief stipend and gathered some sheep and cattle from the villagers for him to tend, for which he had to sign a contract. At first Ralo worked diligently and his house really seemed like a home, but as soon as he had clothes on his back and food in his belly, the seeds of laziness gradually sprouted again. He stopped tending the livestock, stopped working, and went into town to idle around. Eventually his livestock contract was rescinded, and his wife lost all patience with him.

Ralo had been in town for a bender, and after all his money had dried up he returned home to discover that his wife was nowhere to be seen. According to his neighbors, she'd been taken away by Sonam Dargye, so off he went to Sonam Dargye's house to fetch her back.

"This is my home now," she said.

"*Ah tsi*, are you possessed or what?"

"You're the one who's possessed!" Sonam Dargye approached him. "She's my legal wife, what other home has she got except this one?"

Ralo, incensed, started to butt Sonam Dargye with his shoulder. "You'll steal someone's wife in broad daylight?!"

"If you think I stole her then go report it to the police. Then we'll see whose wife she is."

Only then did Ralo remember that there is a place that can subdue tyrants and protect the weak: a place they call "the courthouse."

8.

I took Ralo to the civil court and introduced him, then went back to the office.

The civil court summoned Sonam Dargye and the woman to investigate the matter. "It's true that Ralo and I lived together for a while," she said, "but we weren't husband and wife. If he says we were, then where's the marriage certificate? Isn't it against the law to live together without a marriage certificate? So my marriage to Sonam Dargye is completely legal." She produced a marriage certificate from her pocket.

According to the verdict of the court, the woman was Sonam Dargye's legal spouse. Ralo's lawsuit had about as much impact as throwing a stone into Qinghai Lake.

Ralo now finally realized the importance of getting a marriage certificate. He felt a deep sense of regret that he hadn't sorted out this marriage certificate before. He gave himself a slap on the face, and the snot ran down to his chin.

9.

Ralo exited the courthouse and wandered aimlessly down the street. Coming to the door of a restaurant, he realized that he hadn't had breakfast or lunch yet. He felt a wave of heat in his stomach, which emitted a long rumble. Unable to stop himself, he went into the restaurant. However, while he still had some livestock, he unfortunately didn't have a penny to his name.

A lot of kids these days will eat without paying for it, but Ralo was not that kind of person—in fact, there was one time he returned 4000 yuan he found on the street straight to its owner without a moment's hesitation. No one could accuse Ralo of having sticky fingers, unless they were talking about him picking up cigarette butts out of the teachers' trash back when he was in school.

Ralo stood in a daze, staring at the mouths of the diners. As he stared he found himself thinking back to his time as a monk: the faithful masses would always donate congee filled with more meat than rice, and there would even be raisins and sugar. If ever a family that wasn't so well off substituted dates for raisins, the monks would say "Hey, they've put damn dates in here!" and with no hesitation at all upend their bowls on the table.

"I really didn't know the value of food in those days," he sighed. Ralo swallowed a mouthful of saliva and turned to leave, but from his stomach there continued to come the warning sign that he had to eat something.

"Ah—what can I do? I've got to get some food, no matter what!" Ralo cast about desperately for a familiar face. "In the old days," he thought to himself, "I'd sell a sheep or a cow and drink to my heart's content, then all my classmates and people I knew would be buzzing around me like bees. Where have all those people gone now?" His thoughts turned to the old yak, the one he used to ride. That yak was the only one from his herd of livestock worth any money, as well as his only means of getting around. But what's more important than your stomach? Don't all living things, from the lowest ant to the noblest human, rush about madly just for the sake of their stomachs?

Ralo sold the old yak for 700 yuan. If he had been an experienced trader, there's no doubt he could have got more for it. But as far as Ralo was concerned, 700 yuan was a most satisfactory sum. Never before in his life had he held so much money in his hands.

10.

"I'm Ralo, and I'm rolling in it! Drink, drink, drink . . ." Ralo was a little bit drunk. He was in a restaurant, waving a handful of 100-yuan bills in the air, and drinking beer in the middle of a crowd. "As for Ralo's paternal ancestry and maternal ancestry . . ." he began, snot running down to his chin.

It was dusk, and the restaurant was lit up. A woman kept peeking in through the doorway and looking around. As Ralo was coming back from taking a piss he saw her and stayed outside for a moment to size her up. From the look of her clothes, she wasn't a local.

"Where are you from?" asked Ralo, staring at her.

"Amchok," said the woman, turning round to look at Ralo. She was just over twenty years old, her clothes were worn out and she had cracked lips, but her deep-set eyes gave off a sincerity and a purity that called to Ralo's mind the image of the water-fetching girl from the year before.

"Have you ever been to the Tsechu to fetch water?"

Not understanding the meaning behind his question, she stared at him in bemusement.

"You've definitely been to the Tsechu to fetch water." Ralo interrogated her as though he were a policeman. "What are you doing here?"

"I want to eat something . . . but . . ."

Ralo realized that she must have no money. "I know you. I've seen you before. Just wait a second." He went into the restaurant and whispered a few words to a young man who had the appearance of an official. The man passed him a key, and Ralo returned. "Come on, let's go eat."

The woman was hesitant and stayed where she was. "Don't be afraid," said Ralo. "I know you." He tugged on her sleeve and so she reluctantly went along.

Side by side, they went into a narrow alley.

"There's no happiness in samsara, but you can dispel your troubles!" Ralo blurted out. On top of the proverb, he added: "Let's get a marriage certificate."

"*Ah tsi!* What are you on about? I've got a husband."

"Ah, but after we get a marriage certificate, you'll be my legal wife. Then no one can interfere, whether you had a husband before or not!"

"Really?"

"Really! I had a wife before too, but she got a marriage certificate with some other guy so the court said she wasn't my wife, but the other guy's wife. The Chinese rely on writing, Tibetans rely on their word, as they say."

"Then it's up to you. I can't get along with him anyway. If I could, then what would I be doing all the way out here, wandering around on my own?"

The strange thing was that, in this place, though it was hard to get divorced there were no procedural requirements at all for getting married. As long as both parties consented, then that was it. So Ralo and this virtual stranger went down to the county government and got a marriage certificate, no problem.

Though there was no way that she could be the water-fetching girl, compared to the yellow-toothed partner he had before, she was prettier and a whole lot nicer. So Ralo swore from the bottom of his heart that he would change his bad and idle ways and resolved to spend his days with this honest woman. He even swore off the drink before a lama.

Ralo genuinely fell in love with her. This love was something he hadn't felt at all with the previous two women. For instance, when he went into the county town to buy grain, he wouldn't waste a single second messing around and would hurry back as soon as possible with a new shirt or some sweets for his wife. And as soon as she saw Ralo coming back in the distance, she would rush out to meet him, bringing food and drink with her. Things were going well for the two of them. They used the old tent that Ralo's mother had left behind to store dung, and the brand new one they moved into was filled with the sound of laughter.

11.

Some people said that this woman put Ralo on the straight and narrow. Others even said that she might be the reincarnation of Ralo's mother. Either way, ever since they'd been together Ralo really had become a different person. There was even less snot on his upper lip than there used to be.

However, one day, two men from the public security bureau showed up completely out of the blue and took Ralo and his wife away to the county town.

According to the court, his wife had committed bigamy, so she was sentenced to six months in prison. Ralo cried until the tears and snot mingled together on his chin. Coming up close to him, she said, "Ralo, don't lose heart. Six months isn't that long. I'll always be yours."

What sincere and kind words! These words gave Ralo a kind of courage and hope that he had never felt before. Wiping away the snot and the tears, he stood up straight and called out, "Don't worry, I'll wait for you!"

UNDER THE SHADOW

BHUCHUNG D. SONAM

The bus ride from Delhi to Manali churned my empty stomach into a state of intoxication. I retched until my stomach hurt. Each time I bent to vomit, my head banged against the seat in front of me, but nothing came out other than tired strings of saliva that stretched from my mouth to the dusty floor of the howling bus. I ranted at the driver, who in turn blamed the potholed road, the government, and all the crooked politicians whose names he chanted like mantras. He kept chewing betel nut and laughed sardonically each time he honked loudly at a vehicle in front of him.

The bus conductor was a mustachioed man in faded green pants and shirt. He took out some tablets from his pocket.

"Take these and you will be fine," he said.

I swallowed the bitter yellow tablets, washing it down only with saliva. I felt a little better.

"How long have you been doing this?" I asked the conductor after most passengers dozed off.

"Ever since I was old enough to think."

"Do you get scared of being killed in an accident?" I asked. He was staring straight ahead onto the road, puffing on his cigarette.

"*Ayi*," the conductor said to the driver, "The kid is asking if you want to die." The driver spat out the window, turned his head around and said, "*Arey*, dying, living, driving, all same." I had no more questions.

At around eleven, the bus screeched to a stop and the conductor announced it was time for dinner. The roadside eatery had *charpoys* placed all over. I threw myself flat on one of those frames strung with jute ropes. I wasn't hungry. Besides, my wallet was empty. After half an hour of semi-sleep, the driver shook me to life and the journey resumed.

After passing through numerous half-lit villages, we entered a long dark road. I fell asleep. When I woke up to a terrifying groan of the weary vehicle, I found that the man sitting next to me had his head comfortably rested on my lap. The driver was cursing the potholes and politicians again. My legs were cramped. Everything was dark, except the road directly ahead lit by the two giant eyes of the bus.

Not wanting to wake the man up, I sat still. A car came from the opposite direction, honking madly. It raised a swirl of dust and for a moment I felt that we were floating on a cloud. When the dust cleared, there was an electric pole on the left without a light and then a bridge appeared. In the middle of the bridge was what looked like a deer standing immobile under the bright headlights. Its eyeballs were shining brightly. The driver pushed down hard on the accelerator and the giant, fuming metallic monster roared across the bridge. I heard a low thud.

"*Mathar chod!* Why do they always stand on the bridge?" the driver shouted.

"*Hari Ram! Hari Ram*!" cried the conductor and popped his head out of the side window looking backwards.

"It's fallen off the bridge!" he said.

A sharp shiver shot up my spine. Then I felt numb again.

Early the next morning, a cool breeze gushed through the half-opened window. The sun announced its arrival and chased out the remnant of the night. The winding road of the hills disappeared into forests through which the bus slowly wormed its way, howling loudly each time it made a sharp turn. The sight, and the smell, of trees somewhat eased my head. The man who sat next to me gave me a soft handshake and got down at one of many short stops. Before disappearing into a thin crowd, he looked back and smiled. I sat still waiting for the bus to move again. At the next stop, a woman with a little baby took the place beside me. The faint smell of ammonia and baby powder filled the bus.

When we reached Manali, I got down and shook my dead legs alive. As I walked toward the iron gate of the school, the bell pealed for morning prayers. I saw the tree standing a few feet away from the library wall. I knew this tree well. It had five large branches with many smaller ones shooting outward to create a cool shade underneath. The dark-green leaves were as perfectly round as lids of jam bottles, but they had two-inch long tips, which were extensions of the mid-rib. At the margins of the leaves grew a fine white hair that on hot days seemed to disappear only to become visible when the sun went down or when the sky was overcast. A cluster of ten to fifteen leaves grew on light green stems and at the base of stems were double stipules that hardly ever blossomed into full leaves.

Children were chasing each other around the tree in their blue pants and green sweaters which almost matched the color of the leaves. When the Discipline Master shouted, they rushed into the hall. I went around the tree and ran my fingers down the rough bark. A girl's name was carved on the trunk. The wrinkled bark seemed to have grown old and sad. Some of it was peeling off. The leaves were in full foliage. Young branches, thin like lady's fingers, were shooting up from the base of mature ones. The leaves on the new branches were dark green. I saw caterpillars and the stains of bird droppings on the leaves.

My friend Yeshi was waiting for me. A short, chain-smoking man with an aquiline nose from which watery liquid kept dropping at any time of the day, he was a great guy and a fantastic friend. His only vice was "exaggerated articulation." If he said, "Today I saw a man who was so fat that a tractor went flat when he got on it" he had most likely just seen a heavy man on a motorbike that had a flat tire. Our mutual friends often joked that we had to cut 50 percent from Yeshi's stories.

He picked up my small bag and we went to his quarters. Over cups of sweet tea, tomato omelette, and fresh bread, he told me that the tree was to be chopped down to build a *stupa*, a religious structure representing the Enlightened Mind. I was stunned. I didn't know what to feel. Yeshi had insisted on my visit and one thing that I looked forward to was sitting in the library reading books and seeing the tree, its shadow stretching into the window and its leaves rustling in the summer breeze.

Yeshi told me that the principal of the school, apparently a very religious man but one who had difficulty keeping himself away from whisky bottles, had decided to build a *stupa* so that students could do circumambulation to accumulate good karma. Yeshi despised this portly man, who liked to walk around the school, rosary in hand, ostentatiously mumbling mantras. If you crossed his path he would demand that you bow your head a little to acknowledge his superior position.

In the three years since he had taken over as principal, there hadn't been any visible improvement in the school. The first thing he did was to increase the duration of morning and evening prayers from twenty to forty-five minutes. The classrooms were fitted with a cement blackboard, a rickety table, and a chair for the teacher. Children sat on the floor. The staffroom was bare except for a long wooden worktable and a few discolored plastic chairs. My friend and the other teachers planned their lessons by hand in long notebooks.

The stock of books in the library was dismal. Over the course of the first week, I read most of the publications, which included old copies of *National Geographic* and *Time* magazines donated by an old English woman, and worn out abridged editions of classics such as *Oliver Twist*, *The Adventures of Tom Sawyer*, *Moby Dick*, and *Black Beauty* precariously displayed on two wobbly bookshelves. A locked steel cabinet contained some reference books, including a complete set of hardbound *Encyclopaedia Britannica*. When there was no one in the library, my friend gave me access to this precious cabinet.

Sometimes I played with older children with balls made from abandoned socks. When the stuffed-sock ball fell into the gutter, the boys picked it up, squeezed out the water, and the game continued. Each time the ball struck the white wall, it left a black mark. Occasionally, the Discipline Master would appear and forbid us from hitting the wall again.

The school office was a ten-by-fifteen foot room crammed with five tables for five staff members and two grey-colored steel shelves packed with thick-spined files and other documents. The most amazing sight was the secretary in the office, a chubby, cheerful man in his forties with extremely sparse hair and his "gentleman coat" as the kids called it. Every day he wore blazers of the same color. Like a disciplined soldier, he typed in all school records on an old Remington typewriter. The drumming of keys on the paper was music from another era.

A fortnight after my arrival, coolies marched onto the school grounds one morning with spades, pickaxes, ropes, and a chainsaw. They looked grim and determined. One of them was a frail old man with his wrinkled face set in a permanent frown. When he broke into fits of laughter over some innocuous jokes, he seemed to grow a decade younger. He was the leader of the gang. The rest of the coolies included young men, women, and a bunch of children who played in the area and made a rumpus. Under the stern look of the potbellied principal, the coolies pulled down the low brick fence around the tree. When they pulled out the grass in clumps and dug into the soft dirt, earthworms wriggled out. Some of the schoolchildren picked up the twisting worms and released them into the nearby river.

I watched the execution of the tree from the library with a book in my lap. The tree was two stories tall and some branches swayed so near the window that I could reach out and stroke the shivering leaves. I felt as dark, empty, and tired as if I had been chased to the end of the road by a flock of blackbirds. For the first time, books, and the parallel worlds I lost myself in, no longer seemed precious.

The next day, however, the coolies did not come. They had developed a sprout of rashes on their faces and hands as big as peanuts. The school nurse applied some ointment, but the eruptions did not subside. One woman's pustules were particularly severe. She had eruptions all her over face, hands, neck, armpits and even her private parts, where she wouldn't let the nurse take a look.

The children and teachers speculated that the spirit residing in the tree, outraged by the destruction of its refuge, had caused the inflammations. But why was the plump principal spared these itchy lumps? He had helped as well.

That evening I sat down with an old man who had been a cook in the school since its inception and who had now retired. He had a prayer-wheel lying on his lap and a rosary in his left hand. His eyelids drooped so much that he had placed a chickpea between the lids of each eye so that he could catch blurry images of the world that no longer belonged to him. I needed to ask him about the tree whose uprooting was causing so much trouble for the coolies.

“Do you know who planted the tree?” I asked.

“Boy, it was a long, long time ago. The tree is special, did you know? The spirit who lives here can possess you and send you into a trance.”

“But do you know the one who planted this tree?” I asked again. It took a long time for him to search the labyrinth of his memories. Under the faint light of the 40-watt bulb, he closed his eyes tightly and let out a long sigh.

“His name was Rigzin. A couple of years after the tree was planted he was transferred to South India to be a Tibetan language teacher in a school. When he left, the tree was this tall,” he said lifting his left hand about two feet from the ground. “He recited prayers and burned incense near the tree. He even made a mud incense burner and a wooden flagpole. They were removed when this school was built years later.”

I knew my grandfather spent some time around Manali as a road-builder in the early years of exile. But I never saw him going into a trance. Thoughts cluttered my head.

My mother had died two days after my birth in a local hospital and my father a month later due to a fall from a tractor donated to the settlement by USAID. The only image I have of my parents is a faded black-and-white photograph that we had in our house. My grandfather brought me up.

Grandfather loved to plant trees, and they surrounded our small house in a settlement in South India. He gave them names and often talked to them. “In Tibet,” he would say, “none of these would grow. Only willow and poplar survive there.” On hot days, he would strip down to his underwear, sit under their shade, and recite prayers. Often he pointed to a tree near the entrance to our house and said, “That one is our soul tree. I planted it soon after we got here. But the spirit doesn't come anymore." He was the only family member I had. He was also my first teacher, who taught me to read and write.

Some children came and sat with us. When I shifted closer to the old former cook to make room for them, I caught a good whiff of the rancid odors from his unwashed body which lingered in the air. I was about to ask him more questions when one of the boys said, "Have you seen the spirit?" Before the old man had a chance to answer another boy asked, "Where did the spirit come from?"

"When we came into exile," the old man said, "our protector deities and local spirits also ran away and came here with us."

"Can we see them?"

"Well, we cannot see them, but we can feel them," he said.

"But why did this one live in the tree?" a girl asked.

"Those were difficult times. We were all working as coolies building roads and we couldn't afford to placate the deities with rituals and cakes or offer daily incense and put up prayer flags. Many spirits took refuge in large boulders, trees, and other places along the road. The spirit residing in this tree was one of them."

The children were astounded. I too had wondered at such things, once. How could deities and spirits run away? Did they come hiding in amulets worn around necks or in charm boxes refugees brought with them? Did they fly across the high mountains? Couldn't they stay back in the caves, rocks, and rivers in their homeland? Had any spirits died on the way, as hundreds of people had died on their tortuous flight into exile?

"If the tree is cut, where will the spirit go?" asked a boy holding a tattered notebook.

The old man put his rosary on his lap next to the prayer wheel, rubbed his forehead, and looked at his dirty hand. "It will become a refugee again."

"Can the spirits go back home?"

He had no answer. He stared into the dark sky and then told them to go away and play.

"What did Rigzin look like?" I asked. I wanted to make sure.

"He was a big man with a limp."

My grandfather's right leg was an inch shorter than the left one. An Indian doctor advised him to craft a one-inch thicker sole for the right shoe in order for him to walk normally. This was perhaps the only advice that he ever listened to. For everything else, his response was, "The spirit will guide me." Every time he asked me to pass his shoes to him, I would pick up the right shoe first and say, "This is so much heavier than the other one." He would laugh out loud and snatch the shoe from my hands. During my second year in college, Grandpa got very sick. Doctors performed a series of tests and linked him up to all sorts of machines but they could not diagnose his illness. Grandpa got thinner and thinner, as if someone was pumping all the energy out of him.

In the end he simply refused to take any medication and insisted on going back to our house. He died three months later on a swelteringly hot Indian summer's day far from his home in the mountains. His death left a permanent void in my heart. That year, despite my best efforts and daily watering, the "soul tree" near the gate of our house dried up.

The principal was displeased at the coolies' condition. His astrologer had advised him to finish building the *stupa* before a certain auspicious date. The principal shouted at the contractor to bring in a fresh troop of coolies. However, the smooth-talking contractor reasoned that it was out of the question as the construction season had begun and there was a dearth of coolies. But he promised that the *stupa* would be finished on time.

Five days later, the same band of coolies resumed work. The eruptions on their faces and bodies hadn't healed properly yet and yellowish pus oozed from them. This time, the principal himself took charge of the operation. They used saws, axes, and chisels to chop the thicker roots. The smaller ones were pulled out in a merciless tug-o-war. The trunk was sawed off into three sections. Branches and leaves lay scattered. It was an agonizing death. Finally, when there was nothing left in the deep hole but some stubborn roots, they threw in a bucket of foul-smelling sulphuric acid and common salt to prevent the roots from recovering.

Grandfather came into my dream that night. He was limping worse than a three-legged dog and his face looked as if all the blood from his body had been let out. His gangly body was naked except for a thin white shawl tied around his waist. Grandpa raised his hands, showing a wisp of hair under his armpits, and kept shouting: "Follow the spirit!" I woke up in the dark room. My friend was snoring hard.

During the following nights, there were reports of mournful voices heard all over the school campus. One of the boys apparently saw a tall figure cloaked in elaborate attire walking around the empty hole left by the felled tree. "Looked like he was dancing! Hands raised in the air and his feet kicking the earth!" the boy told the headmaster. Soon the entire campus was abuzz with various tales. The children were scared to go to the toilet at night and many wet their beds.

They mourned the tree's removal. They could no longer chase one another around it or compete to slap the highest leaves. The boy who had scratched the name of the girl he loved on the trunk was particularly upset. For his misdemeanor, the Discipline Master had made him do one thousand prostrations in the assembly hall. He had become a hero among the boys.

The teachers talked amongst themselves, agreeing that it was absurd to destroy the tree to build a *stupa*. The money, they complained, could have been used to buy computers, books, teaching aids, skipping ropes for girls, and balls for boys. No one, however, openly raised a dissenting voice for fear of repercussions from the principal who had a reputation for not sparing anyone who opposed him. All watched the tree fall. Guilt hung heavily in the collective conscience.

Eventually, on the spot where the tree was murdered, a *stupa* was built and an elaborate consecration ceremony took place. The school invited seven monks from the local monastery to perform rituals, including rites to subdue spirits. The children were treated to small ritual cakes and sweets. "Don't waste your time playing games or running around. Instead circumambulate this holy *stupa* to accumulate merit," the principal lectured them.

Old people came for daily circumambulation and the principal joined them with great pride. The birds, however, sang less and less and the children kept away from the new edifice. The library got hotter. Though the weather was perfect that summer, it was a traumatic holiday for me. The days passed slowly, and the evenings drudged by. I sat in the library gazing out the window as if the tree would return.

I had salvaged one leaf and pressed it between the pages of my notebook, in which I wrote: "Days I see not / Nights I feel not / Only confusion reigns / Chaos to lunacy." Sometimes clouds in the eastern sky gave some shade, but the shade only made me sink deeper into melancholy. An image of the glass-eyed deer falling off the bridge flitted through my head and the sound of Grandpa's "Follow the spirit!" echoed in my ears.

I saw thousands of pigeons in my mind. Amidst the flapping of their wings came the sad music of the dry, rustling leaves. The music grew louder and louder.

When the flapping of wings ceased, a clear silence rang. I became restless. Unable to bear the stillness building up inside me, I chased the fading light of the evening to the bridge across the river flowing east of the school. The horizon darkened, as the last rays of the sun receded over the hills. I stood in the middle of the bridge and let the dried leaf I had salvaged drop from my hands. It was carried away by the never-ending waves.

A moment later I followed it.

THE AGATE AND THE SINGER

KYABCHEN DEDROL TRANSLATED BY TENZIN DICKIE

The singer's name was Yangchen Pema and before she died, there were many stories told about her. People said she had an abortion at some hospital, that the child's father was some big shot county chief who bought her an apartment to make up for it, and that his family's tantric master, a black magician, had blown puffs of air into her mouth that sweetened and strengthened her voice, not to mention that while stealing another singer's lover, she had also stolen the singer's voice, and so on.

Last New Year's, when she sang a song called "My Sweetheart" at a concert organized by the TV station, this song not only spread from cities to towns to rural villages but there was even a young man, a youth who gambled the whole day away at hotels, who said, "If I could only sleep one night with Yangchen Pema, I wouldn't regret it even if I had to die the next day." When a trader told him, "I am financing Yangchen Pema's next album," he followed the trader around for many days, serving him like a lackey, and the incident became rather famous.

If you listened to those who worshipped her passionately, they even told how if you were to call her name from the rolling pastures or from the canals dug into the fields, she would appear in front of you like a divine goddess versed in the art of enchantment.

A herder named Tsering had a dream in which a goddess carrying a golden vase suddenly appeared beside a clear stream. Upon waking up, he said that he found himself reciting the songs of Yangchen Pema. About a week after he told this story, this herder named Tsering fell prey to a sudden and serious illness from which he emerged speaking like an idiot. At times he would say, "Yangchen Pema is my wife. Our child's name is Yangtruk." At other times he would utter, "Don't let me go. I can't go alone." He abandoned his herd and became a beggar, crying out "Ki hi hi!" and telling unending stories outside a dance hall where Yangchen Pema had once performed.

At any rate, by the end of a spring in which many men's desires grew wings, every household in the land had a DVD of Yangchen Pema's songs, and the phones of those who rode horses and those who rode motorcycles, of businessmen as well as workers, were full of photos of Yangchen Pema.

One day, a college student named Dorjee lay asleep late into the afternoon, sleeping off the previous night's intoxication, when someone pulled at his blanket. Waving his hand, he said, "You bastard—go away. I need a little more sleep." Then he felt a cool, silky hand stroking his hair and heard a woman's voice in his ear saying, "Wake up and see. It's going to be a new day today." Blinking the sleep out of his eyes, he saw that there was a woman in a red shirt in his room. Her smile brightened the whole room like a ray of light. With a sense of panic like none he had ever felt before, he rose to his feet and the woman vanished.

Saying that the woman was Yangchen Pema, he became the first person since the spring to claim to have seen her.

After that incident, people argued and discussed why Yangchen Pema had gone to the young man's room and most of them agreed that it was because of a precious nine-eyed agate stone that had been in Dorjee's family for many generations.

According to the wanderer Tawang, if Dorjee's family were to lose its agate stone to Yangchen Pema's tantric master, then

Yangchen Pema would transform into the goddess Saraswati in this lifetime and the music of Saraswati's sitar would enchant the people of the world and even cause them to sing their words rather than speak them. Tawang's story spread swiftly from one person to ten people and from ten to a hundred till it reached the ears of Dorjee's mother. She spent a long night in doubt and anxiety and then hid the stone under one of the stakes of the family tent.

Dorjee was majoring in mathematics. The night he saw Yangchen Pema, he thought that the numbers that had made him suffer for so many years had nothing else to do but bother people like the flies that hovered around toilets. He felt that the sum of all that accounting had no basis, the way the joy derived from intoxication had no basis, because no amount of addition or subtraction could produce something like Yangchen Pema. Thinking these thoughts, feeling as if he had lost the heart in his ribcage, he got up and thought about taking a walk, but it felt like there was no longer anywhere to go.

His schoolmates surrounded him and asked him various questions about Yangchen Pema until finally he said, "To be honest, I was sleeping at the time. I saw her only in my dreams." A female classmate, consumed by jealousy, said, "Why are you all gasping in surprise? Yangchen Pema is also a person. Do you know what a person looks like? A person has a mouth, a nose, and a tongue, like Dorjee." Dorjee flushed from head to toe at the mocking laughter of the students, and, head down, paying no heed to the teachers, he walked past the school gates with his bag and left.

This is what the female classmate wrote in her journal about Dorjee's departure from school: "When he left, it didn't look like he was walking on two feet but rather, that he was on all fours. Will he still have two hands when he comes back?"

All around the perimeter of the school lay a large field that looked like a chessboard, and the sunlight, which could not be gathered again, instead dispersed like powdered color over the crops that grew in the field. Much like the four-legged animal that his classmate described in her journal, Dorjee sought out his destination but found himself circling and circling the same area. He grew thirsty and felt a desire in his body that he had never known before. When he thought of Yangchen Pema as he had seen her that day, it seemed as if her red shirt held the dew drops that could slake his thirst and he felt that were she to touch him again, he would surely lose his seed.

That evening, he reached a town where dogs were barking. He asked for lodging from a local family. Their walls were decorated with Yangchen Pema's pictures. His cross-eyed hostess said to him, "This woman's fame has spread far and wide. But there's a thread running from her back and at the tip of this thread is a fat man, and were it not for him, who knows if her beauty would dim and even her words fail her." He thought that this fat man could be none other than the tantric master that he'd heard others speak of.

When he was getting ready for bed, his hostess gave him a blanket as dark as the night, and all night long, he felt as if the dark was pressing down upon him. When it became difficult even to breathe, he thought about getting up but found that his body lacked the strength. He realized that the house he was staying in was a juncture where the real world met the dream world. Just then, he saw the fat man his hostess had mentioned. There were many wrinkles on his face, and he had fat lips with a flat nose and extremely tiny eyes. His left hand gripped a thread as his right hand clutched a fistful of notes.

No matter which way Dorjee looked at the thread, it flowed and gleamed deceptively like an endlessly long river. He could not see the end of it. The fat man said, "Look here. At the tip of this thread hangs Yangchen Pema. And in front of her there are all the people of this world. Ha ha ha." He looked far into the distance and continued, "Young man, don't you see? That dark shadow up there is your family's black tent. Beneath one of the stakes holding down that tent, your mother hid that which Yangchen Pema has lost. Your people may have thought they were keeping it hidden, but it looks to me as if they just left it out in the open."

The fat man made Dorjee hold the thread and led him to the tent, where he pulled the stake from the ground and snatched the agate stone underneath. He wiped the dirt from the agate and then, taking out a silver needle, stabbed each eye of the agate stone, cleaning out the defiling particles. He brought the agate to his mouth and blew, and then there was a sweet sound of music as if the wind were helping him. Yangchen Pema appeared before them and the thread in Dorjee's hand went slack. The fat man gave her the agate stone and said, "Daughter of Brahma, you have suffered."

Dorjee held on to the thread for a while until there was nothing at the other end but a woman's skin.

He woke up at that point. The day's newspaper carried the following headline: "Famous Singer Yangchen Pema Dies Suddenly." At the scene of her death, the police found a Louis Vuitton bag. In the bag were a plastic brush, a small mirror with the photo of some famous singer on the reverse side, a CD of her latest music, the lyrics of a song titled "White Snow Mountain," an eyebrow pencil, and some lipstick.

THE NEW ROAD CONTROVERSY

TAKBUM GYAL TRANSLATED BY LAURAN HARTLEY

Nagshar, as everybody knows, is a remote village in this county. It used to be that no truck load could ever make its way there, because there was no road.

Concerned about the backwardness of life in Nagshar and the absence of any conveniences, higher authorities made the decision last fall to construct a road to the village.

Once this news had spread, Nagshar was in an uproar. Aku Yontan and Dolo were the first two men to speak.

"Our father's land is a valley of milk and honey, without a single enemy except for the prairie rats and moles. And now, this year . . . old man that I am, I have never agreed to even a furrow being dug in this soil. There's nothing left now for us old men, but to die before our time."

"Yes. And after we go, how will the young people carry on? This is our birthplace, the land where our umbilical cord was cut. What are we going to do with a road? Where was this road when our ancestors were here? You're still going to live here, aren't you? If we wander down some road, where will it take us?"

"Yes. It's just like the two of you say. I feel the same."

"Of course. Everyone feels the same."

A few other older men concurred with Aku Yontan and Dolo. Because Aku Yontan was the only articulate speaker in the village, everyone thought of him as some sort of village official. But, he had never been granted any formal position. The young men of the village too were emboldened by his speech and the next morning, just as the sun's rays began to shine on the fields, each and every family member in the village gathered in Nagdangdo to form a "militia." Everybody appeared holding slingshots and Tibetan nunchuckas. When the village head returned, it was quite late in the afternoon. As he neared the outskirts of the village, he was surprised to see a great number of people and horses amassed in the forest at Nagdangdo. "What happened?" he wondered. Thinking that maybe they had been fighting again with another village, he goaded his horse with a quick kick of the stirrups and rode straight to where the "militia" was gathered. Not even taking the time to tether his horse, he let the rope fall to the ground and hurried into the crowd. The village head asked out loud what had happened, but everybody was too angry just then to pay him any heed. With nothing left to do, he made his way to the center where Aku Yontan stood with trembling lips and asked the old man about the situation. "What exactly happened?"

"Hmmph!" Aku Yontan glared at him with angry eyes. "You haven't heard yet? They are wringing the very essence out of our father's land. Haven't you heard? Neither our fathers nor their forefathers ever had a road and there is no need for one now! We are two hundred families strong in Nagshar village and we firmly oppose planting this so-called flag of opportunity where there's never been any opportunity by building a road here now."

When Aku Yontan reached this point in his speech, the village head understood what he was talking about and relaxed. He smiled.

"Oh. You're talking about *that*?"

"What else would I be talking about? What's so funny? Think about it. Why can't we live the same way our ancestors did? If we suddenly wander along some road, where will it lead us?"

"They are concerned about our village. We need to realize this. And so . . ."

Seeing that the village head was about to make a speech, Aku Yontan started jumping up and down.

"Concern?!" He glanced around. "And if our grasslands are destroyed, will they be concerned about that? You tell me. Whether it's building a road or whatever, didn't our fathers always say: Plowing any old which way destroys the essence of the water and the land? You're the village chief! Why should you be the village chief if you don't pay attention to this issue?"

"This decision was made by higher authorities. There's nothing I can do." The village chief was looking a little perturbed again.

"Of course! It was the higher authorities who made you village chief." At this point, Dolo also confronted the village chief. "We'll deal with this, even if you—the village chief—won't. There is no way we'll let them build a road here."

"Hmmph!" Now the village chief too was highly incensed. He started to leave in a tantrum, mounting his horse. "Let's just see if you can stop this!"

And with a quick yank on the rein and kick of the stirrups he rode off.

Within a few days, a great horde of laborers, trucks, and equipment had arrived in Nagshar village. Some laborers had previously marked the land with white chalk. They now began to plow following these lines with all sorts of machines. As they began to work, the "militia" of Nagshar village ran toward the workers—some carrying slingshots, others carrying Tibetan *chakors*. Having no idea what this was about, the road crew quit their machines, got into their trucks, and fled the site immediately in great fear. Feeling even more heroic, the Nagshar militia attacked the now abandoned bulldozer with stones and their metal nunchuckas. Once the glass had been smashed and the metal body completely wrecked, they left the site shouting "*Lhagyal lo*!" When they reached their camp, Aku Yontan's face glowed with victory. "This was something we had to do. A few more times, and they'll have had enough. They'll have to leave then." As he spoke, everyone nodded in agreement, their hearts filled with confidence.

It was unbelievable. Within two days, the township head arrived leading several men from Public Security. He had a few of the young men in the village arrested and then proceeded to severely criticize the village chief. Finally, he began to lecture the village residents: "People! My brothers . . ." The district head stood amidst the people with his hand raised high. "This recent affair is a mistake. You should be happy that a road is being built. The higher authorities were concerned about this on *your* behalf. Our village is still backward because it doesn't have a road. Think about it. As it is now, whether you're going to the county seat or to the township center, everyone has to transport things by yak. Those who have horses ride them, but for those without a horse, it takes two days to go by foot. *Two days*!" He held up two fingers. "It's exhausting, no? With the road, you will be able to go by truck and get there within one hour. So a road is something to be happy about. This opposition we have here is a real mistake. Don't you think?"

Not a single villager—old or young—agreed, but they knew it wouldn't be wise to talk back to the township head. Rather, they signaled their disagreement by standing with their heads averted as if they weren't listening.

"So that's what we'll do then," the township head continued. "Your recent destruction of the country's equipment is a breach of the law. If there are still agitators who aren't happy about the situation, they will most certainly be arrested. You'd better not learn any lessons from these bad sorts. Construction of the road will be resumed starting tomorrow."

With these closing words, the young men under arrest were herded into a truck and driven away. At the sight of the young men being taken away, the people of Nagshar village felt afraid. Everyone stared dumbfounded after the truck—eyes wide, mouths open.

"Maybe . . ." Several moments passed. It was as if Aku Yontan had just emerged from a deep spell of thought. "Maybe we didn't handle this quite right. Now we'll have to think of some other tactic."

Everyone nodded their heads and appeared to agree, but no one came up with an alternative plan that day. They returned home and tried to think of something.

Within three days, construction was resumed.

That day an old man called Chaglog, who was typically rather dull-witted, thought, "Anyway, they would never take a human life." Feeling heroic, he walked into the demarcated work site and lay down in front of the bulldozer. The road crew stopped plowing for a while and gathered round to watch the spectacle, asking out loud, "Is he insane?" A few people walked up to him and made various motions to signal that he needed to clear the road. The old man remained silent without stirring. However, within a short while he started as if remembering something and quickly unwound the belt from his waist. As he pulled his *chupa* up around his head, the construction workers could do nothing but shake their heads. Chaglog stayed this way for the entire day and the road crew was unable to continue their work.

"Now *this* is a tactic!"

"Right. They would never take a human life."

"No. Who has the right to take a human life?"

Seeing what Chaglog had done, everyone in Nagshar figured this was a good strategy. They became inspired again.

"So, that's what we'll do." Aku Yontan finally said. "Now, we'll do it like this. Each day we will take turns one by one laying down at the work site. I'll go tomorrow. Dolo will stay there the next day. Then, we'll see."

On the fourth day, Aku Yontan set off early at down and at the same spot where Chaglog had lain down the day before removed his belt. He took off his shoes. He pulled his *chupa* up around his head and lay down. When the road crew arrived for work, they were amazed to see that yet another body was sleeping on the same site as yesterday. The captain of the crew paced back and forth, smoking all the while. He thought. Finally figuring that it was not possible for there to be so many crazy people, he decided, "Anyway, if I can scare him a bit, then we will know for sure." He drove the bulldozer up alongside where Aku Yontan lay. Still, the old man didn't stir. But when the road crew captain planted the bulldozer shovel deep into the ground and prepared to lift Aku Yontan and the patch of earth where he lay, the old man was frightened. He threw aside his *chupa* and rolled over several times. Then he got up forgetting even to put on his shoes and fled the worksite.

"Oh, it's really a sign of bad things to come." When Aku Yontan returned both eyeballs were rolled upwards in fear. "They are as brazen as an old bull tearing up the land with its horn. They were even ready to tear off a huge chunk of land and carry it away. Honestly, they even might be stronger than a wild yak."

"Is that possible?"

"Why not?" The village head gave a condescending smile and surveyed the group. "Anyway, it would be better if you didn't attempt a stand-off with the machines. They know no compassion."

Everyone slowly turned toward the village head and nodded their heads automatically . . .

Nagshar Village, as everybody knows, is a remote village in our county. But with the completion of the road this year, many trucks loaded with wool and whatever else now frequently roll by and the people of the village are elated.

NYIMA TSERING'S TEARS

WOESER

TRANSLATED BY JAMPA, BHUCHUNG D. SONAM, TENZIN TSUNDUE, JANE PERKINS

It was one of those hot summer days in 1999. As usual the Tsuglakhang was packed with pilgrims and tourists. And, as usual, Nyima Tsering was at the entrance selling tickets and ready to give tours in English or Chinese to visitors from far away. This was his job. Unlike other lamas, he was called a "tour-guide lama" in the press or on TV. Yet he was not only a tour guide, he also held many other titles, such as Member of the Standing Committee of the People's Assembly in Lhasa. So, in the news on Xizang TV and Lhasa TV we often saw a young monk in his maroon robes sitting amidst taciturn-looking officials in their laymen's clothes. He always looked calm, sensible, and self-assured.

On that day, someone suddenly told him to submit two photographs to the department that handled passport applications. Nyima Tsering was told that he was to fly to Beijing a few days later, where he would join other officials from various government departments to attend an international human rights convention in Norway. Norway? Wasn't that the country where the Dalai Lama received his Nobel Peace Prize in 1989? Nyima Tsering felt slightly excited and uneasy. When he went to submit his photographs, a man there noticed his strange expression and said: "Relax, the people you will be traveling with are all high-ranking. They won't be like the officers in Lhasa who know nothing."

Soon Nyima Tsering boarded an airplane alone to Beijing. Of course, there were people who saw him off and received him at both ends of the flight. He couldn't quite remember who he met or what he said. Two days later he was on board again with another ten to twenty member delegates heading to Norway. He could barely remember anything on the way. This was Nyima Tsering's first overseas trip. However, compared with human rights, other matters were just not that important to him. What else but the convention could have concerned him so much? After all, he was the lone Tibetan coming from Tibet and the only lama in monastic robes.

The people with him were indeed different. They were older than him and, unlike the Lhasa officials, they looked well-educated, had good manners, and were not loud-mouthed nor bossy. To this day, Nyima Tsering still remembers an official from the Committee for Nationality and Religion, at an embarrassing moment when he couldn't hold back his tears, quietly asking, "Are you feeling unwell?" Finally, when he did burst into tears, no one demanded any explanations. That was a kind of understanding that Nyima Tsering appreciated very much.

These days, whenever the convention is mentioned, Nyima Tsering tends to avoid talking about a lot of details, such as the convention's proceedings, participants, contents, its background, environment, atmosphere, or the gatherings, discussions, and sightseeing that took place outside of the convention. In fact, the incidents that Nyima Tsering remembers come out of nowhere, from deep in his heart where they can no longer be suppressed. The first incident that he remembers occurred when the morning session of the first day was over, on the way to a lunch party at the Chinese Embassy. The worries Nyima Tsering had for so long were receding, since nobody had bothered him or asked him questions that were hard to answer. It was pleasant to watch the elegant Scandinavian street scenes pass by as they drove and Nyima Tsering began to chat with the foreigners sitting next to him. Gradually, he seemed to have returned to his confident self who was used to leading foreigners around the Tsuglakhang. Therefore, when the car suddenly stopped and its door was pulled open, the sound of people, oh, that sound of people, that sound of many people, was just like sudden thunder coming face-to-face with Nyima Tsering. He felt like he had been hit. It was like the aftershock of a big explosion in his head. He almost lost consciousness and could barely move.

"Gyami" . . . "Gyami lama" . . . "Communist lama" . . .

Outside the embassy, scores of angry faces had features that couldn't be more familiar to Nyima Tsering; scores of mouths were shouting in a language that couldn't be more familiar. These were men and women of his age, and these people shared the same blood as Nyima Tsering. The only difference was that they were exiled Tibetans; he and he alone was the "liberated Tibetan" from Tibet. However, at that moment, in the city where the Dalai Lama had received the Nobel Peace Prize in front of the Chinese Embassy, he and they were like two completely divided formations.

Also, they came with several banners on which they had written "Chinese, Give Us Back Our Home" in Tibetan, English, and Chinese.

Everyone else got out of the car, ignoring the scene, and moving straight ahead. But he couldn't move. How could Nyima Tsering do that? Afterwards, no matter how hard he tried he just couldn't remember how he had negotiated that short distance between the car and the building. Yet, it was certainly the longest and most difficult path he had taken in the thirty-two years of his life. His Tibetan monastic robes were like a brightly blazing flame, the disgusted looks of the protestors were like drops of oil or boiling butter, making the fire more intense. Those splattering drops of burning butter scattered on his bowed head, his bent back, and his shuffling legs.

Nyima Tsering's voice became sharper, and he said, "What could I do, what could do, I was wearing this . . ." Tugging at his burgundy robe, which looked so brilliant under the sun, he quietly kept repeating this as though talking to himself.

"Since then," Nyima Tsering recalled, "I was never able to feel light-hearted. For four days I came to understand what it means to be an ant on a hot pan." The hot pans were everywhere and there was no cool place to hide.

By the time Nyima Tsering had finally walked that short path of ordeal, he was completely wounded. He felt deep scars of pain, the deep marks of a branding iron. This branding iron was so painful that he wanted to cry, but there were no tears. The other people in the embassy pretended that nothing had happened, or, one might say, they were used to looking but not seeing. No one mentioned the drama. They were all talking about something else. While everyone was politely chatting and eating, only Nyima Tsering couldn't swallow, as though a fish-bone was stuck in his throat. This was the first time he had seen so many exiled Tibetans of his own flesh and blood in a foreign land. Though they were only a few feet away, it was as if they were separated by ranges of mountains.

Many people must have said things to Nyima Tsering. Yet, none of it mattered or was of any consequence. He listened to them without real attention, listened and forgot. His heart was wounded and he had lost his spirit. And yet he remembers that besides the sympathetic glances of the foreigners in the car, there was an official from Beijing who quietly asked, "Are you feeling unwell?" Nyima Tsering nearly nodded his head. The man looked gentle and polite. No sooner had the worries that accompanied him for days vanished than they appeared again.

The worries that had been growing in his mind since he left Lhasa were hard to allay, and now more concerns had been added. "What if I step out of the door and run into them again, will they despise me, ridicule me, feel sorry for me? Oh no, now I am a 'Gyami lama', a 'Communist lama' in their minds." Nyima Tsering smiled bitterly.

So when he forced himself to cautiously step out of the embassy, still feeling unsettled, he sighed with relief. Yet, he suddenly felt lost. The agitating fellow Tibetans who had earlier gathered were gone, leaving the place empty. Where had they gone?

The second day went smoothly.

On the third day, Nyima Tsering gave his speech, which was the real purpose of sending him to the convention. Because the voice of Tibetans had been missing from the previous meetings, the reasoning from the Chinese side about human rights conditions in Tibet always sounded very weak. The presence and testimony of Nyima Tsering was supposed to prove that Tibetans had human rights and that their human rights were protected. However, who would know what the dilemmas were in Nyima Tsering's heart? How to speak? What to speak? What should be spoken . . . and what shouldn't be spoken? He was really troubled. Although he was aware that he, in his burgundy robe, was no more than a stage prop, he didn't want to sound too out of tune or go beyond what was proper. Quietly, he asked the opinion of a foreigner whom he had begun to trust. The foreigner also quietly told him to talk in general terms and avoid mentioning anything concrete.

Nyima Tsering thus went on reciting the speech that he had prepared according to "the text" or, more precisely, according to "the text" of newspapers, radio, and TV stations. It was completely in tune with ideas that often appear in the domestic media—such as that the culture of the Tibetan nationality is fully protected and has progressed, that Tibetans have religious freedom, and that the monastic masses are patriotic. Everyone in the convention listened to him in silence. Only one person from the audience, an American, asked in English: "If that's so, why don't you have the freedom to meet with the Dalai Lama?" Nyima Tsering was dazed. Although he had already prepared himself for questions of this kind, on hearing the name Dalai Lama, as he did on the first day when someone pointed out the place to him where the Dalai Lama had received the Nobel Peace Prize, he was still dazed. But he immediately regained his composure and cleverly responded, "This is a political question, I refuse to answer." "What kind of political question is it? Can a Tibetan, a lama, wishing to meet his Dalai Lama be a political question?" No one else asked any questions, as if everyone at the convention understood his situation and his feelings. The fourth day finally arrived. Nyima Tsering had thought that the days of torture would soon be over, but the biggest blow fell on the fourth day.

Since it was the last day, an arrangement was made for the delegates to visit a famous national park. The parks in Norway were very beautiful and full of the charm of harmony and co-existence with nature. This cheered up the young lama, who had grown up on the rooftop of the world. While he was looking around, a young woman approached. Despite the way she dressed in a T-shirt and jeans, no different from the foreigners around, Nyima Tsering recognized at first sight that she was a Tibetan with a typical Tibetan face, Tibetan aura, and Tibetan character.

The woman walked toward Nyima Tsering with her arms outstretched and looking as if she'd run into a long-lost friend. All of a sudden Nyima Tsering was in a trance, thinking he had met and known this woman before. He too couldn't resist holding the woman's hands. But, very unexpectedly, the woman not only refused to let go of his hands but began to cry loudly. With tears flowing, she said to him in Tibetan, "Kusho, what are you doing here? What are you doing with these Chinese? You are a Tibetan, remember you are a Tibetan, don't be with them . . ."

Nyima Tsering was embarrassed, nervous, and felt very sad, but he was neither able to withdraw his hands, nor could he find any words to say. A crowd began to gather. They were all foreigners, very curious at a monk in his red robe being clung to by a crying woman. None of the delegates intervened. Instead, they quickly moved away, looking as though it had nothing to do with them, which could in some way be a kind of sympathy and understanding. The man who had been sent by the embassy to follow Nyima Tsering for these four days opened his mouth: "Let's go, Nyima Tsering. Leave her."

Of course the Tibetan woman couldn't understand Chinese, but she could guess what that meant. She got angry and was trying to shout at him in English. Nyima Tsering hurried to stop her while repeatedly saying to her, "I know, I know, I know . . ." The Tibetan woman kept weeping and said, "If you really know, then don't go back." By now, with great difficulty, Nyima Tsering blurted out what was really in his mind. "How can I not return? Our home is there. If we all leave, to whom will Tibet be left?" As he said those words he could no longer hold back his tears. They drenched his eyes.

Eventually some people came to help them out of their predicament. These were Tibetans who had been sent by their work units in Lhasa—such as the TAR Academy of Social Sciences, Tibet University, and the library—to take short-term advanced courses in Norway. Nyima Tsering didn't know them, but he could tell that they were just like him—Tibetans from Tibet.

But even to this day Nyima Tsering wonders why there were so many Tibetans from different backgrounds gathered there that day. Of course, at the time he couldn't think that much. In a big hurry, he pulled himself out of the grip of the woman who was still crying. He quickly dried his tears with his robe and rushed to rejoin the delegates.

"Kusho," one of the mediators stopped him and kindly advised him: "If anyone asks you what has happened, just tell them someone from her family has passed away and that she asked you to light butter lamps and do some chanting for her dead relative in the Jokhang once you get back to Lhasa." Nyima Tsering quickly nodded his head and felt that stabbing pain again in his heart. No one glanced at him or even said a word when he was approaching them. It was as if nothing had happened, nothing worth talking about.

Finally, it was time to leave Norway. But not right away. The delegation had to wait for a long time at the airport—more than two hours. The leaders and cadres from the embassy, including the man who had never been apart from Nyima Tsering for the previous four days, had already left after dropping the delegation at the airport. In those long hours in the bright, spacious, and comfortable airport lobby, people sat, stood, or moved around. No matter which country they were from, everyone looked free and relaxed. Nyima Tsering also strolled around freely. No one seemed to watch him particularly, which made him feel that he could go anywhere he wanted. In a flash, an idea popped into his mind: "What if I don't go with them? After all, the passport is with me and I have enough money. If I go to buy another ticket for somewhere else . . ."

Of course, the idea was just a flash. As I mentioned earlier, Nyima Tsering was always calm, sensible, and self-assured. So, in the end the ant on the hot pan went back with the delegation.

Returning to where he had come from seemed like the best arrangement for him. Yet, while the flight slowly departed from Oslo Airport, and while Norway—the symbol of the free world—was gradually left behind, two streams of tears silently ran down Nyima Tsering's bony cheeks.

HUNTER'S MOON

JAMYANG NORBU

He went over the ridge at midnight. The moon was low and gibbous and cast a mean furtive light over the gray and wasted land. Crouching low, he padded softly over the hard earth taking care not to be silhouetted. The stacking swivel of his rifle jingled softly as he ran. He stopped against a dark boulder and peered into the night for the patrols that he knew were there. But he saw nothing. There were only wavering shadows in the sick moonlight.

He thought of the eager young soldiers with savage eyes, burning in the darkness, watching his every move, waiting. He was old and very tired. His broad chest heaved with the agony of the long run and warm beads of sweat trickled down a face that looked like a lost battle.

In the far distance a flight of sarus cranes flitted past the falling moon, and he remembered the stories he had heard as a child . . . "Did you know, boy, that whenever the little marmots had to move to new lands, their king would summon the cranes from the great marshes, and every gopher would rise on a crane (much as you and I would ride a horse) and fly, far, far away?"

"I wish you could carry me away from here, bird," he whispered through his dry and cracked lips. "But only death is around here tonight," he thought, smelling the breeze that blew up to him.

He remembered, with some bitterness, that long night when they had walked into the ambush. There was a great deal of confusion and the old man could not remember much. Only a few stray, dislocated images lingered on in his mind: the pin-points of muzzle-flashes, like momentary constellations on the dark mountain side, and the black outline of a rearing stallion against the brightness of illumination rounds and dashes of fiery tracers.

The whole company, about a hundred and twenty guerillas, was wiped out. Only ten managed to survive and break out through the trap.

They fled north. There was no other way to go. In the days that followed they were hunted by patrols on horses and on foot, patrols of young and cruel soldiers, skilled, untiring, and enjoying the hunting of ten tired men who were running nowhere. The first to die were the ones who could not run—who lay down with useless legs and bursting lungs—and shot themselves in the head. Death also came unexpectedly in bursts of rifle-fire, when the small group was exposed on some open stretches. Finally, only the old man and a muscular boy from Kanze had survived. But the hunters were relentless. The boy had died near a large patch of rocks on the side of a craggy hill.

"He died badly," the old man thought. "But who can die with dignity when a bullet has torn open his entrails?"

From the darkness below the ridge, a faint clatter—falling rocks—drifted up the still night air. The old man listened. No further sound came from below but he knew they were there. He spat silently on the ground in disgust, and sat down to consider his next move. He wiped the sweat off his face with the frayed sleeve of his grimy jacket, and pulled out a small waterskin from his pack. He swilled the cold water around in his mouth, to warm it before swallowing.

"Rest a bit . . ." he told himself, "you can't go on now. Those sly young devils have sneaked up ahead of you, and you didn't hear them or smell them. You're getting old." He closed his eyes in defeat and exhaustion. Yet after a little while he got up, flicked the safety off his rifle, and ran, ducking low, along the side of the ridge. Descent on either side would now mean a certain death or capture, and he knew his only chance of surviving the night was in keeping to the heights and getting to the end of the long ridge.

It was difficult to move along the slope, and the old man was careful not to slip or kick any loose stones that might signal his presence. After about an hour he stopped to rest. The soles of his feet had been, for the last few days, blistered to bloody shreds, but he had ignored the initial pain and so now only a dull ache still persisted. There was never time to clean the wounds, and his feet were now stuck to his boots in a mass of torn flesh, dry blood, and pus.

The old man remembered the time he had gone down to India. He had met some of his old acquaintances and relatives, but there was no pleasure in the meeting. The people had changed. A few of them were reasonably prosperous and had advised him to leave the mountains and to leave the Chinese alone, and to settle down in peace. He recalled his anger at their words, and also his own inability to tell them why he was still fighting. It had seemed to him that exile had sucked away their manhood and turned them into strange empty *pretas*, without hatred, without pride, and without love. He had remembered the brightness of their eyes before—and the present blankness troubled him. The next day he left and went back to the mountains.

"Why do loved ones have to die and go away? Why do friends have to become strangers?" His thoughts rebelled against his resolution, and the solitude overwhelmed him more than his pain and exhaustion. "It is as if they had never existed . . . as if they were never real."

The moon fell below the horizon, and he got up. "But I am real, the enemy is real, and maybe the darkness that protects me is real."

Suddenly a streak of light arched into the night sky and a star-shell burst silently in the darkness, lighting up the harsh terrain for hundreds of yards with a scorching white glow. It remained suspended in the sky like a new angry sun and after a moment it descended slowly, very slowly. The wind carried the flare and its parachute toward where the old man lay. The relentless light coming from it pored over every rock and pebble, scratching into every gully and depression and tearing away the dark scabs from the very scars and erosions on that hard frozen earth. The old man hugged the ground and lay as still as the rocks around him. "They are hot on my trail now," he thought and smiled a little at the fuss they were making over him. "Just an old man, ready to die, even if they left me alone . . . They could have taken me a long time ago. I guess they must want to stretch out the pleasure of the hunt a bit, but it can't last too long now."

As soon as the flare burnt out, the old man jumped up and began to run. But another brilliant star-shell rocketed up the sky and for a moment he stood there exposed. Bullets whined all around him and one struck him in the right leg. He fell down but managed to roll over behind a large boulder. For a few moments the air around him was filled with the mad screaming of ricocheting bullets and he felt his back being peppered with flying flakes of shattered rocks.

The old man lay very still and after a little while there was a lull in the shooting. The rifle was still in his hands and as he pulled it slowly up before him, a sharp stab of pain coursed through his right leg. Reaching down, he felt the warm blood trickling out of the jagged wound, and realized he would not be able to walk.

"But where did you expect to go?" he asked himself angrily. "Do not be foolish. This is your last night and your last moment. Use it well."

He nestled the worn stock of his rifle between his cheek and shoulder, and felt a momentary glow of comfort at the reassuring heft of the gun. Below him he saw a few vague moving shadows, and lining up the barely visible sights as best as he could, he squeezed out a round.

He felt certain he had hit one of them, but before he could draw back the bolt, a bullet slammed into his shoulder. The shock threw him sideways, and a burning pain surged up his broken bones, tearing the flesh and muscles around them. Darkness entered into him and he wanted to close his eyes and submit to it, but a lifetime's habit of defiance willed him to consciousness. The old man struggled to his knees, painfully raising himself erect, and as another star-shell burst above him, he threw back his head and screamed his last battle cry.

The bullets tore into him, penetrating skin and flesh, cutting arteries and veins, slicing muscles, shattering bones; and as they left him, blasting open his back, they scattered the down stuffing of his old jacket and created a minor snow-storm of white feathers in the air around him.

He dropped to the ground and rolled slowly down the slope, picking up speed till he hit the bottom and lay sprawling on his back . . . very still. There was a long silence after that, disturbed only by the muted roar of the small landslide that followed his descent. But after the last pebble had clattered into place, it was very quiet.

He did not hear the boots softly crunching the ground toward him and he thought he heard his wife's voice calling him in from the field, but he could not recollect her face . . . he could not remember. The warm metallic taste of blood flooded into his mouth, but he managed to whisper the sacred mantra: "*Om Mani Padme Hum*. Hail the Jewel in the Lotus."

The sky was faintly tinged with the coming dawn, and from the east a single white crane winged its way overhead. The old man looked up and then closed his eyes . . . he knew it had come to take him away.

THE FLIGHT OF THE WIND HORSE

PEMA TSEWANG SHASTRI

TRANSLATED BY PEMA TSEWANG SHASTRI AND TENZIN DICKIE

From very early times, among the many unique customs of Tibet, one of the most conspicuous and ubiquitous was the flying of prayer flags, or what the Tibetans called *lungta*. Lungta literally meant "wind horse" in English. The lungta symbolized either individual or collective luck, fortune, or positive potential. In the neighboring country of India, there was even a popular expression, *"Jahan janda hain/ wohan Tibati hain."* Where there are prayer flags, there are Tibetans.

The Tibetans put up yellow, green, red, white, and blue colored prayer flags, printed with the heart mantras and prayers of Avalokiteshvara, Manjushri, Vajrapani, Amitabha, Tara and Guru Padma Sambhava, in addition to many others. They first carved out the prayers on wood blocks and then printed them onto colored fabrics. Then, they strung the flags together. The five colors symbolized the five outer elements of earth, water, fire, wind, and space and the inner elements of flesh, blood, warmth, breath, and consciousness. The Tibetans flew these flags on top of the trees and high mountains in order to prolong their life and enhance their merit, wealth, health, and fortune. Sometimes drawings of the garuda, the horse, the tiger, the dragon, and the snow lion were printed on the flags as representations of space, wind, fire, water, and earth respectively.

On a day in September a little over ten years ago, a sizeable crowd of people gathered in the courtyard of Tamdin Khangsar's house, located on the right side of Yuthok Street, in Lhasa, the capital of Tibet. The crowd was very boisterous and noisy. The majority of those gathered here were youngsters. The people walking on the street could hear Tibetan and Chinese songs coming from the party. The crowd was celebrating the thirteenth birthday of Tamdin's daughter, Lhadon. In the past, common Tibetans did not celebrate their birthdays. The only birthday celebrations were grand ones like the celebrations for the Dalai Lamas' birthdays. But these days, the trend of celebrating children's birthdays was becoming more popular in Tibetan society, both inside Tibet and in the diaspora. This was the fifth time that Lhadon had celebrated her birthday.

On that day Lhadon, who was in a playful mood, wrote a note in a beautiful Tibetan Uchen script, "My name is Lhadon, and whoever receives this balloon may please contact me at the following address." She added her home address, tied the note to one of the thirteen helium-filled yellow balloons and released them into the sky. Lhadon's friends also wrote notes and messages on other balloons. Some wrote their own names, some scribbled various drawings and others wrote prayers for Lhadon's long life on the balloons. After blowing the candles and cutting the birthday cake, they sent more balloons in the sky. All the balloons floated slowly up into the sky and after a while they disappeared from view.

Two weeks later, a yellow balloon sailed across the beautiful, cloudless sky in the Otok nomadic village of Lithang in Eastern Tibet. Dolma, the wife of Denma, was milking the *dris*, their female yaks. Her daughter Lhadon was helping her. While both mother and daughter were busy with their chores, the yellow balloon fell on the ground in front of Dolma. Dolma merely grabbed the balloon and put it down near her. But Lhadon became curious, picked up the balloon and looked at it carefully.

She saw the note and read the following message in Tibetan: "My name is Lhadon, and whoever receives this balloon may please contact me at the following address." She saw the Lhasa address. "Mother, look at this. How strange, my name is written on this balloon!" Lhadon said, with a funny look on her face. Dolma replied, "What are you talking about? Just do your work, Lhadon, instead of talking nonsense." Dolma continued milking the *dris*. Lhadon insisted, "Mother, I swear, I am telling the truth. Just look at this!" and showed the note on the balloon to her mother. Her mother, still disbelieving, glanced at the note and said, "Now don't try to be funny and childish. You must have written this yourself and you are just trying to trick me." Her mother did not pay any more attention to the balloon and carried on with her chores.

But Lhadon took the balloon into their yak felt tent and copied down the Lhasa address in her notebook. She thought the strange incident of the balloon over. She was the only person in her village called "Lhadon" but the address on the balloon was definitely a Lhasa address. How strange to believe that a balloon could fly all the way here from distant Lhasa, she thought. She reread the text written on the note. She wondered, could this be a dream or an illusion? For a week she kept thinking about the balloon, where it was from, who it was from. It was not an illusion. The balloon could be seen with the naked eye and touched. The writing on it was not hers.

She decided to write a letter to the address: "Dear Unseen Friend Lhadon, we haven't met each other. But I received the yellow balloon that you sent into the sky. My name is also Lhadon. I don't know whether your address written on the balloon is a true address or not. Anyway, if you wish, you can write me back. Your unseen distant friend Lhadon." She sealed the envelope and wrote Norsang's address on the back of the envelope. Norsang was a businessman who ran a grocery shop in Otok village. She had to use Norsang's address because her own family moved every now and then to look for good pastures for their herd.

About two weeks after Lhadon mailed the letter, Norsang called on their family and gave Lhadon a letter saying, "There is a letter for you from Lhasa. It came to the shop." Lhadon thanked Norsang and immediately opened the letter and began to read it. The letter said:

"My Dear Namesake Lhadon la, My name and the address are all true. Right now I am thirteen years old. I sent that balloon into the sky on my birthday. But I never imagined that the letter would end up with my namesake in Lithang. Maybe it's just coincidence but maybe there's a karmic connection between us. Judging from your handwriting and the content of the letter, I believe that you're also a school student like me. It would be nice if we can correspond with each other and be penpals. What do you think? Your namesake Lhadon."

Lithang Lhadon became very excited and happy to have the opportunity to correspond with someone in Lhasa who was not only of the same age but also her namesake. So she immediately wrote back a long letter mentioning how happy she was to have a pen friend in the holy city of Lhasa. She wrote about her life, how she helped her mother in herding the cattle, milking the *dris*, and selling butter, cheese, and wool in the market during her school holidays, how a variety of beautiful flowers bloomed on the turquoise-like meadow of Lithang during the summer when the popular Lithang Horse Races took place, and how a huge crowd of festive people gathered together to picnic, burning incense, singing, and dancing and taking part in the horse race.

In response, Lhasa Lhadon wrote back about her life in Lhasa, about her parents and her little brother. She also wrote about the history of the majestic Potala Palace, explaining that it was formerly built by the Dharma King Songtsen Gampo in the seventh century as the Red Palace, and later on expanded by the Fifth Dalai Lama. She mentioned the Jokhang temple and Sera, Ganden, and Drepung, the three great monasteries near Lhasa, where streams of pilgrims and tourists visited every day. She described the spectacle and the constant crowd in Lhasa Barkor, Lhasa's main market. She also mentioned that when she told her father that she received a letter from her namesake in Lithang, her father jokingly repeated the popular Tibetan proverb, "Oh, Ba and Lithang are the places of thieves, but we dare not say that as it is the birth place of the Dalai Lama."

And so in this manner, the two Lhadons continued to keep writing each other for a long time.

After three years of the girls' friendship, the family of Lithang Lhadon arrived in Lhasa for a pilgrimage and a meeting was arranged between the families of the two Lhadons. On the day of the rendezvous, when the two Lhadons met each other and came face to face for the first time, both the girls were stunned. They stood frozen and speechless for a few minutes just looking at each other's faces. The reason was that the similarity between the two girls was so striking and unbelievable. In fact, the only difference between Lhasa Lhadon and Lithang Lhadon was that the former spoke in U-tsang dialect and the later spoke in Kham dialect. Otherwise, in terms of their height, facial features, skin color, hair color, demeanor, and even their movements, they were exactly alike. The two girls embraced and touched each other's hair and faces, exclaiming all the while. Their family members watched them. Tamdin, Lhasa Lhadon's father, and Dolma, Lithang Lhadon's mother, remained speechless for quite some time, looking at each other and remembering the past.

LETTER FOR LOVE

TSERING WANGMO DHOMPA

Letter writing was no simple task. Take, for instance, Mr. Dorje, who received money for his daughter's education even after she'd stopped attending school. "She has no brains," he explained to Karma. His daughter had twice failed the fourth grade. He suggested they avoid the school topic. "Just write about the weather and how China is destroying us," he said. He was a widower and a cook in a monastery. He ministered over gigantic aluminum pots of food with a ladle in one hand and a bottle of home brewed *chang* in the other.

Then there was Mr. Tendor. He had been a chieftain in Eastern Tibet. As evidence, he still wore his hat and his Tibetan dress, even while lounging at home. When she wrote letters for him, Karma learned details of a country she would never see: lavish offerings to mountain deities on hills, week-long summer picnics where men shot at targets while standing on their horses, the electric air of stupefaction after a thief's tongue was lopped off.

Mrs. Gombo owned a noodle restaurant and had more money than all six families that lived in the apartment building she owned, yet she still had use for the $400 she received every year from a man in Florida and so she needed Karma's help to thank him. She had a Samsung television as tall as herself, a row of ceramic five foot-tall snow lions, and a leather sofa in her living room. She had resorted to dressing the sofa with a plastic cover because she did not trust her husband's relatives—an older couple from Tibet who had been living with them for a few months—not to ruin the leather. Pinching her bony arms together, she complained that she worked hard but never prospered. Karma, who was only helping these people write letters to keep her mother, Tsering, happy . . . and even then, not for any other reason than good returns in future lives . . . nodded her head slowly.

Then there were the Trinleys: Mrs. Trinley's face was thinner than the electric poles on the street. She had a mole on the ridge of her nose, and it was as though the mole, glossy and plump, sucked all the fat from her body. A hardworking woman who earned a few hundred rupees a day spinning wool for a carpet factory, Mrs. Trinley got right to the point when writing to June, her daughter's sponsor in Portland, Oregon. When exactly was the next check coming? Was it possible, for June, to send used clothes for her daughter as other sponsors did?

Her husband was not so direct. In his letters, he gave lectures, even on birds. "You are father and mother to my family," he would instruct Karma. "Write that. The sun is peeping out from the clouds like a new bride," he'd quote, with a grin. "Write that, too." In school, Karma had learned to stick to a format. Beginning. Middle. End. But if she protested, Mr. Trinley would remark that a good writer adapted to myriad styles.

Mrs. Trinley said Americans were kind people. Americans went without ice cream and movies in theatres in order to send little refugee girls to school. They were not crooks like the Chinese or the Tibetan and Nepali shopkeepers, who used unreliable weighing scales. She wanted to be reborn in America, even as a cat or a dog. Mr. Trinley said Americans had no shame; they had absolutely no control over their bodies. Americans farted as they strolled the streets of Kathmandu. "Just like that. In broad daylight and in public."

"I bet," he added, "their president lets out gas in front of his secretaries."

Karma had recently graduated from high school. Tsering, her mother, had decided English would not work in her favor unless it was used to help the elders. Earlier in the day her mother had taken Karma to a neighbor's house. She had pointed to the English letters on matchboxes, snuff bottles, sodden biscuit packets and to instructions on medication bottles ablated by fingers and time into a blur of lines. She had noted the expiration dates on vitamin jars; the elders saved everything even when they did not read, she had muttered. She had picked up two unopened letters. One letter implied the sponsor would visit in a year. That was propitious news and begat the next question: would Karma help translate when the sponsor came?

"Of course, she will. She has six months till she joins college," Tsering had said.

Writing letters would improve her English and her karma. But Karma had wished she could have said, "Thank you very much. I can find other ways to improve my English."

Now they were to compose a letter to a Mr. Gregory Hill for her mother's friend Pema. "You must keep everything in perspective," her mother said, leading Karma into Pema's house. Karma understood this to mean she was not to get ideas about writing similar letters. Pema was not yet old but Tsering explained her situation was delicate, required swift action, and that nobody else could be trusted with the task.

"This is a 'special friend' letter," she said.

"Love letter from Pema to this American man?"

"Is that all you girls learn in school these days? Love letter she says, and not even eighteen years in age," Tsering exclaimed.

"We must address Mr. Greg cordially, not too warmly," she continued, after a minute.

Dear? My dear? Dearest? Karma wrote the three words down on a sheet of paper.

"Dearest is too much," her mother said. "It will give him ideas."

Pema ran a shop at an intersection where everyone coming or going in three different directions was vulnerable to her gaze. Older girls from Karma's school said Pema was a forty-three-year-old widow with panties clogged with ideas.

"Strangers and government officials, even, are addressed as Dear,'" Karma explained.

"All over the world?"

"Yes, all over the world."

"Okay 'Dear Mr. Greg' then," Tsering said. "Mr. Gregory Hill. Like a movie star's name," she added softly.

Tsering had assumed the role of intermediary. She understood the story that was to take place and because she still had her husband, she was trusted to select the appropriate tone. She stated that the first letter would establish the direction of Pema and Mr. Greg's future correspondence. None of it mattered to Karma so she wrote, "Dear Mr. Greg."

"He lives in California," Pema explained. "He's tall and has feet the length of a Lhasa Apso. He is in tip-top shape and other than a filling in one molar, he's disease free." Pema's eyes were on Tsering as she spoke. Karma had never known her mother to have female friends but for the duration of the evening Tsering and Pema appeared close.

Tsering had not seen Mr. Greg but having studied plenty of American tourists, she said she had no trouble conjuring an image of him. And, she added, he had never married.

Karma suggested mentioning the week-long festivities of the approaching Tibetan New Year. Tsering said it wouldn't do to make Mr. Greg believe Pema was having too good a time. "A widow should not come across as a hedonist," she said.

It would be best to portray Pema as a responsible, respectable woman, but one who was capable of jollity, according to Tsering. Letter writing was Karma's craft but this was her mother's project. Karma could not write a word without Tsering checking on the potency of each syllable.

"Every word is a weapon," Tsering said, winking at Pema.

The first letter was cordial. There were questions about the size of the town Mr. Greg lived in (did any famous person live there?) and enquiries about the vegetables and fruits available in the market. What kind of deities did people worship in his town? Karma held her tongue to keep from answering the questions. To balance the ordinariness of the letter, she slipped in a sentence on the lingering reach of jasmine in the last hours of the day. Then, unable to help herself, she wrote about the dawn: how the opaque mist smeared itself so thickly it allowed people to believe it would burst like a balloon if poked with a finger.

She knew what her mother's response would be if she read the unauthorized sentences, "Why would Pema stick her nose into jasmine plants when she knows men are pissing into them every day?"

The letter done, Karma thanked Pema for the tea and rushed toward the door. Mr. Greg would have to respond and then they would take the next step. He would receive the letter in two weeks. If he wrote immediately, they could hope to see his letter in four weeks.

Karma was aiming to get home before 6 p.m. to catch a TV program on birds of the Himalayas. She had learned, a week ago, that the pigeons she found so dull and ungainly had originated in southern Asia several million years ago, even before humans had appeared. This fact, compounded with the idea that pigeons with white wings were not white but without color made her regard them with the same interest she kept for the tourists who came in shorts all year round. What did it mean that the white pigeon was not really white? It sounded like a conundrum the lamas would toss around in a conversation. The question, asked to nobody in particular, came into her mind several times a day when she encountered white objects.

She waved to a friend as she walked by her store on her way to the *stupa*.

"Meet my cousin Rinchen. He's here for the summer. He's a final year college student. You can ask him about college and stuff," her friend said.

"Hello, Rinchen," Karma said distractedly.

How many pigeons would it take to cover the *stupa* in pigeon droppings, she asked herself as she took a round of the *stupa*. A hundred or more beggars were scattered around the walking path of the *stupa*, their palms disciplined to receive. Tomorrow they would be elsewhere. Karma did not know how to speak of the destitute when she saw them in such large numbers; this was their country after all. Just the other day their milkman had said Tibetans were lucky bastards.

"If you were in your own country, you too would be selling your milk instead of drinking it," he said to Tsering. Tsering responded that it was harder for a poor Tibetan to live in Nepal than it was for a poor Nepali to do so. "We walked across desert and formidable mountain passes to get to this country. We walked without a map and without a name to your city." The milkman said he wished he were a refugee: perhaps then he would get a sponsor.

The milkman was knobby at the knees but nobody sent him money so he could stay home and play with a prayer wheel all day, he told them. He left his village at three in the morning and arrived at Karma's house at six with the final two liters of milk and a thin coat of perspiration on his forehead. Even his cow, he said, felt the pressure of producing. Some of his customers had switched to pasteurized milk in plastic packages that were carried from the factory in a truck.

"How would you like to battle with a truck?" he asked Tsering. His cows aged each year. They were no match for Green Valley Dairy Ltd. whose milk was advertised to be, "as pure as the milk from the cows in your grandmother's village."

"Hello, Rinchen," Karma repeated to herself, in an effort to recall how she had sounded to him.

Over dinner Tsering explained that Mr. Greg had a father, and a stepmother who was Chinese, not Chinese-Chinese but from Taiwan. A few months earlier while holidaying in Nepal, he had stopped at Pema's shop to ask for directions to a monastery and Pema, lacking English words to explain the road's circuitous path, had made a customer watch the shop while she walked him there. The next day Mr. Greg had returned with a bottle of Pond's Shampoo.

"Head shampoo. Why would he give her head shampoo?" asked Tsering's husband.

"A practical gift. First class choice," Tsering explained to him.

Mr. Greg had then gone trekking in the mountains for three weeks and upon his return to Kathmandu he had brought Pema a bag of dried apricots.

"This proves he is a man with sense. Common sense is very important in a man," Tsering said, directing her gaze at Karma.

Tsering had been fifteen when her marriage had been arranged in Tibet. She had first seen her husband on the afternoon of her wedding day. Whatever she saw she had accepted, she had once said. Karma heard her parents address each other by their first names, not "Daddy" and "Mummy" like some couples.

Three and a half weeks later Pema visited before the morning tea had boiled. She feigned nonchalance as her fingers fiddled with the envelope in her hand. Tsering said Pema must be embarrassed to be so eager about something she would have preferred to keep secret. But the letter had to be read.

Pema said she'd just come from arguing with Mrs. Trinley. People in the area, and Mrs. Trinley included, dumped plastic bags full of refuse right across from Pema's shop, which over time and under the blatant gaze of the sun, turned into putrefying sticky lumps of green and purple.

The stench made Pema nauseous all day. She had requested people to take their garbage out of view, to the big trash bins half a mile down the road, but nobody paid her any attention. She was now surprising people into shame. She had caught Mrs. Trinley just as she was about to let the plastic bags slip from her hands.

Might Karma or Tsering drop some hints about hygiene when they went to the Trinley's next, she wondered? She held a photo out.

"Oh," Tsering said looking at Mr. Greg, "Oh."

He had begun his letter with "Pema" —no dear, not even hello, just "Pema." The word, all by itself, was a rebuke. In a Tibetan letter the salutation could take half the page, even to a stranger. Tsering said they had to continue to address him as "Dear Mr. Greg."

"We can't go backwards," she explained.

Greg wrote that his father and stepmom lived an hour's drive from him, and that he met them every alternate Sunday for dinner. He was a postman. He walked a lot. It was not the same as walking in the Himalayas but it was preferable to sitting in a stifling cubicle all day. He lived in an apartment complex, alone. The fog was thick where he was, he wrote. There were days when he imagined it was an alien swallowing his car as he pushed through.

Tsering said he was a sensitive man. Why else would he mention the fog? Her cheeks were red as though she'd been in the kitchen kneading flour.

They decided to respond to Mr. Greg's letter the following morning. "Think about what you want to say," Tsering called after Pema, who left to get her photo taken at a photo studio.

All morning Tsering fussed over the gray in her hair. Did she look older than Mrs. Chonzom who lived down the street? Mr. Tsering said she looked older than Mrs. Chonzom because she *was* older. Tsering said she had not asked him for his opinion.

Karma never saw her parents lean or rest into each other when they sat side by side. She never saw any clues to intimacy but at night she often heard sounds escape their room: whispers, assenting laughs, conspiratorial pitches.

When Pema arrived the following morning, she laid a photograph on the table. Karma recognized the studio from the backdrop. Pema's hands were folded in her lap; the camera had caught her just as she was rounding off her smile. Her face was shaped like an acorn. Her features were small and grouped closely together. Her neck was an unsteady branch. Only her hair, black and thick as a log, triumphed, down the center of her spine. It was the sturdiest column on her frame.

Tsering told Karma to ask Mr. Greg if there was anything he missed about Nepal.

"This will give him the chance to say he misses Pema," she said, with a sparkle in her eyes.

"So this is how the game is played," Karma thought to herself. She had brought her fountain pen. It had a nib that allowed delicate machinations to letters. She had been saving it for two years but recently had come to the realization that if she didn't use it her mother would give it away. Everything she owned was prey to her mother's generosity. *I sit in my shop all day surrounded by perishable goods. All day I watch people and feel so much happens in their lives. Day after day, I sit in the one spot, watching them.*

Tsering was pensive after Pema left the house. She asked Karma to buy a calendar, one with space for notes. Karma had heard her mother tell guests more than once that she had no need of a calendar. Everything was in her head, she would say. Karma selected a calendar with birds on every page. She took the longer route on her way home. She did not see the college boy in her friend's shop. She could not recall his name. Her mother made a big red circle on the day they had mailed the first letter. She put a blue circle on the day Mr. Greg's letter reached Pema and hung the calendar in the kitchen.

Over the next week Karma overheard her mother ask Pema on the phone if she had heard from "him." During the day she called out to Karma with ideas for the next letter: the king was visiting the U.S; four of her favorite biscuits were manufactured by the same company in Nepal; nasturtiums were covering the walls; Pema was not willing to go to the internet shops and have Karma send emails because she didn't trust the boys who ran those computers; green was her favorite color (green was *Tsering's* favorite color.) Tsering said Pema had Mr. Greg's photograph in a photo frame under her pillow. She said she could calculate quicker in her head than anybody on her street but this letter writing business stretched over many weeks was bewildering her because she couldn't foresee or calculate the outcome.

Mr. Greg wrote that he missed the monkeys and the way they swung from the temple bells and hissed at dogs. He missed the urgency of mornings in Jyatha and Asan Tole when everyone was out in the narrow streets at the same time. He said he had not seen his neighbor for a month. The only proof of the man's existence was the echo of his shoes falling to the floor in resounding thuds, at the end of the day.

"How is your son?" he wrote.

The two women grinned at each other.

Pema wanted to speed up the correspondence. Seal the deal. But Tsering said the tactic in hand was a good one. Spitting letters at Mr. Greg wouldn't do the trick.

"You're not a young girl. You have to wait for him to say something," she advised Pema.

I know the world through neatly marked cans and bottles in the shop, Karma wrote. *Dried milk powder from Holland, beer from Denmark, sugar from India and pink toilet paper from China. The chocolate bars from America always include nuts or caramel. Do Americans dislike simplicity?* Karma went back and forth in her mind over using the words "humble" or "simple." Tsering debated whether to mention Pema's mastery of every item in her shop and her genius in eliciting a profit on each sale. She decided that they should write instead about the significance of fate.

After dinner, Tsering peered into her cupboard and declared that custom and obligations had taken over her wardrobe. She only attended weddings and funerals. "I was so happy the year you were born," she said to Karma. She had been twenty-five, her husband had found a job, and they had rented two rooms from a family friend. They had adopted a stray dog and bought a gas stove. She said the steel trunks they still used in the house to store their extra blankets had been purchased that year. She had imagined happiness to grow from that moment. Through the years she wondered how her husband had kept his happiness, sitting quietly across from her every day, never saying much, never demanding. In all their years of marriage he had never cooked a meal but he had never complained about anything she had fed him. His contentment was a burden, Tsering said. His happiness made her feel wronged.

She caressed Karma's cheeks and announced she was going to bed. She called out to her husband to lock the gate.

He said, "So early?"

"Why? Am I going anywhere that I have to stay up till midnight?" It took her whole face to suggest the sarcasm; her skin furrowed into an assemblage of delicate crimps around her eyes and lips. There was little to hope, from the lines, that youth would make a comeback even with offerings to lamas and foreign creams; for the first time Karma saw her mother as an aging woman.

Mr. Tsering told Karma her mother was getting to be like grandma, who never had any answers, only questions to questions.

He asked to be called Greg. He found himself searching for Pema's letter when he opened the mailbox, even on Sundays, he wrote. He recognized her handwriting. Her photograph was in a simple wooden frame at his bedside. Fate sounded so much like faith to him. His father was a landscape gardener who believed in trees, his mother exercised every day, even on days when it rained. Greg had studied Greek literature in college but had floundered at a profession so he had become a postman. He had entered it as a short-term job but being a man of habit he had sunk into its routine.

Come to think of it, letters are perhaps the most original and accessible forms of literature, he wrote. *Do chance and fate mean the same thing?*

Pema said Greg was too smart for her. Could Hindi film magazines be counted as literature, she asked Karma? Tsering fretted they had used the wrong word: they should have written karma, not fate. It was Karma's fault, she said. Young Tibetans attending English schools often thought of fate and karma as the same. The two are different; she exclaimed.

"If you write good letters and help people, you will reap good karma. Fate does not work like that, it is not in your hands. Why do you think I tell you to be good to everyone and write properly?" she said.

She wanted to know what Greg did in his spare time. Did he do calisthenics? Did someone come to cook for him? Did he play the guitar? What about badminton? Did he drink tea?

It seemed to Karma that her mother was willing to believe Greg could be the man for Pema—and the momentum of the letters from him made her believe that he was also willing. The word love had not been mentioned so far. Love, its absence or its imminence, was not to be a deciding factor in this project. Pema's first marriage had been arranged by her parents and there had been no mention of love.

"When your parents choose a man for you, they pick someone who will make a good husband and your duty is to find a way to love him," Pema said when Karma asked if she had loved her late husband.

"Even if you've only seen him once and don't know anything about him?"

"What is there to know?"

"But what if love doesn't come?"

"Idiot!" Tsering interrupted, adding unthinkingly, "It has to come. Look at me." She pointed toward Pema as though she had been referring to her.

Pema said perhaps the letter could now be signed, "with love."

Tsering said they should wait for Greg to do so first.

What chance was there that these letters, entrusted into one of the most unreliable postal systems in the world, would bring about love? Then a third letter was announced, in the third week. And then, defying all previous calculations came weekly postcards from New York, San Francisco, New Orleans, Dallas. The arrival of each postcard led Pema and Tsering to study the map for the distance and meaning between places.

The rains came and lingered shamelessly for weeks, drowning the shape of the roads. Garbage traveled around and clung to cross streets much like the thin teenage boys hooked on glue and local *arrack*. Tsering had signed Karma up to volunteer at a free health clinic organized by a Tibetan Women's organization. Rain or shine, Tsering said, the free clinic would run. By the time Karma reached the clinic, her feet were covered with mud. She washed her feet from the water that dripped from the roof's awning and settled down at a desk. Two hours went by in a blur as she took down the names of all the elders and their ailments. Every time she called out a name, the elders asked her to repeat herself.

"Is this your name and are you here with this ailment?"

"Yes."

"Then it is you."

Someone said hello. It was Rinchen, the college boy. Caught off guard, Karma asked if he was hoping to see a doctor.

"Maybe," he joked.

He asked if he could get her some hot tea. He returned with a glass of tea and a packet of glucose biscuits for her.

"Rinchen Zangpo. We met briefly at my cousin's shop," he said.

"I'm Karma."

"I know."

He was wearing shorts with rubber chappals like those worn by the little boys who played in the field behind her house. There were drops of water hanging from his glasses.

All day long, people came up to her with questions: were the doctors qualified? Would they give free medicines as well? Were they eye doctors? Most men said little, they held their bodies loosely beside their wives, just in case they were called upon to respond.

Rinchen said his cousin lived across the street and he had nothing to do. The rain, he said. He had an ease about him that made Karma aware of her own discomfort. She had spent most of her life accompanying her mother around elders. She was used to building a case against young men almost as soon as she spoke to them. Rinchen asked questions as though any response would be the right one, he teased the elders and made them laugh. He seemed careless—or was it carefree? She could not decide.

By late afternoon she was exhausted from defending the credentials of the doctors, the quality of the free medicines, and the continuing rain against the suspicions of people who persisted in finding flaws in an outwardly well-orchestrated day.

Rinchen asked if he could call her, if they could meet for tea before he left for college. Struggling for a polite way to mask her inexperience, she nodded instead. She left her phone number with him and rushed out into the street without opening her umbrella.

Greg signed the letter: *with love.*

Pema slapped a palm against her thigh and smiled. She and Tsering spoke at the same time; their voices peculiarly shrill. Pema said she was finally getting a sense of where things were going. Tsering, flushed in the face and neck, said she was pleased with the progress in these epistolary exchanges.

The commonplace was fertile grounds for exchanges. Questions were good tools. She cautioned Pema against brash emotional admissions and insisted the letter continue to be signed, "yours." She said she would consult the Tibetan calendar and time the letter to be signed "with love" on an auspicious day.

They had been exchanging letters for five months. In five months the post office had closed for ten public holidays, a twenty-year-old monk from a nearby monastery had eloped with a married Nepali woman, and the country had seen two prime ministers. The new party in power announced they would restore order to the country: they would bring electricity back and ban all strikes. Pema had trouble getting sugar and rice in stock because there was trouble along the India-Nepal border. It was a transportation strike, she heard on the radio. She wondered if Maoists lived in the jungles of America. How often did the electricity go off there? Was the public forced to observe curfews—no shops to be opened some days, no cars to be driven other days?

Rinchen called to say he was leaving in two days.

"Can you meet me for tea?"

"Now?"

"Whenever you are free."

"Ok. I'll meet you in an hour at your cousin's shop."

Karma had never met a man alone. She wondered if he would take it as a signal of her interest. Was she? Interested? Maybe he saw her as a sister or a good friend. She had never been asked to tea. Maybe college boys did this all the time. He was sitting in the shop on his own when she arrived. She told Rinchen of the letters she was writing for the elders, leaving Pema out of the narrative. She asked if college was difficult. He said not so difficult if you were organized and a little diligent. He offered to pick her up at the airport and take her to college when she joined in a few weeks.

"I am not that sort of a girl."

"What sort?"

She felt stupid. "I do not meet boys regularly for tea."

"I know," he said.

She found herself beaming, to his smile.

A few months ago the lights in the city went off for an hour. Everyone walked out of their offices and around the block as if they were in a ghost town. Nothing worked. No computer or subway trains. You could not buy tea or coffee even if you had money because the cash registers went dead. It was a very strange feeling to see everything at hand and yet have nothing.

Would you consider moving to America?

Tsering took the letter from Karma's hand and looked at it for a long time.

Was that an American marriage proposal, she wanted to know.

"Greg hasn't mentioned marriage," Karma explained.

"Well, not directly," her mother said clasping the letter to her stomach. "The question is indicative of intention."

Pema said she'd have to find out where a second cousin lived. She was afraid to be the only Tibetan in town. How was she to communicate with Greg once she got there? Should she start selling her furniture? Who could she entrust the shop to? What sort of gifts should she buy for his family? What if he did not like her once she got there?

"Married couples don't need to speak much to each other," Tsering said. "There will be plenty of things to do. Don't you see in the foreign movies, how people are always rushing here and there with big brown bags in their arms? You don't see them lounging around street corners or having tea on doorsteps, chatting with people as we do here."

The reply took three hours to script. *My husband who is no more will be happy to see me with a good man. A young boy needs a man to look up to. It is karma that brought you to my store. You could have just as easily stopped to ask Mr. Tamang for directions,* Karma wrote, obeying her mother.

Tsering was pleased, "Now we've tackled the whole problem of whether he is asking for marriage or not. We just assume he is. It's easier this way," she said. She said there was no going back. "America will be good for you, Pema." Pema could start again there and her son would have everything: a good education, a future, and he would care for her in her old age.

The letter galvanized them into frenzied outings. What were the colors for a new country? What did American men like? What about a different hairstyle? Tsering did not have the answers: she had known only one man as lover. For twenty years she had folded her hair into a tight bun and carried it behind her head. She suggested a green sweater for Pema. Green was a good color for a fresh start, she said. Pema bought two seaweed green sweaters, one for herself and one for Tsering. Pema cut three inches off her hair, all around. She coaxed Tsering to trim hers. Just two inches, she pleaded and Tsering allowed the hairdresser to release her hair from its habit of a clenched fist. Her hair was shampooed, cut, and dried. It was Tsering's first time at a hairdresser's. She said she left the salon feeling as though she'd lost four kilos from her head. Her scalp tickled, her hair felt weightless.

Alone in the kitchen with Karma, she wondered, "America is a long way to go for a man. Can a woman be happy in a new country half-way through her life? What if the man's a crook? Or already married?"

I am trying to memorize everything familiar here so that when I am there in California, I will not feel so far away. I will miss my friend Tsering. We both cut our hair and took a holiday. We even stayed in a five-star hotel. When you stay in a hotel, you feel different. Soon, I will see you. I feel my heart a stranger with so many emotions. How will America be I wonder? How will you be? I have never sat in a plane.

A few days before she was to leave, Pema brought over photos of lamas and her half opened packets of rice, cooking oil and lentils to Tsering.

"I'll keep them for you. One day you will need them again," Tsering said.

Pema laughed, "You are sending me to America and then you want me to return before the oil goes bad?"

"You are not coming back."

Tsering held Pema's hand all the way to the airport and attempted to joke. When they got to the departure entrance, Tsering offered a scarf to Pema and hugged her tight. Karma had never seen her mother cry for anyone outside the family. Pema was weeping noisily.

"Better stop or you'll be looking like an old lady when you reach America," Tsering teased. She waved till Pema's face became a tiny dot in the air. She did not speak on the journey home. When they passed the entrance to the *stupa*, she said she wanted to get off and do some prayers.

"But it is warm now," Karma said.

"It will be alright. You go home."

Karma excused herself from her letter duties a month before leaving for college. Rinchen had called her four times in the past month. After each call Karma tried to remember his face. Pema wrote that people were so carefree in the U.S. She said you could see in their walk that they felt unencumbered by duties. *It does not come easily to me, this levity. Americans do a lot of things because they feel like it, not because they must, like us. I think of you every day. I look at the time and say, Tsering must be having tea now, Tsering must be walking around the stupa in her blue shoes.*

Pema was learning English from the television programs made for children. Every afternoon at three sharp, she took her tea and sat out on her small porch. She listed what she did: once a week she sliced beef in thin slices and dried them in the garage; she made Tibetan butter tea in the electric blender; she made flat bread every morning. She kept an altar. Half of the goods were from China, India, or Sri Lanka. Even the salt came from elsewhere, she wrote.

Karma was surprised to hear the announcement over the speaker that she had a visitor. She walked out of the women's hostel to find Rinchen sitting on a wooden bench under one of the cement umbrellas built in the last year. He stood up when Karma walked toward him. He looked different from her memory of him. He held a small box of pastries toward her. She asked if he wanted tea and got up to walk toward the college cafe without waiting for his response. She took her time at the counter. Had she combed her hair in the morning? She should have worn her jeans. She did not know how to walk back to him.

When Rinchen said he should get going an hour later she wondered if she had bored him. Walking him to the gate she tried to think of questions. What could she ask him now?

"Thank you for the pastries," she said.

"Can I come visit you again?"

On weekends they toured the city. Rinchen always had a plan and a back-up plan. He walked briskly. He laughed easily and loudly. He coaxed Karma out of her tendency to weigh small decisions as though every outcome would be damaging. Yet Karma had still not mentioned him to her mother. In the beginning, she had wanted to wait till she was certain that their meetings had a feeling of longevity to them, and then too much time passed by and she did not know how to bring the subject up. On a few occasions she had practiced breaking the news to her mother and then Tsering had spoken about other feelings, of some sort or the other. Just a week ago, she thought there was too much wind in her body, causing her to be unbalanced. It was as though she was half-awake. She could not shrug off a feeling that she'd left a life behind. Was that possible, she had asked Karma on the phone? Karma had not spoken up.

Rinchen was in his last year of college. He was considering going to the south of India for a Master's Program in Geology. He wanted to know if Karma would transfer to a college there. Karma realized it was too late to seek her mother's advice. She tried to find the right time to insert the story of her attachment casually, every time her mother called.

Tsering said the neighbors to their south side were adding a story to their house. All day long, workers filled the house with music and construction cacophony. She said that she spent afternoons with her husband, just sitting and drinking tea in his office.

It was time for Karma's class. Tsering said she'd call the following week. "Eat all your meals on time," she reminded her and hung up.

Two days later, Tsering called to say they had received a wedding proposal for Karma from a family friend. The boy was studying in Toronto. Tsering said he had always done well in school and was a good boy.

"Maybe you can write to him," she said.

Karma said she was not interested.

"What's the harm in writing?"

"I don't want to?"

"You don't have to marry him. You only have to write to him."

"I like somebody. His name is Rinchen."

Tsering said nothing for a long time.

"Where is he from?"

Karma imagined her mother tapping her fingers against her hip as she spoke.

"What is he like?"

"He is nice. He brings me soap and flowers."

Tsering said, "Thank god he's Tibetan."

Knees, her mother said. Her knees were acting up. The most she had walked in the recent past was on the afternoon Pema had flown away. She had walked all afternoon and her knees had not bothered her that day. Now she struggled to get over a few stairs, she said.

When Karma visited her parents for the winter break, she noticed the calendar in the kitchen was still open to the month Pema had left. Tsering didn't take Karma around the neighborhood to the elders. Tsering said she hadn't replied to the last two letters Pema had sent and asked Karma to write for her before she returned to college.

English is taking so long to come to me and yet it's already conquered my son.

Pema had given up making bread. There was so much of it in the market, Pema wrote. She was no longer wearing *chupas*. She wore trousers and T-shirts with the names of cities emblazoned across her chest, which Greg brought back for her when he traveled out of town for office retreats.

Almost a year has passed and all I have to say can fit on one page. Is this happiness?

Karma reread the line out loud. Tsering said it was harder to evaluate happiness with age. Maybe a new place and new life turned things upside down. Or perhaps happiness was only recognizable when it was replaced with something else. She said she had never demanded happiness for herself but she had prayed for Karma's happiness every single day. She said the first time she had thought of her own happiness had been the day Pema had flown away.

She was hoping to have a big wedding for Karma. Perhaps their relatives from Tibet could come?

"I am not ready to marry yet."

"Very few people marry because they are ready."

"I want to finish college, get a job. I will wait till I am certain."

"Certain of what?" Tsering asked. Karma said she would know when she knew.

"How?"

"I don't know right now."

"Remember the day Pema left and I got off the taxi to walk?" Tsering asked.

Karma remembered it had been a warm afternoon and her mother had insisted on walking. Tsering said she had gone to her husband's office that afternoon certain of her feelings, but facing him she had not found the words.

"I examined my life as I stood before him and could not recollect my life as a seamless series of events. And yet, the future was full of desire. I wanted to leave. For a place I did not know."

She had been silenced by that strange certainty in her uncertainty, she said. Late at night, her husband asked if she was alright. She had seemed different in the office.

"I told him it was not important. I had stopped by because I thought I had lost something. I told him it did not matter anymore. The idea of happiness existed all on its own and outside of me. Where could I have gone to look for something that I didn't have a face to, or a name to?" she asked Karma.

Karma imagined her mother studying her face carefully in the mirror the afternoon Pema had flown away. Perhaps for the first time she had looked at the slight swelling under her lower eyelids, at the three lines on her forehead, and had looked into them for signs of options other than the life she lived.

She had seen Mr. Greg write, "Would you like to come to America?" in clear Times New Roman print.

She had whispered: *yes, yes.*

Two faint creases had criss-crossed her forehead, two tiny spots had appeared beneath the eyes. *Yes,* her mother had repeated to the image in the mirror.

THE CONNECTION

BHUCHUNG D. SONAM

"You have a background," said the police inspector.

It was the first thing he said after ordering me to sit down in the chair in front of his desk. He knew me from my many previous visits to the police station.

"I . . . I . . ." I intentionally fumbled. Having read enough detective stories and crime thrillers, I knew what "background" meant, especially when used by a senior police officer.

"Young man, go on, what do you say to that?" he said.

"Sir, I don't understand what you mean," I answered respectfully. I had found that things often worked in my favor when I used polite language and lots of "sirs" around government officials and policemen. These *saabs* liked authoritative language to reinforce their positions of superiority. On the white wall behind the inspector's head was a map of India on a rusty nail and a two-year-old calendar.

Perhaps the calendar was kept there for its image; an intimidating painting of the four-armed wrathful goddess Kali extending her tongue to her chin and adorned with a necklace of human skulls.

"Kabir, *pani lao*," the inspector commanded his peon. A little later a man appeared with two glasses of water. He placed them on the table, bowed a little, and left the room.

"Think . . . think about where you travelled and who you met over the last year," said the inspector, pushing one of the glasses toward me. I was taken aback when he said "year." I thought about how I should respond.

"Sir, I just came here to ask about my Identity Certificate. The police inquiry has not come through yet. It's been two years since I applied," I said. In fact, it had been more than two years. An IC is the yellow booklet issued to Tibetan refugees as a travel document, in lieu of a passport. It was a complex and laborious procedure to get one. When I called and got through to someone at the Regional Passport Office about the status of my IC, the lady who answered directed me to go to the local police station, since the necessary background clearance must come from there. The police had to issue a No Objection letter and send my file back to the passport office. If the slow-motioned bureaucratic juggling went well, the travel document would be issued within a few years. But any forward movement in the process would not happen without a letter from the local police station. And this was how I landed at the police station.

"I know. We have your file in there," the inspector said. He pointed to a cupboard packed with rows of spineless yellow cardboard folders each containing forms and handwritten observations clamped together by a neatly knotted white string.

He took a long sip from his glass and made a phone call most likely to someone of equal rank as himself. He mentioned Case Number Twenty-Five a few times and said that he had no new leads. I stared at the files and at the computer. The keyboard had turned yellowish from age and overuse and the Logitech mouse looked tired. There was a distinct mark of index fingers on the right click button. A 3D text screen "With You, For You Always" revolved slowly on the monitor. The CPU swished as the system fan blew out hot air from the hard disk. I felt anxiety building inside me. The phone call ended with a Hindi maxim that could loosely be translated as "the fish will land in the net."

"So, tell me," he said. The inspector rose from his chair, cracked his fingers and threw a few punches with his right fist into the open palm of his left hand. I knew about police beatings. But the inspector did not look like the type who would use his belt. His oil-soaked hair was carefully parted from the left to the right side of his head and his thick black moustache was disciplined downward into two horn-tipped ends, touching the edges of his mouth symmetrically. He wore gold-colored spectacles and had two pens sticking out of his shirt pocket. He looked like a seasoned teacher, except for his khaki uniform. Nevertheless, I was scared.

"Sir, I don't know what to tell you," I said. "I was a college student and I applied for an Identity Certificate. I hope to get a scholarship to study abroad."

"Good. That is good." He paced around the office. It was a hot day. The ceiling fan creaked as it circulated stale air. All the windows were closed. The room was suffocating.

"Tell me about your friends."

"Sir?"

"Your friends, tell me about your friends," he repeated.

"I have many friends, sir." Now I began to see what this was about. I hesitated, "Sir, you want me to name them?"

"Go on then."

"Tenzin Dhargyal, Sonam Paldon, Roger Walters, Hari Prasad, Abul Khayr, Ravi Verma—"

"Yes, yes. Abul Khayr," he interrupted, "Tell me, how do you know him?"

"He was my classmate in college," I replied quickly.

"Where is he from? What do you know of his background?"

"Sir, he is from Kashmir. That is all I know."

"We know that. Tell me more."

"Sir, what more can I tell you?" I said. This was false. Abul Khayr was my friend. We became close on the first day of our class at Narmad College. He was tall, incredibly intelligent, and strikingly good looking with his deep blue eyes, dark eyebrows, and fuzzy beard. He loved poetry like me, and Neruda was his favorite. He was born in a tiny village very close to the Pakistan border, where his father was headman. After his elder brother became a militant pledging allegiance to the Kashmiri separatists, his father sent Khayr to a school in the neighboring state of Himachal Pradesh and later to Narmad College. At the beginning of our second year there, his brother was killed by the Indian security forces in an encounter. Khayr wanted to go home for the funeral but his father said no.

I never heard Khayr talk admiringly about his brother. But his death had had an impact. I told him about the death of my own brother when I was ten in a protest that he organized. My brother was leading a group of villagers on a march to the local Party headquarters to protest against the pollution of the local river by a large mining company. The police opened fire onto the unarmed villagers. My brother was shot and then clubbed on his head. The police did not give his body to our family. Khayr and I filled each other's loss like hands in a glove. Nevertheless, the sports-loving Khayr became less visible on the playing fields. He spent more time reading. Once, by chance, I saw a brief quotation in his notebook: "O Allah! Make strong and firm the Muslim freedom fighters in Palestine, Chechnya, Kashmir, Philippines and in all places. Aameen." I never thought twice about it. Khayr always copied phrases he liked from the books he read.

That year we had planned to go to his home in the hills for our summer break. We made plans to trek the mountains and to tour surrounding areas. However, Khayr's father wasn't keen to have an outsider coming to his home. He wrote to Khayr that our plans of trekking and touring local villages were "foolhardy" in an area infested with separatist militants and a heavy military presence. Furthermore, he advised Khayr to go to his uncle's house in Hyderabad. Thus, instead, I led a group of Israeli tourists to go trekking in the lower ranges of the Himalayan mountains in Ladakh to earn some money. I was their guide and cook. Khayr went to his uncle's house. At the railway station, while we were waiting for his train, he recited an Urdu poem by Faiz, out of which one line became imprinted in my mind: "The dusts of old chapters have opened." The inspector now sat in his chair with a brown file in his hands. As he spoke, he flapped the pages.

"You are young. Your future is bright. Tell us what you know about Abul Khayr's activities."

"Sir, we were classmates and he is from a small village in Kashmir."

"You already told me that! Tell me something else."

"Sir, that is all I know. We were not that close, really."

"Really. Tell me more!"

"Sir, I don't know anything more."

"*Achha!* So you won't talk? *Hain!*" He threw the file on the table and stared at me.

"You know what happens when you refuse to talk?" he shouted, turning his head to his right where at the corner stood a *lathi*, a foot-long stick made of wood and studded with metal at the tips. He stood up kicking the chair backward with his right foot, walked to the corner and picked up the stick.

"*Jiski lathi, uski bhains.*" So saying, he lifted the stick high with his right hand and brought it down on the side of the table, cutting through the air with a thwacking sound. The brown file nearly fell off the table. A sharp twinge shot up my spine.

"A few whacks and you will pee like a baby. Now talk!"

"Sir, we were very good friends. But I haven't heard from him for a long time now," I said. This was partly true. After graduation, he went back to Kashmir and I lived in Delhi. During one of our phone conversations, he complained that his village had only a single phone line that often went dead, and the electricity was on for only a few hours a day. The local security forces turned up and routinely interrogated him and his family members. At one time he was locked up for three days in a police station. He sounded terribly frustrated.

"You know that his brother was a terrorist, don't you?" the inspector said.

"I know his brother was killed in an encounter with security forces, sir. I don't know if he was a terrorist."

"Tell me, when was the last time that you met Abul Khayr?"

"Sir, we met for the last time in Narmad College. That was in May." This was false. Khayr and I met in September in Pokhara, Nepal, when I was leading four Americans for a thirty-day trek to Mt. Annapurna Base Camp. I had dinner with him at a lakeside restaurant. The two of us sat together talking well into the night. Our conversation revolved around our days in college, but we did not talk much about what the future held for us. He wanted to be a teacher and I had a vague idea of becoming a writer. "We should just let life happen," I said. Khayr told me that he had come on a business trip with two of his brother's friends. He left the subject there and we switched to Neruda. When the night grew old, and the world sank into a deep slumber, we recited Neruda. Khayr's favorite was "Tonight I Can Write." He began to recite and I followed along. When we were halfway through the poem a plane roared across the silent sky. The sound echoed in the giant mountains. We saw faint ripples move across the lake under the bright sulphur lamp and our voices trailed off at. . .

> The same night whitening the same tree,
> We, of that time, are no longer the same.

"Do you know where he is now?" the inspector shouted. A lot of things cluttered in my head. I must stick to one line and not say too many things, I told myself.

"Sir, I don't know where he is."

"We have reasons to believe otherwise." The inspector had put his feet on the desk and reclined back in his chair. The soles of his highly-polished brown leather shoes blocked my view. I couldn't see his face. The numbers on the soles of his shoes were nearly worn off.

"In September you went to Nepal. Did you meet Abul Khayr there?"

"No . . . no, sir," I stumbled, wiping the sweat from my forehead. I was baffled that the authorities knew I went to Nepal in September. What else did they know?

"Young man, think carefully. Your friend is a suspected terrorist. He might be involved in the hijacking of an Indian Airlines plane from Nepal. So, tell me where he is or we can make things very difficult for you." He got up and pushed a file toward me. It contained newspaper clippings about the hijacking.

"I went to Nepal as a trekking guide and was with the group of Americans the whole time. Sir, I did not meet Khayr." I tried to sound as truthful as I could.

"We believe you met Abul Khayr in Nepal and that you know where he is now," the inspector said. "So do yourself a favor. Tell me, where is he?"

"Sir, I don't know. I haven't seen him since college."

The inspector just looked at me. He picked up the lathi from the table and placed it at the corner from where he picked it up.

"Sir, I really don't know where he is," I insisted. "We don't keep in touch. We lost contact after college. Sir, have you asked his family? Maybe his father knows."

The inspector said with a sardonic grin, "Vikas Bhai. Does the name ring a bell with you?" He smiled at my reaction. I had been hot and sweating in that office, but now I shivered for the first time.

Vikas Bhai was a muscleman and student leader with good political connections. He was my classmate and a friend of sorts. "You have any problem, come to me," he would say. When Bhai learned that I was going to Ladakh during the summer break, he asked me to bring him five *tolas* of hashish from Manali. I reluctantly agreed, partly because he paid more than five times the purchase cost.

After my trek, I bought hashish from a small shop behind the bus stand. The shop had only a few rudimentary items prominently displayed. This was a cover; since its real business was selling hashish. I put the stash in my dirty socks, rolled the socks into a tight ball and put it in a small black polythene bag. Once inside the bus, I left the plastic bag in the overhead shelf separate from my luggage. If there was a search, I could deny that it was mine. I boarded the bus first and got off last.

Bhai said that the stuff was excellent and wanted me to bring more the next time. So even after I left college, I was supplying him more than he ordered. If the police had gotten Vikas Bhai to talk, my life would be reduced to a dot in prison.

"I see you know that name," the inspector said. "Vikas Bhai was very helpful, very helpful indeed."

"Sir . . ." I said.

"Yes, go on," he prompted.

I had to think fast. I did not want the inspector dragging me into the Vikas Bhai affair. The plane hijacking had caused acute embarrassment to the Indian Government. It had the police and other agencies working on every lead. I must get out of the net set up to catch bigger fish.

"Sir, I met Khayr in Nepal." The words flew out of my mouth.

"Good, tell me more."

"I met him in Pokhara one night." The fan kept on creaking. The inspector's armpits were wet. My mouth was dry. I had to swallow before I could speak again.

"Khayr told me that he came with his brother's friends on a business trip," I added and sighed. I held my head in my hands, squeezing out the heaviness. That didn't help.

"Yes. Go on." He took a pen and a brown notebook and nodded for me to continue.

"We had dinner together and talked for a while."

"Go on," he said without writing anything.

"We talked about our time in college, our friends, books that we read, and we recited some poems."

"Did you meet him after that?"

"Yes, sir." My heart was beating fast. I stared at his desk and a small yellow sticker pasted on the glass top stared back at me. It said "Truth is my god—Gandhiji."

"When? Where?" he demanded.

"About fifteen days ago at New Delhi railway station."

"Where was he going?"

"He boarded a train to Hyderabad."

"Where is he now?" he asked without looking at me. He was writing furiously in his notebook.

"I don't know, sir. That was the last time I saw him." This was true. Khayr did not tell me where he was going. We did not speak much. The railway station was a mass of human traffic. An air-conditioned luxury train halted and disgorged hundreds of well-dressed passengers. We stood near a magazine stall. A small boy with a trained monkey came and the monkey danced. Khayr's beard had grown long and his eyes seemed gloomy. A little later the Hyderabad Express came and jerked to a stop.

Khayr looked around and seemed uncomfortable standing under the bright light of the stall. We moved to a bench behind a pillar. A large rat picked up a piece of bread from the garbage heap and ran into the shadows.

Khayr and I sat on the bench silently amidst the cacophony of the bustling station. People went in and out of the train. Coolies shouted. Babies cried. Music blared from a radio. A woman made high-pitched announcements through invisible speakers. When the train whistled and the green flag was raised, Khayr took out his notebook from his shoulder bag and gave it to me. We hugged. I tied a *rangzen* band around his right wrist. As he got into the slowly moving train he said, "*Phir Kabhi . . .*"

The inspector put his pen and brown notebook on the desk. He scrutinized me and called out to the peon.

"*Do cup chai lao!*"

A little later the peon put two cups of tea on the desk and left the door open. A surge of air rushed in. I nervously sipped from a white cup. The inspector made a phone call, probably to someone senior as he spoke very politely. He made a detailed report on the interrogation with special emphasis on Abul Khayr and Hyderabad, mentioning each several times.

A few weeks after my interrogation in the police station, a policeman in civilian dress came to my apartment. He asked me to show my birth certificate and other documents to prove who I was. It was the police inquiry relating to my travel document.

Shortly after that I read in a newspaper that two men suspected to be involved in the hijacking of an Indian Airlines plane from Nepal had been arrested in Hyderabad. The story said that the police declined to give the names since the matter was under investigation. The photograph showed police leading two men in black hoods with their hands tied behind their backs. I could not make out if one of them was Khayr. I threw the newspaper down and stared into the blank wall of my rented room. For a week, I could neither sleep nor eat.

Five months later my IC arrived. They had printed my name wrong.

LIGHT

TSERING LAMA

We live in an old city with almost no electricity—but every so often a charge comes, and we hear the hum.

It was winter, the dry season, and load-shedding meant only three hours of power each day after lunch. As Mother reminded us endlessly, this was just enough to store the charge for the electric lamp, run the water pump, and put on a pot of rice in the cooker for dinner. As a consequence, we watched TV the way we used our taps, turning it on only at the right moments. This was, I know, as difficult for my mother as it was for my cousin and me. Most evenings, with hours to go before we could fall asleep, Cousin Norzy and I would lie around in the TV room, draped over the sofa's armrests, a candle stuck on an empty jam jar between us, while Mother prayed in the kitchen. Of course, even as paperless refugees, we weren't strangers to this country. We were born in this brick and dust valley and were used to waking up to find uncharged cell-phones and light switches that were indifferent to our repeated pokes. And like the neighbors, we too spoke longingly of the 1990s when the power only went out every other day—or so we recalled.

But it was boredom, not the darkness, that eventually got to us.

That night, I remember making a few predictable, lazy suggestions: we could henna our hair, or read Norzy's ex-boyfriend's letters again. But my cousin only made a few low grunts barely audible over the crickets, stray dogs, and Popo's prayers.

Popo, my father's father, was visiting at the time. Though my father passed away many years ago, Popo was as strong (and short on words) as ever. He still lived in the Tibetan settlement a five-hour bus ride away in Pokhara where my parents met as children, fell in love, and built their first home together with stones and a bamboo roof.

My mother tried for many years to convince Popo to come live with us in the capital, saying that it wouldn't be a financial burden, but he refused. Instead, every year around this time, he came to the capital to renew his Residency Card (something they stopped giving out before my cousin and I were born) and stayed with us as he made many trips around the city to get the right stamps and signatures. The rules changed often and I always sensed in Popo the fear that he wouldn't get the paperwork done that year, that he might somehow lose his place in the country.

Over the hum of Popo's prayers, we could hear the neighbors cooking and fighting about their landlord's wife. Norzy and I tried to make out the details but the pressure cooker always hissed at the worst times. This was its way. A few cars and motorbikes honked at each other in a small traffic jam nearby, crunching the gravel as they wedged themselves out of the narrow roads in our neighborhood. They set off a stream of barks from the white Pomeranian who lived on a balcony next door, just as the last hammerings ended at the construction site nearby.

In the kitchen, Mother was reading aloud from an old newspaper she had placed under a candle stick. Despite my pleading, Mother refused to throw chipped tea saucers away, and instead used them as stands for candles.

"U-r-u-g-u-a-y. Ur-ghee."

"U-ru-guay," I said, straining my neck, toward the kitchen door.

"U-ru-ghee," my mother repeated.

Norzy and I didn't pass the Class Ten exams (she due to laziness, and I due to money—though my mother said for many months: *please just go to school, we'll borrow what we need*), but we knew a lot more about the world than her. We knew perfectly well that there were no jobs waiting for us in this country. The moment someone asked us if we were Nepali, if we had official papers, we were done for. We didn't even have any rich relatives with carpet factories to hire us. Still, Mother liked to tell us that we were too immature for girls in our twenties.

"Where's Nepal on this thing?" Mother asked from the kitchen.

"Lost, lost!" Norzy said with a giggle. "Forget it, *Ani*. Learn about the big countries instead."

I rolled over and slowly let my body slide off the sofa onto the carpet.

"Norz," I said through the wool burning my skin. "Going crazy here. Tenants went on pilgrimage. Turn on the TV."

Our tenants downstairs also used our electricity reserve— as a result of Mother's bargaining after they threatened to leave and take away our only steady source of income. This meant that we couldn't watch TV most nights or we would run out of stored electricity.

"There's no cable anyway," Norzy replied.

"No, there is now," I said. "I overheard the shopkeeper saying our cable company is using a generator."

"Okay. But this better not be one of your fantasies again."

As Norzy approached the TV, she said a little prayer, "*Om mani padme hum*. Please work."

When she pushed the deep-set black button of our old TV, the inverter shrieked and the light in the hallway—the only one left on at night to ward off thieves—dimmed and then returned.

Through the static on the screen, we saw a man's face flicker. The cable really was working, somehow, that night.

I knelt beside Norzy before the TV. Not too long ago, we were given twenty-two channels by the cable-man—thanks to Norzy's flirtation. But later it turned out that half of them were useless news stations showing the same faces every day. We were tired of those men in their suits and pointed hats, taking photos before signing agreements that meant nothing. Norzy flashed past Sagarmatha News, Kantipur News, Nepal News, Mountain News, and finally reached the good channels like Zee TV and Star Channel.

Then we saw in perfect, saturated colors, the living room of *Kasauti Zindagi Ki*—a bonafide, juicy Indian soap opera.

I heard Mother push back her chair in the kitchen and come rushing into the living room.

"Is that . . . *Kasauti*?"

This was my mother's favorite show. She sat down on the sofa and patted on the seat. "Come away from the TV screen. Your eyes . . ." We receded to the sofa but kept our gaze fixed on the screen.

The hero appeared. He was walking up the grand staircase to his new bride. Meanwhile, his mother stood in the foyer with an evil self-satisfied expression—clearly having brewed some trouble for the new bride in her home.

"Horrible woman," my mother said, shaking her head. "Turn up the volume!"

The hero then entered the grand bedroom where his new bride awaited his return. She was sitting on the veiled four-post bed, her delicate fingers caressing a photo of her family. The bride didn't notice that her husband was in the room: he came and sat gently beside her.

"Do you miss your home?" he asked with a knowing smile.

She turned to him and showed her eyes, full of tears.

"Isn't she beautiful?" I asked Norzy and Mother, but neither replied.

I clutched my shirt and scanned her face as the tears streamed down my face. Poor girl. Poor poor girl.

Just then, Popo came running through the hallway—shawl flapping at his waist, prayer book dangling from his hand—and went straight for the TV. We pulled back in disbelief, speechless as Popo flipped through all twenty-two channels, back and forth, back and forth. He muttered some complaint about how many channels we had.

"What are you looking for?" Mother asked.

Norzy and I bit our nails and bounced our legs at the thought of all the precious *Kasauti* moments passing by.

When a news anchor popped up on the screen, he stopped. It was channel three: Kantipur News, a channel we could always get.

"Popo!" I cried out. "This is a local channel. It's just a local!" Startled by my shouting, Popo accidentally changed the channel. He quickly went back to Kantipur News and flailed his prayer book in my direction

"I'm seeing about the strike," he finally said.

Popo had meant to return to Pokhara any day, but a few days earlier someone called an indefinite countrywide strike. Every third day, it seemed someone would call for a strike. As a result, only pedestrians, cyclists, and rickshaws were allowed on the roads. Everything from schools to shops had to be closed as well—though the smaller shops would open partway, and close their shutters when strikers came by. This was the way of the country now.

The news anchor was in mid-sentence: "—marked new protests begun by the hotel unions. The hotel manager has cited difficulty in meeting the demands, saying that occupancy has been at a ten-year low due to a lull in tourism— "

"So best not complain now!" The newly appointed minister of energy flashed on with an unrelated press conference.

Ever since the Maoists had kicked the old king out, it was one new official after another, making grand speeches before being replaced by another politician.

"If the king and his useless bourgeois minions had planned things properly years ago, I wouldn't have this mess on my hands. I don't want anyone here saying this and that if they don't understand the history of this country. So put the blame where the blame belongs because my sight is clear and my hands are clean!" He smiled and showed his palms to the reporters who laughed, nodded, and scribbled onto their pads. "The government is also announcing that from tomorrow on, electricity will be cut up to fourteen hours a day due to shortages and the poor conditions of the hydroelectric dams. After that, the power cuts will be sixteen hours a day. Thank you. That's all."

"*Six*-teen?" I whispered. That meant four hours of electricity during the day, and four hours in the middle of the night.

"Eat shit!" Mother blurted out at the TV.

Soon, it was clear that Popo had no intention of releasing his deathly stare at the news anchor. As the woman read the usual news of killed journalists and kidnapped activists, he listened intently, blinked, pretended to spit, and groaned like she was selling him pork when all he wanted was dried yak meat.

"Roads, roads! When do they open? Tell me something useful!"

The three of us sank into the sofa and I thought about when I was little and all I wanted was to be a news anchor. To wear a smart business suit and lipstick. To read the English news in a British accent. My father used to tell me that I'd be the first of our kind to be on the news. That everyone would watch me and listen to me. And he would be proud because he would know that, finally, one of us had made it onto the television, which was the only way to be heard.

But now, for nearly half an hour, while *Kasauti* and every other worthwhile show was ending, Popo cursed the news anchor, her family, and her dog. He blocked the entire screen with his face, and kept his massive, wrinkled thumb on the channel button.

That was when the idea occurred to me. Turning to Norzy with a most serious expression, I told her that we had to go watch *Ghajini* right away, that night, before the cinema also stopped having power. This was the latest Aamir Khan flick, already the movie of the year though it was only a few weeks into 2009.

"You're right, cousin!" she said.

"I am, aren't I?" We were both a little surprised at how forward thinking I had become.

Mother, completely put out by Popo, reached into her blouse and pulled out her change purse for us. We went into our room where the battery-powered radio was always on, and began to get dressed. Norzy put on her red and white striped socks and white loafers. I put on my red hoodie and put my bed sheet on the floor. Then I laid down on it to iron my hair.

Norzy already looked amazing due to her new perm so while I tried to get ready, she dialed up our friend Sriti who worked in the cinema box office.

"Packed house tonight!" Sriti scolded us through Norzy's phone, which had been stuck on speakerphone for a few months.

A week after its release, nearly everyone in Kathmandu had seen *Ghajini*. It was the biggest film of the year with the biggest Bollywood movie star ever. My aimless cousin Changchub had seen *Ghajini* three times. And I even heard from him that

Aamir Khan, due to his magnificent looks and incredible talent, would soon get the Key to India—which they apparently wanted to *invent* this year, *solely because of this film*.

"Sriti, please!" I shouted into the phone. "Put two tickets aside quickly, quickly. I need some lightness." As I tugged my pants up over my leggings—I lack a curvy butt so I wear extra layers down there—I added, "Fatty please, don't be like this. Remember when I made two dozen dumplings just for you?'

"*Ke*? What?" Sriti replied, "I can't understand you." She was making fun of me, because even though I was born here and would probably die here, I still spoke Nepali like a Tibetan—which is to say, very poorly. But then she told us to meet her at the box office's side door in twenty minutes; she would arrange for some tickets.

"You, Sriti," I said, "are the best damn Nepali girl I know. If I had a brother, I swear, I would suggest he marry you!"

"Okay, good. That would double my dumpling supply!" she said and hung up.

In the taxi, we were euphoric, bouncing in our seats and gripping the door handles as we moved through the dimly lit city streets.

"There's everything in *Ghajini*," said the young driver. "Fighting, danger fighting, at the end!"

"I don't like fighting," Norzy said and flashed him a smile from the rear view mirror.

I checked my watch and hoped we would make it in time.

"Ah, romance too, sister. Aamir Khan's made himself an amazing body. He worked out for a year and a half."

"Wow!" I said. "Drive faster, brother!"

The first time I saw Aamir Khan, I was a little girl. I remember vividly the scene in *Qayamat Se Qayamat Tak* when he sang in a beautiful grand room at a party as his father watched.

The lyrics of the song were about a father who had high hopes for his son while the son said he needed to find his own path. As Aamir strummed the guitar and gave high-fives to all of his friends in the room, his father watched, filled with pride.

It was just after my own father passed away; the movie was playing in a small tin shack near our house. Mother sent me and Norzy there to get us out of the house because every day for forty-nine days after his death, our house was overtaken by monks who helped my father through the process of discovering his death, of letting go of the world, and of finding a new life.

Although Mother had gotten rid of Father's photos right away to ease the letting-go, the monks needed to burn a photo of him near the end of each day's prayer. After a day of all of us searching the house, I found a picture of my father in my clothes cabinet, tucked into an envelope folded into a pair of jeans. It was from our trip to India when I was just a baby—from one of our few family vacations. Father is standing with a field behind him, and I'm at his side, my hand in his. He looks worried because my right foot is shoeless. I had just lost my shoe on the bus ride to the picnic site. I saw it slide off in the crowded bus when he was carrying me, but I didn't tell him. I wanted to see if he would notice because he was always giving me his attention. But he didn't see the shoe fall off, and I didn't say anything about it to him—even when he asked me where it went.

Every night for a week, I went to see that Aamir Khan movie. While Norzy slept in her seat beside me, I watched Aamir Khan and his father deal with separation, with new love, and with an uncertain future. I cried secretly in the cinema, wiping my tears like a heroine in the films, arching my fingers like a peacock wing and using only my index to wipe. I cried for Aamir.

Oh, and in the song, the one at the party where Aamir Khan sings, his skin was so fair. His black hair was parted down the middle, so shiny, so bouncy, just like my heart had felt for a moment.

When the taxi reached the cinema, we rushed to the box office. The crowd was already filling up the narrow entryway.

As we stood before the hall doors, Norzy begged me to get whatever was left at the concession stand. She said she hadn't eaten all day since Popo poked at her potbelly.

"A samosa, a burger, or a chili chicken. *Anything*, my darling."

I am unusually tall and often the task of getting things in crowds falls to me: tickets, food, directions. So I began to shove past all the average sized people until I was at the counter. The samosas and burgers were gone, but I grabbed a bag of masala chips, Cheese balls, popcorn, Twix, a Kit Kat, a Coke, a Sprite, and the last veggie wrap in the rotating plastic display. Looking into my wallet, I realized that I would only have twenty rupees left from Mother's money after this. We would have to walk home. Still, I decided it was worth it to walk since we might not have a night like this again for a long time.

"Are you feeding the entire row?" said some voice to my right.

"No. Just me and Norzy," I replied, not even bothering to look at him.

My mother was always happy with my standoffish attitude toward boys. She often swatted at Norzy for laughing too loudly in public, telling her it attracted the opposite sex.

"Who is Norzy?"

I turned my head to see the face of this person who clearly thought he was something special and deserved to know all of my business. Then I realized who it was.

Yes, he nodded and silently said, Yes, it's me. Aamir Khan.

Standing just an arm's length from me, impossibly near. I kept my eyes fixed, fearing that he would leave, but I could see that no one else in the theatre was paying him any attention. No one seemed to notice who was standing beside me, even as Aamir Khan's hair was shaved just like in the movie poster for *Ghajini*—with the curved scar from his forehead to the tip of his scalp. His character, a romantic business tycoon, gets amnesia after being struck in the head with a metal pipe. That's why he had the scar.

It was as if the rest of the world was behind a thick pane of frosted glass, and somehow I was given entry to this secret space. Standing in front of him, staring, I felt like a crow. Ready to be shooed away.

"Norzy's my cousin." I finally managed to form the words. "She's only four foot nine so she gets ignored at the concession stand."

"That's very short. Compared to you," he said.

"Yes, I have to hunch when I'm with her. It's embarrassing. I'm like a beast."

"You are a fantastic height."

"Really? Wow."

"Will you share some of the food with me?" he asked with a smile.

I looked down at my hands and saw that I had dropped the popcorn on the ground. But the veggie wrap was still there, resting on my palm though I couldn't feel its weight.

"Would you like this?" I asked hopefully. Then I turned to the counter where the masala chips sat, along with all the other things I had bought. They were all glowing but I couldn't focus my eyes to see what was what. "Or any of these?" As I reached for them, the veggie wrap slipped from my hands. It was as though I had no bones, I was so nervous.

But as the wrap plummeted toward the ground, Aamir Khan knelt down and saved it just before it hit the tiled floor. I was speechless. He was the same as in the movies.

Standing up, he smiled again, showing his small jaw and the naked inner corners of his mouth. I immediately felt embarrassed; I had seen such an intimate part of him—a part that even he couldn't see at that moment.

"Are you laughing at me?" he beamed, the hollow corners of his mouth gleaming like headlights.

"Laughing at you?" I sputtered.

No, I wanted to say. Aamir Khan, I would never laugh at you. I want to be a business tycoon so I can make my own movies for you to star in. I want to go to journalism school and be the only journalist in Nepal good enough to interview you. I want to hide and rest inside your sweater, and then let you hide inside mine. If I ever laugh at you, Aamir Khan, let me turn into a fish that is caught and left to rot on a dusty table in the market, eyes graying as I wait to be bagged and deboned.

"How do you like it here?" he asked, changing the subject.

Aamir was a natural conversationalist, unlike Popo and my mother and all the adults here who get that faraway look in the middle of talking about life.

"Here? Oh, god!" I said, nearly dropping the Kit Kat bar I wanted to offer him.

He had put the veggie wrap back on the counter—likely because it failed to live up to his standards.

"As my mother says, 'Our life here is just darkness, day and night.' I cannot wait to leave and go somewhere else—" But as I said this, his smile faded. Dark circles appeared under Aamir Khan's eyes. Just as the white sails on boats I'd seen on television collapsed when they reach shore, his bright expression dropped.

Quick, I thought. Quick! Say something else to him. But what? What? Selfish idiot of a girl. I'd managed to drop a fat water buffalo onto this sweet pot of yogurt. I'd taken away Aamir Khan's iridescent aura. I was not just surrounded by the groans and moans of this depressed place, I was infected. I had nothing but darkness coming out of me.

The concession worker to my right started to shout at me to pay—*pay!* A rush of noise came from every direction. The glass between the world and us was quickly disappearing and the crowd was coming back in all its force. I was desperate to stop it. But the doors for the theatre opened and the crowd became louder than ever. The usher started fumbling with people's tickets, tearing each ticket with gusto and slurping the spit around the flashlight stuck in his mouth. I heard my name called out in the hustle and bustle. Norzy was buried somewhere in there, in the crowd that was moving around together like seaweed, which I'd also seen on TV. Both heavy and light, held down to the ocean floor though always pulling away.

I looked at Aamir Khan and told him, nearly overcome with tears, "I have to go."

"I understand," he said, adding, "my heroine."

"Am I really? Me?"

"You are. Always have been." At that moment, he caressed my chin just as the hero in *Kasauti* did to his bride.

Then, *without any words*, he told me that he was happy he'd come here, to this country, tonight, for me. He said he forgave me for yelling at first. He said he wanted me to enjoy the film. And that he would watch, hidden behind the curtains, for all of my reactions.

"I will show you," I promised.

Inside, feeling his gaze on me in the darkness, I laughed and clapped for Aamir Khan. But the crowd around me leapt out of their seats and cheered him on even more. They hooted, they mimicked his blows as he fought the villains. Behind me, a woman who already knew all the songs sang the lyrics by heart, a few beats ahead of the hero and heroine. I even heard Norzy cry beside me when Aamir Khan's girlfriend was killed by the villains. I had never noticed how noisy the theatre got. How many people were in there, other than me.

And I remembered that outside, the city was dark. I thought of Mother and Popo, probably sitting in their rooms, spinning prayer wheels or counting rosaries. I thought of Mother opening her change purse earlier that night, and all those nights after my father's death. I thought of all those times she had given up watching *Kasauti* or any other thing for Popo and me and Norzy. It would be a beautiful night on the verandah. Even if that was all I would ever have, it would be beautiful to sit there while my family spun and chanted in the rooms nearby.

THE SEASON OF RETREATS

TSERING NAMGYAL KHORTSA

He had come to the Catskill Mountains to study at the feet of a Tibetan Lama and to finish what he had hoped would be the final draft of a novella about Tibetan Buddhist "crazy wisdom." He had also been practicing meditation of late, especially in the mornings. And that particular morning, he had had a typically restless sitting session. His mind kept traveling to Iowa City, where he had spent two years in graduate school working on what became the first draft of the book while consuming what seemed, in retrospect, the entire local brewery. Disillusioned with campus life, he had written to the lama of his intention for such a retreat—as far away as possible from the women, wine, and what he thought of as the rather pointless and loud music festivals of the Midwest. And the lama, an old family acquaintance, had invited him to stay there, at no cost whatsoever.

Following his morning ritual, he decided to go to the dining hall for breakfast. Normally, it was retirees who greeted him as they ate their meals. But today the scene was slightly different: he saw a beautiful young woman sitting at the table. She greeted him. She looked even more charming when she was talking, her unusually large dark eyes speaking more than her words. Wearing a long black dress, she had a loud and ready laugh. She was a medical student from a prestigious university in the nearby state of Connecticut. A beauty with brains, he thought. But at a Buddhist retreat?

"Here to volunteer for six weeks," she said firmly and matter-of-factly while playing with her phone, "and learn more about Buddhism."

For him, her response raised more questions than it answered. She had her own questions for him. As soon as she learned he was from the Tibetan community of India, she asked him, amongst other things, about the human rights situation in Tibet and the Chinese government's latest policy on the reincarnation system. As if that was not enough, she wanted to know about democracy in the Himalayas. But he was in no mood for such discussion before breakfast, especially today.

"I thought we were at a retreat," he told her, much to the shock of a bespectacled, greybeard sitting next to them. "Are we really allowed to use phones here?"

"I am not really using it to call people," she responded." I am just using it for my Facebook."

He didn't know what to say. She told him she would like to visit Dharamshala, and wanted to know what would be the best time to go.

He still wasn't convinced that she was interested in studying Buddhism, definitely not in any serious way. And what would she do here among the monks and retirees? Listen to the teachings? Meditate? Write? In fact, yes. She told him that she, too, wanted to write poetry. She had also signed up to volunteer in the main shrine room during her six-week retreat. She said it with such conviction, as if all the Buddhist deities in the shrine room had somehow collectively hired her for the summer.

He had come here three months ago specifically to get away from such distractions and focus on writing. He had been productive. The pine trees, the verdant valley, the big blue sky above reminded him of the Himalayas of his youth but the general laid-back atmosphere was not unlike graduate school. Yet, unlike in Iowa City, there were no bars—at least, not as far as he knew. For the past several years, he had spent far too much time traveling in Asia and in the universities of the West (including a stint at a British university). At the retreat he had so far stayed off social media, and had been able to concentrate on the final draft of the book. But now that she had appeared, his focus was no longer the same.

In the barren sexual landscape of the spiritual retreat, she looked like a veritable feast of flesh at a table of hungry ghosts. Her colorful appearance and the sheer economy of her clothing always caused much excitement among the crowd in the dining hall, making them forget, for a moment, that they had come here to get rid of desire and attachment, not increase it. All eyes collectively followed her movements. One aging artist and world-traveler announced: "She must have been a Goddess in her previous life."

The woman was rarely out of his sight. She seemed to be everywhere. Meanwhile, the food was getting predictable, as if to remind him of the repetitiveness of meals in the Indian schools of his youth, which had served rice and dal seven days a week. This meant he went to the dining hall a lot less than before. In a few weeks, he lost at least four pounds.

He soon went into hiding to focus on his book. He tried to keep to himself, spending most of his time writing in his room. Whenever he took a break, he usually hung out with a senior Bhutanese monk who also resided there. The monk, who had a passion for spicy cooking, also found the food in the mess rather bland. "Salads are for Westerners," the monk told him once, "Himalayans eat differently." The monk often invited him to dinner, which usually consisted of a particularly hot dish made of Sichuan pepper and dried beef, the last of which was imported all the way from Thimpu. They ate rice and beef and drank tea while sharing their views on politics and the royal family in Bhutan, and they often burped loudly together after the meal. After they finished their dinner, he would return to his room to write.

He also sat on his cushion and tried to practice meditation, which basically entailed following his thoughts to wherever they went and making attempts, usually unsuccessful, at bringing them back to his breath. He wasn't really convinced that it helped calm him down. He was even conscious of the fact that this kind of practice was straight out of the generic beginner's guide to meditation sold in college bookstores. His mind often behaved like a particularly hyper-energetic monkey: perpetually in motion, jumping from one place to another, completely undisciplined and random. Restless, his mind traveled places, often in quick succession—to the Himalayas, to his social media pages, to the plot and characters of his novel, and how he would—or should—end it. His mind drifted to his friends, to the jobs he had held over the years, and to the people he had met along the way, on three continents around the world. Now, his mind seemed to travel exclusively to the woman at the retreat. What was she doing now? Who was she talking to? She must be in the shrine room. He knew he was in trouble. What would happen to the book?

He tried to avoid her, but the retreat center was a tiny community. It was like an extended family living in a small hostel with an immaculately designed temple attached to it, above which resided the lama. One evening, he was eating with the Bhutanese monk, his mouth burning with spices, chatting about Bhutanese politics and electoral rights in the Himalayas when they heard a gentle knock on his door. She came in hurriedly. The monk had to look away, for her cleavage was clearly visible. She sat down near the monk.

She turned and asked him if he could help translate for her. She wanted to know if she should drop out of med school and go to India to study Tibetan medicine.

His jaw dropped. "Are you nuts?" he said. "That is not medicine—that's traditional healing."

"I like traditional healing," she responded, without a hint of irony.

"So you'll leave Yale—just like that?"

She wanted to help raise awareness about the human rights situation inside Tibet, to teach English to Indian kids, to take lessons in Tibetan cooking, to study Ayurveda and yoga, all the while studying ancient Tibetan healing. She had done all the research on the Internet.

He was left speechless. He just stared at her face. She was attractive in a movie star kind of way, a consequence of a mixed parentage and, she confessed, a lot of sports from a very early age. His skepticism did not diminish. Still, he reluctantly yielded to her request, after she held his hands and begged for his help.

The monk took a scripture bound in fine silk out of his cupboard. He threw dice, and looked up some lines in the scripture. The verdict of the divination was that medical school actually did not look very attractive in the long run.

He turned to her and said: "The monk says: Drop Out!"

She immediately jumped on her feet and high-fived him.

"You see, my intuition was right. You've got to listen to your heart."

She was following her heart by swapping a highly selective and prestigious medical school for a course on Tibetan herbal treatment in the Indian Himalayas. He wondered if she was mentally sound. But then the monk told him that that it was quite hard to come across normal, functioning people in the decade that he had been in the West. "Relationships and mobile phones," the monk said, "combine these two and they make people completely crazy."

Two days later, he received an email from Iris. In her first email since they had parted ways six months earlier, she asked him how he was progressing on the book. She had been hurt by his decision to leave behind the beer, music, and anti-depressants that were supposed to ease him through the travails of graduate school and go to the mountains. He wrote back that it looked like his path to creativity and simplicity was not without its challenges. Furthermore, he was sad to announce that there had so far been no signs of spiritual liberation for him, nor had he achieved much headway in his literary endeavor. He didn't know if he would be able to finish the book. She wrote back that he should have gone for a doctorate degree, which might have helped him find a fellowship somewhere. "But now you sound like you are at the wrong summer camp!"

And in the meantime, the young woman had now become a book unto herself, a permanent fixture of his impermanent life. He saw her in the reading room and in the shrine room during his morning prostrations. She would be there offering butter lamps, dusting off the cushions, mopping the floor, or simply meditating in a corner, silently reciting mantras. He saw her, of course, during his visits to the dining hall. They often found themselves eating together. He would generally keep quiet, his mind obsessed with his book. But it was difficult.

More questions followed: Why do Tibetan statues depict deities embracing each other in such reckless abandon? Why does he think Tibetans are self-immolating with such frequency? Does he consider himself Tibetan, Indian, or Chinese? Her questions turned every meal into a press conference. She paid little heed to his statement that in fact he was not in a position to speak with any authority on these issues. He had spent most of his adult life working outside India, far away from the local politics, far away from the Tibetan community. If she had more questions about Tibet, he told her, they should best be directed to the lama and other relevant specialists. Her questions, however, persisted to the point that he once warned her that if she asked him one more question, he would burn himself right then and there! "Silence is golden," he told her more than once. "Speech is bullshit."

Time flew by. The summer gave way to autumn, and it was already quite chilly, even during the daytime. His meditation practice seemed to be helping him concentrate better. And he had made some progress in his writing. Now he pretty much knew the arc of the story. He wanted to finish the book at a sacred site in India, which would serve as the end point of his fictional pilgrimage.

One evening, he walked up to the building where the lama lived and gathered enough courage to tell him that he had changed his mind. He had done more meditation in the past three months than most people would do in their lifetime. And he did not think he should do the three-year retreat that he had originally planned. Since he already had doubts about the retreat, it was better not to begin it at all than to leave in mid-session, which would reflect very badly on his character, especially because so much preparation went into the program.

This must have come as good news for the lama who was skeptical of what he must have considered as a rash decision by a young man. The lama immediately agreed and gave him approval to leave the retreat. The lama even called in his assistant, a garrulous and cheerful lady, to help book his bus and airline tickets back to the city and onwards. He thanked the lama and offered him a scarf that the Bhutanese monk had given him. The lama advised him that since life was short and impermanent, he should devote himself to serving others, which was the secret to happiness. Nothing existed in and by itself, he was told. And then the lama gave him some real advice. Forget writing and get a wife, he said, adding that there were plenty of Tibetan girls in Dharamshala. One of the lama's relatives, volunteering at Tibetan Youth Congress or Students for a Free Tibet, had even met a girl from his own Tibetan region there. He was quite impressed with the lama's advice. He had never imagined that his teacher's spiritual advice would include terminating his literary ambitions and joining a political movement to find a wife from the same Tibetan region. Anyway, he thanked him and left.

When he walked out of the building, he saw the woman sitting outside on the stairs, playing with her iPhone.

"I heard you're calling it quits," she told him.

The assistant had apparently already started spreading the news. He told her he was going back to New York City to work at an NGO. He didn't tell her he was actually flying straight to India from New York.

She told him that her dad was quite unhappy about her decision, but his threats and warnings had done little to dent her enthusiasm for India. She said that one of the aging artists had already been tutoring her pro bono on every nook and corner of Hindustan. The seasoned traveler—who apparently had been kicked out of India several times for overstaying his visa—had even given her a thick, old copy of *The Lonely Planet Guide to India.* She was reading the section on Dharamshala and had already made furious notes in the margins. She had memorized the distance from Delhi to Dharamshala in kilometers.

She asked: "Do you think I should stay overnight in Pathankot when I travel to Dharamshala?"

He spent the next week adding the final touches to his book. He wrote to his friends and family in India about his decision to return there. He updated his Facebook page to make an announcement: "Done with the Retreat. Off to India." He immediately earned several likes and comments. Over a particularly spicy dinner, he told the Bhutanese monk that there was more to life than silent meditation in upstate New York. The monk pointed out that he had already spent three years writing the novel. That evening, he bid farewell to the monk: his one true friend at the retreat, a pillar of support, and a trusted partner in clandestine Bhutanese cooking, a completely unexpected high point of his American retreat.

The next morning, he quietly hired a taxi to the Greyhound station. He thought about the young woman. He felt strangely vulnerable after the retreat and he was already beginning to miss her presence. He was almost resigned to the fact that he would surely run into her somewhere in India and that she would become part of his circle, or his mandala, as Tibetans would call it. He was drawn to her and she, with her strong passions and flawless looks, was a formidably interesting character. Still, the novelist in him realized that she was far more interesting as a figment of his imagination, best envisioned from a distance, than as a real person crowding into his daily life.

The bus ride to New York City felt very quick. Navigating the maze of tunnels underneath Port Authority, he hopped onto the train to JFK. Before checking in at the airline, however, he thought he would eat something. He walked into a Korean restaurant. After three months of fiery Bhutanese food, the spice in the kimchi noodle failed to register on his tongue. But he did enjoy his first Heineken in three months, which actually made him feel quite meditative. On the plane, he tried to watch a Bollywood film but fell into a deep and peaceful sleep right after the first song. Soon enough, however, he had a nightmare which woke him up—he dreamed that he was frantically and repeatedly adding the woman as a friend on Facebook.

He drank some water and tried to clear his head. And if he did run into her in India, he decided, it would be no mere coincidence, but a sign that she was meant to be in his life—to be part of his story. Or, at least, his story about that season of retreats in the mountains of New York.

THE DREAM OF A WANDERING MINSTREL

PEMA TSEDEN TRANSLATED BY TENZIN DICKIE

1.

Tsering the Wandering Minstrel traveled the road in search of a dream.

2.

One night during the spring when Tsering turned fourteen years old, he had a dream. A girl appeared in the landscape of his dream. Tsering already knew his alphabet by then and at times even wrote simple lyrics. Here is the entry in his diary detailing his dream:

"Yesterday, a girl appeared in my dreams. I have never seen her before. I still see her image clearly in my mind. She was around the same age as me. She had a fair and round face with a green mole on her chin. Her hair, pulled into tiny plaits all over her head, looked very pretty. She said we should play catch and she ran in front of me as I chased her. I ran until I was exhausted and out of breath but no matter how I ran and ran, I couldn't catch her. We were lost in our play for a long time. And then she left. I felt as if I had known her in my real life. I don't know her name or what village she's from. But I'll never forget her."

The next day when Tsering recounted his dream to his father, his father laughed at him and said, "When you grow up, you can take this girl of your dreams as your bride."

Tsering sat lost in thought with a smile on his face.

The girl appeared in Tsering's dreams many more times. Each time, they played catch. Each time Tsering wrote down the details of his dream and narrated the details of his dream to his father, and each time his father laughed and said to him, "When you grow up, you can take this girl of your dreams as your bride."

Each time he struggled to understand what the dream meant and sat lost in his thoughts with a smile on his face. Who could have known then that this dream would turn into the search of his life.

3.

> The sun had nearly set. The sky became blurry as dusk fell. At the end of each day, Tsering had no idea where he would find shelter that night.

All these years, his dream and his *piwang*, his fiddle decorated with a dragon's head, clung to him like a second skin. Who knows how many plains, mountains, and valleys he had crossed in search of his dream and who knows how many more plains, mountains, and valleys he would still have to cross? During this endless journey of his, he began to feel his senses failing one by one and sometimes he felt so tired in his body and mind that he thought he just couldn't go on. But he kept following the road and continued his journey, facing countless challenges, searching for the dream. He wondered whether his dream was true or not but then he remembered this quote by some unknown person, “Why do people come to this world but to search for a dream?” and his heart filled with hope and faith again, and he continued on his way in search of the dream.

4.

> As Tsering grew up and became a young man, so the girl in his dreams grew up and became a young woman. She still appeared regularly in his dreams. As the girl grew up, Tsering’s heart became as unsettled as a summer lake. They had long stopped playing catch with each other. Tsering kept a record of each dream just as he had done before, but he stopped sharing his dreams with his father. For a period of about two years, he dreamed the same dream each time. Below is a record of this dream.

“Yesterday she appeared again in my dreams. Her face was as fair and round as ever and she had the same green mole on her chin. She looked like a goddess come to earth. As I looked at her breasts and the peaceful and gentle expression her face, I couldn’t help realizing that she had now blossomed into a sixteen-year-old girl in the full flower of her youth. Her lovely eyes were fixed on me, and I felt and understood the secret hopes and dreams hidden in her eyes. Her mouth parted, her soft and lovely lips moved but she never spoke a word. I still had no idea what her name was and she never asked for mine. I asked her gently to tell me her name but she just smiled and gave no answer. We stood in front of each other, not moving, not touching, just staring at each other with desire. I reached out my hand to touch her but no matter how I reached for her, I could never touch her. Then I woke up.”

5.

Tsering the Wandering Minstrel felt a great fatigue. He stopped walking, slipped the dragon-headed *piwang* off his shoulder, and set it down on the ground. He turned toward the west and stood staring into the distance.

The sun had gone down over the distant horizon. The evening clouds, pierced with the remaining rays of the red sun, appeared bloodshot. In front of Tsering flowed a river. He did not know its name. It was a river running in the opposite direction. Tsering had first come across this river a month ago when the edges of its waters were still frozen. Since then, he met this same river again and again. Spring had arrived but the grass and greenery had yet to sprout and everything was white and barren as if it were still winter. Blocks of ice that had broken off from the bank drifted in the water following the current. A cold breeze rose from the water, and Tsering couldn't help shivering.

Tsering rose, slung his dragon-headed *piwang* onto his back, and set off toward the water. As he neared the water, he felt a sudden thirst and hunger. He squatted on his haunches, pulled out his wooden bowl and *tsampa* bag from the fold of his *chupa,* and placed them on the ground. Then he opened his *tsampa* bag, grabbed some *tsampa* with his fingers, and poured it into his mouth. With his bowl, he scooped up some water, drank, and chewed the *tsampa* in his mouth. After he ate his fill, he put his bowl and *tsampa* bag back into the fold of his clothes. He looked out at the water and thought about his dream. After some time, he stroked his dragon-headed *piwang* and began to play it. In his soulful baritone, he sang a sorrowful song.

Love of my dreams,
Where are you?
In search of you,
I cross countless mountains, valleys, and plains.
Love of my dreams,
Where are you?

He was eighteen when he wrote the song. It was a song he loved to sing. Its haunting tunes echoed across all the towns and plains that he passed through.

The wind carried away the refrain of the song into the far corners of the world. Tsering ran his fingers over his *piwang*, looked off into the distance, and gave a deep sigh.

6.

The dragon-headed *piwang* was Tsering's only inheritance from his father. Tsering's father had been a famous minstrel who not only knew many episodes of the great epic of King Gesar by heart, but also knew a great number of folk songs from Amdo, U-tsang, and Kham. Because he possessed the dragon-headed *piwang*, his fame travelled far and wide like thunder in the summertime. This *piwang* was given to Tsering's father by his own father at the time of his death. Tsering's grandfather had also been a famous minstrel. On his deathbed he gave the *piwang* to his son and said, "This dragon-headed *piwang* is an instrument that comes from the time of the Fifth Dalai Lama. It is made of sandalwood and more than ten of your ancestors have died for its sake. This *piwang* shall turn you into a minstrel without equal." At that time Tsering's father had no idea how to play the *piwang*. Tsering's father had never even touched the *piwang* in his own father's hand. When he touched the strings of this instrument, carefully

> and with wonder, a strange music he had never heard before sounded in his ears. At that very same moment, a feeling that he had never experienced before spread through his body and he felt as if he had suddenly become a skilled musician. From then on, he began his wandering, traveling from place to place with the invaluable *piwang* on his back.

When Tsering's father was around thirty, he came to Kham. It was a hot summer. Seeing the blazing green pastures and the white, red, and yellow flowers blooming across the grass, he fell in love with the place and stayed there for a month. Plucking the strings of his dragon-headed *piwang* and speaking in a sweet and melodious voice, he told the tales of King Gesar of Ling to the people who had lived on these fields for generations. He sang them many sad and sorrowful songs. His music and his songs brought much joy to the lives of these people who had heard no music till then and also won him the heart of a girl. That girl was Tsering's mother. When his father left those pastures behind, the girl left with him. In a year's time Tsering was born, and not long after that, she passed away. Tsering's father bottled up the sorrow in his heart, took up his *piwang* again, bundled Tsering into the fold of his *chupa*, and set off once more to be a solitary traveling minstrel. Whenever he heard a small cry from Tsering, he felt a gladness in his heart.

7.

> One day, Tsering the Wandering Minstrel was resting after the day's travel when he found himself singing that same sad little song again in his baritone. Whenever Tsering sang this song, his thoughts went immediately to the dream that he still sought.

He lifted his head slowly and looked into the distance. It was almost dusk. The mountains in the distance, cloaked in approaching darkness, began to grow indistinct. A strong, cold air rolled in stealthily from all four directions, making him restless. Every now and then, a bird or two flew over his head. Tsering stroked his dragon-headed *piwang* and thought about his dream again.

After some time, he took out his little notebook from his *chupa* and began reading it. In this notebook were the written records of every single dream that he'd had since he was fourteen years old. Because it was almost dusk, the words on the pages were blurry and indistinct. But he deliberately turned over every single page. Every word he had written on these pages, every page, was like a picture carved into his brain. Even without looking at the book, he could still see each dream appearing in front of him like a vision. He read the notebook several times, turning all the pages this way and then that way, before tucking the book away again in his *chupa*. He lifted his head again, looked into the distance, and thought again about the dream he sought.

8.

The girl grew into a gorgeous young woman throughout each of Tsering's dreams. This was a time of great pain for Tsering, as he was pierced with sorrow by his desire and longing for her. During this period, the girl only entered Tsering's dreams a few times. A deep sadness haunted him, a sadness he had never known before. He saw her image all the time as if she were really standing in front of him, and he never knew a moment's peace. He recorded his dreams during this period in his greasy little notebook without neglecting a single detail, and he never let his father or anyone else look at this notebook. He always found a secluded spot where no one could find him and he read over the dreams he'd written down in his small notebook again and again, at times forgetting to snap out of them. His dreams during this period were almost always the same. What follows is the record of a dream he had during this period as it was written down in his greasy little notebook:

"She was grown up, there's no doubt about it. Now there was no trace of discomfort or uneasiness on her face. Her cheeks glowed with the luster of youth. The green mole on her chin was still there, and she looked lovely and illuminated. She looked at me with wide eyes, dark and deep, and I saw hiding in them a burning love and passion, and her sorrow etched between her brows and her loneliness. Her chest rose and fell with each quick breath and I was seized by such an overpowering feeling of lust that my own breathing ceased. She was seized by the same lust—her soft lips trembled as she said something. We moved slowly toward one other. We gazed longingly at each other. We could hear the sounds of our hearts beating. Now there were only two or three steps remaining between us. We stopped walking, staring silently at each other with eyes open and blinded by love. After an unbearable interval, we went to kiss each other as our lips trembled. But just then, there was a terrific rumbling sound like thunder and the ground under our feet cracked and broke in two, opening a deep, unfathomably deep ravine between us. We stood at the opposite edges of the ravine, watching each other with despairing love, wanting to call out to each other but unable to do so, silently looking at each other like dumb fools."

9.

It became dark. The shroud of night covered the land near and far so that the only thing visible was a blanket of darkness. As before, a cold wind blew unceasingly from the four corners of the world. A bright white light shone and shivered on the river where slabs of ice crashed against each other, sending up splashes of water, the ice melting and running as the river fled away into the distance.

Tsering the Wandering Minstrel stood on a boulder. After setting his dragon-headed *piwang* on the ground, he leaned against the rock and closed his eyes. The hard day's exhaustion stealthily stole upon him like an altar rat, covering him like a cloak, and binding him body and mind. He thought the time had come for him to rest.

10.

Tsering's soulful baritone voice, resonant with love and longing, was not a voice that came to him naturally but one he achieved later with his training. Ever since Tsering was a young boy, he loved music and his father had high hopes for him. His father used to tell him, "Your voice is not good enough, but that does not mean that you can't become a great minstrel. You must learn and practice with great dedication."

When he was tormented by his dreams, he pushed his sorrow and his anguish deep inside himself, kept them in a ball in the pit of his stomach, and threw himself into his lessons with his father.

Overcoming the scorching heat of three summers and the icy chill of three winters, through the angry thunder and fiery breath of a thousand dragons, he studied and mastered range and register, the highs and lows, the depths and hollows of sound and music such that at the end of each day's practice, he was too bone-tired to move and his throat was raw with blood and pus.

One night after Tsering had finished his practice when he was in his seventeenth year, he heard in his dream a strange and gentle tune coming from afar, a tune that he had never heard before. A sadhu with white hair and a white beard appeared before his eyes and placed in Tsering's mouth a tiny white conch that coiled to the right. The sadhu made him swallow the conch and he said, "Listen, my child. As you desire, you will become a great minstrel. Bring joy to the hearts of the people of this land with your sweet voice."

And again a sweet tune sounded from the distance, and then the sadhu disappeared like a rainbow in the sky.

When Tsering woke from his sleep, it was bright outside. The night's dream came immediately to his mind. He sat up with wonder and remembered his dream, mulling it over from start to finish. He felt as if there were a small change in him but he didn't know what this change was.

A sudden desire to sing rose in him and the unbelievable thing was, his voice was no longer his voice of old—he now had a soulful baritone, a voice resonant with love and longing. He felt as if he had miraculously received a divine blessing and, unable to contain himself, he jumped up and down. In awe and delight, he closed his eyes to invoke and praise the deity that had so blessed him.

His father, who was saying his Mani prayers outside the tent, heard this beautiful song and, not trusting his ears, came inside the tent to ask where this song came from. Tsering laughed and sang the song again. His father couldn't believe his ears and just stared at his son. Tsering then told his father exactly what had happened in his dream.

Tsering's father listened to his story in shock, without moving. Then, a great smile broke out on his wrinkled face and he exclaimed, "*Azi*, my dream has come true. My dream has come true." That year, death came for his father and took him away to the beyond.

11.

In a short while, Tsering the Wandering Minstrel fell asleep and traveled to the land of dreams. In his dream, the girl was hurrying toward him from a distance. Her hair was wild and tangled and her usual peaceful and gentle expression was nowhere to be seen. In the blink of an eye, she was standing next to him. There were several steps between them, now. She moved her mouth as if she wanted to say something. As her lips quivered, the green mole on her chin also quivered. He moved toward her and he wanted to ask why she was so upset. He opened his mouth but could make no sounds. She looked behind her in terror and kept hastening toward him. Now there were only four or five steps between them. A tentative smile came to both their faces and they stopped walking and just looked at each other. But when they started to take another step to move in even closer, they found they couldn't move their feet. They were as stuck as if they were statues. They tried hard to move toward each other, but the distance of four or five steps remained steady between them. Then, very slowly, the distance began to lessen. He put out his hand toward her to comfort her and she moved her lips and raised her hand toward him. But again, just as their hands were about to touch, with only a finger's width between them now, they found that they could not move, that they were as stuck as if they were figures in a drawing.

With eyes full of hope, they looked at each other with great desire. Anguish filled their faces, and doubt and confusion. Suddenly, there was a terrible sound and a great wave of water came out of nowhere, rushing between them and sweeping the girl away in its wake. He ran after her. He shouted for her but no sound came from his lips. He kept running after the wave of water. Suddenly laughter rose from the waves that made the hair on his neck stand up and then, abruptly, everything was gone without a trace.

Tsering suddenly woke up from this terrible dream. His face was white, his breathing quick and ragged, and his body was covered in sweat.

Day came but Tsering couldn't shake off the terrible dream. His face remained white and his breath still ran short.

After some time, he sat up and slowly looked into the distance, fixing his gaze on the horizon. He tried to think of other things in order to get out of his terrible dream.

Slowly, Tsering calmed down a little. No matter how terrifying his dream was, Tsering thought he still ought to record it in his notebook like usual. Recalling the dream, he wrote it down in his greasy little notebook, trembling as he did so.

12.

It was during Tsering's time of happiness, after he had received the divine blessing, that his father saw the greasy little notebook. He read the notebook and he became uneasy. On the one hand, he was happy that Tsering had been blessed by the gods, but on the other hand he worried that the dreams were making his son unhappy. His father's wrinkles etched deeper and deeper into his face and his body became thinner and thinner. On a night when the cold wintry gale was blowing more fiercely than ever, his father left behind this mundane, karmic world.

When his father lay dying, he held Tsering's hand tightly and said to him, "You must never search for your dream. The dream is empty."

Tsering just looked at father's wrinkled face without saying a thing. His father looked at him with love in his eyes. Then, slowly, the light faded from his face and his eyes closed.

After his father's death, Tsering embarked on his solitary travels and became a lone wandering minstrel.

During his lifetime, Tsering's father had known countless human joys and sorrows and walked many straight and crooked paths. His father understood the best and worst of life and so he said what he said—so Tsering thought to himself after his father's death.

13.

The sun burned red in the distant horizon. A scattering of black clouds drifted this way and near the sun's edges. After a little while, the clouds had swallowed the last rays of the sun, making the sun look white like the moon.

Tsering, the Wandering Minstrel, went on his way as before. He kept thinking about the terrible dream he had the night before. Agitated and distressed, he found no peace in his heart. That day, he was once again following the same river, the river whose name he did not know. The water was not clear like usual and the ice floating at the edges of the water had all vanished. The surrounding fields were filled with hay and fodder. Seeing this, Tsering felt even more miserable than before.

The sun began to set. The black clouds hovering on the horizon still drifted gently across the sky. Then he saw in front of him a blurry and indistinct village and he felt joy. He hadn't come across a village in many days. Because a village meant people, whenever he came across a village, he felt a spontaneous joy in his heart. He usually stayed in such villages for two or three days. People fell in love with his music and showered him with gifts when he left.

The river, whose name he did not know, flowed from the direction of that village, so he continued walking along the river toward it.

As he neared the village, he saw that a crowd of people had massed by the nameless river. They were all talking in high voices. He stopped walking and watched them for awhile before he slowly started toward them again.

As he came upon them, one man among them caught sight of him. He turned toward him and then watched him in astonishment.

Tsering stopped walking, put his hands together in greeting and asked, "Why are you all gathered here?"

"We came to see the girl that the water has taken," the man said. He still watched Tsering with surprise on his face.

"What kind of girl is she?"

Tsering, feeling a sudden fear in his heart, asked this question in some haste.

The surprise left the man's face and he began to tell his story without hesitation, almost as if he had been commanded to do so. "It will be hard to believe. Who would believe that this was a body brought in by the water? There's still a color to her cheeks as if she had just woken from sleep, and her whole body is so clean—not a speck of dirt on her. Ahh—she had a green mole on her chin. Ahh, she was such a beauty . . ."

Tsering's brain went dark for a moment and he couldn't hear any more. He gave a great cry of sorrow and said, "But she's the dream I have been searching for!"

The crowd in front of him turned around as one to look at him in great surprise. Their bodies grew blurry in his eyes. Slowly, he walked to the front.

It was dark when Tsering left the village. He sat on his haunches in front of the river, the river whose name he did not know. He took out his greasy little notebook, tore out the pages, and flung them one by one into the river and watched the water carry them away. He sat and watched for a long time. Then he fixed his gaze into the distance, and plucking the strings of his dragon-headed *piwang*, he sang in a sweet, low voice filled with pain and sorrow.

> Love of my dreams,
> You are no more.
> In search of you,
> I crossed countless mountains, valleys and plains.
> Love of my dreams,
> You are no more.

THE FIFTH MAN

TENZIN DORJEE

It was October, the best month for camping in Dharamsala. The rainy season was over, although the tail end of monsoon season dragged right through October, flooding our tents on more than one occasion. There were about fifty of us, Tibetans, Indians, Canadians, and Americans, gathered on the Thakur family estate in lower Dharamsala, brought together as members of the same community of political activism. The Thakurs were an Indian family of uncertain aristocratic ancestry with connections to Tibet dating back to the 1960s when Tibetan refugees first arrived on the scene. Their estate was a sprawling farm of acres of greenery and great versatility. The nearest neighbors were fifteen minutes away.

You could walk from mango trees at one end of the farm to a plum garden and pepper plants at the other end, while encountering sleeping cows and fighting hens and barking dogs all in the same compound. During the day, we took our Patagonia ropes to the Deodars and trained at climbing, a skill we would deploy to scale towers and hang banners to promote the respective causes we worked for. We sat in endless workshops discussing the differences between tactics and strategies, between protest and civil disobedience, between conversion and coercion. In the evenings, we sat around a campfire with a couple of guitars and sang everything from classic rock songs of the sixties to Hindi oldies of the seventies to Tibetan pop songs of the nineties.

Throughout this weeklong camp, I found myself drawn to

one particular tree. We called it the magic tree. It was a small tree, a very small tree, no taller than a tall man and barely worth being called a tree. It was actually more of a shrub, a yellowish pigmy all but forgotten amid the giant and proud Deodars that populate the hillsides of Dharamsala.

The tree, or rather the plant, bore these small green pearl-like things that tasted like grass but smelled like marijuana. My friend Kodo Sawaki, an American whose Zen Buddhist master renamed him after the legendary Japanese monk and whose real name was Chuck MacAdams, was with me. We both lived in New York and the two of us used to smoke up in my apartment in Flatbush. We were curious about the green pearls. We placed a small dose of the pearls in a pipe and smoked it. The pearls burned just like tobacco but smelled much better. We were thrilled. The green pearls gave you a good high.

And then it started. I began to see things. On the second evening of the camp, the classical singer Chusang Kyipa performed for us at the campfire. She had the most exquisite voice this side of the Himalayas, and her melodies ebbed and flowed like waves in the sea, evoking memories of our land on the other side of the mountains. As the darkness of the evening thickened into the blackness of the night, she concluded her singing and we all thanked her and said goodbye. A few of us including my friend Kodo Sawaki went to escort her to her taxi, which was waiting in the parking lot of the neighboring nunnery.

We walked in single file through the narrow path in the bush. I was second from the last. I had a flashlight with me, one that I had expressly bought from Marshalls just before I left New York, but the guy walking behind me did not. I kept pointing the flashlight forward and backward so that we both could see in the dark. Once we got to the taxi stand, there was more light coming from the nunnery compound. I turned around but the person walking behind me wasn't there any more.

"That's weird," I said to the others. "There was one more guy behind me but it seems he just gave up and went back to the campfire."

"No, Palden la," said Bablu, the charming son of the Thakur family, who disappeared in the daytime but reappeared without fail at the campfire sing-alongs. "There was no one behind you, it was just the four of us to begin with."

At first I thought Bablu must be mistaken. But he insisted that it was just the four of us all along—himself, Kodo, Chusang Kyipa, and me. I could see from my friends' faces that they all felt a little bit uncomfortable, but we didn't talk about this incident any more. We were all quiet on the way back to the campfire. I don't remember who walked at the end of the line this time, but it definitely wasn't me. We stayed close together, bumping frequently into each other. The walk back seemed to take much longer.

The next day, in the very late afternoon—actually it was more like early evening—I walked by where the Thakur family kept their cows. I was trying to be alone for a moment to clear my head between trainings and workshops. I saw one of my colleagues, Tsomo, by herself under the plum trees, holding her face in her hands. I couldn't see her face clearly, but her shoulders rose and fell as if she was sobbing. Yes, she was crying, there was no question.

I walked toward her. I wanted to ask her what was the matter. If I couldn't help, I could at least comfort her. But as soon as I started walking, I stopped. Maybe she wouldn't want the intrusion. Maybe she just wanted to be left alone for now. Yes, of course, give her some space, I told myself and walked away.

The following day, Tsomo seemed completely fine. So I was right, all she needed was some space and privacy to find her footing. Whatever the cause for her tears, she was now back to her normal happy self.

"So, Tsomo, what happened? Why were you crying yesterday?" I asked. Since I had already given her some privacy the day before, I couldn't resist being a little nosy now.

"What?" She had a genuinely confused look on her face.

"It's ok, I won't tell anyone," I said. "I saw you there under the plum trees yesterday evening."

"What!" Her confusion turned to astonishment. "It must have been somebody else."

"No, I was there. I saw you, and you were crying quite seriously. I came over to talk to you but then I didn't want to disturb you, so I left."

"Okay, guess what, Palden," she said, shaking her head. "Either I'm losing my memory, or you saw someone who was not me."

I felt a sudden chill. *Or you saw someone who was not me.*

I hadn't seen her face but the crying girl had looked exactly like Tsomo. If it really wasn't Tsomo, then who was it?

I never found out who it was. Neither the man walking behind me when we were escorting Chusang Kyipa to her taxi, nor the crying girl who looked like Tsomo but wasn't her.

But it wasn't over yet. On the last night of camping, I stayed at the campfire well past midnight. I was one of the last people to leave the campfire every night. When everyone had gone to bed, I poured a bucket of water on the fire, buried the embers, and separated the half-burned pieces of wood from each other.

I had pitched my tent close to a thicket of bamboo trees. I unzipped my tent and crawled inside. I had been drinking beer. Unlike most Tibetans, I had a pretty high tolerance for alcohol so I was clear-headed but I felt good and I fell asleep immediately. It was a dreamless sleep, which I liked much better than a sleep full of dreams, because dreaming took up so much energy. I preferred to be awake when I dreamed.

That night, I was awakened from my sleep by the sound of light snoring. In the faint gray skylight that penetrated the thin skin of my tent, I saw a man sleeping next to me. I was in my usual sleeping-Buddha position, with my head placed on my right hand. As a schoolboy at Upper TCV, I had consciously slept that way, in the position the Buddha had chosen for his long, unending sleep. I was no longer a believer in the conventional sense, but it had become a habit for me to sleep like that. I blinked. The man was lying right in front of me. I could clearly see his left profile. It was the face of a middle-aged Indian man, thin and dark, with a white-and-gray stubble that looked like he hadn't shaved in a few days.

But what the hell was he doing in my tent? Was he a drunkard who had lost his way and stumbled into my tent? There were a few Indian villagers in the neighborhood, I was aware, some of whom must surely have drinking problems and smart wives who refused to open the door if their husbands returned home too drunk too late.

Or maybe I was hallucinating. I had smoked a small portion of the green pearls from the magic tree that day. That must be it. That had to be it. I was certain. In which case, the man was not really there, he was just a projection of my own mind. So I closed my eyes for a long moment. The prayers that I used to say in school came back to me and I repeated the mantras silently, knowing that the hallucination would be gone by the time I reopened them.

After what felt like a lifetime, I opened my eyes. The man was still there. He was sleeping in the same position, with his face turned upward to the sky, as peaceful as a baby, snoring so softly that he should not have woken me at all.

Well, there was only one way to prove that I was hallucinating. I would have to touch him with my hand. Let me prove it, I told myself. I was intrigued by the possibility of catching my own hallucination red-handed, my own sense of touch proving its superiority over my sense of sight. The command traveled from my brain through my nerves to my muscles for my hand to obey.

But before I could move my hand an inch, something stopped me cold. "What if?" It was the small voice of reason, or unreason, in a remote corner of my mind. What if the sleeping man was neither an illusion nor a real person? What then? My caution wrestled with my curiosity, and I lay there, silent and unmoving, except now my heart was suddenly beating loudly and wildly in my chest.

At that moment, I noticed something odd about the man's face. He seemed to have no nose. Indeed, there was a dent where his nose should have been. But his noseless face was still the most peaceful face I had ever seen. My own peace had been shattered, however, and I would have given anything at that moment to force myself into the oblivion of sleep. In spite of my heart racing like death and beating like a drum, I miraculously managed to fall asleep by sheer will power and concentration.

It was morning and blindingly bright when I woke up. I was alone in my tent. To my right was my black suitcase, extra-large and taking up too much room in the tent. There was no space even for a cat to lie down, much less for a man to sleep. So I had been hallucinating after all. It was clear. All that sweat and fright for nothing, I thought.

Later that day, while saying goodbye to the Thakur family, I shared a cup of tea with Bablu. I jokingly told him that I saw a ghost in my tent last night. He laughed cheerfully—he seemed incapable of doing anything cheerlessly—and said, "Where did you pitch your tent by the way?"

"Just below those bamboo trees, not far from the camp fire."

"Well, now that you're leaving, it's Okay to tell you," he said. "Someone died in the bamboo trees a while ago. We didn't know him. I think he was a local nobody from a nearby village."

"How did he die?" I asked, blowing lightly on my tea to cool it down.

"They say he got in a fight and the other guy smashed his nose in with a cricket bat. He died on the spot."

A lump grew in my throat. I put the cup down. I could hardly breathe for a moment.

"Is something wrong? Now *you* look like a ghost!" laughed Bablu.

He clearly did not believe in ghosts. Of course, neither did I.

WINTER IN PATLIKUHL

TENZIN DICKIE

It was the winter I stayed at Patlikuhl, my Tibetan boarding school in rural north India, a small, isolated school tucked in a narrow valley between the hills of Nagar. The nearby town had only one nameless road going through it. I say "stayed" but what I mean is I was left behind. My parents couldn't come to get me because winter was their busiest season but they had entrusted a man who was coming to get his own children with the task of bringing me as well. Unfortunately there were two Tenzin Lhamos in Class Five. The man ended up taking the wrong girl home. My parents felt bad sending her back, so they kept her for the winter. It sounds crazy now but that sort of thing happened more often than you might think. So I stayed at school for the winter with all the orphans and other children whose parents were either in Tibet or were too poor to fetch their kids for the winter holidays.

It felt like the freest time of my life: no parents, no teachers, no prefects. We still had dorm mothers but we could ignore them. The old peon still rang the school bell but it had lost all its old tyranny. Breakfast, lunch, tea-time, dinner was all the bell meant now. It became almost comforting. During term time, we woke up at 5:30 a.m., put on our uniforms, and made our beds quickly, making all four corners of the bed sharp with military precision. After breakfast, we cleaned the dorm, dusting and sweeping until it was time for our one-hour study period. After that we had morning assembly and then classes finally began for the day. But there was none of that in the winter. We woke up at a later hour, only cleaned the dorm once a week, and best of all, we turned on the TV whenever we wanted. Our dorm mother let us have the run of the place. That was the winter her oldest son was back home, released from the hospital because there was nothing more they could do for him. He wore a Kullu shawl over his kurta, like an Indian, and walked up and down the corridor, a silent specter of a man, getting gaunter and gaunter each week. He had the same vacant expression on his face every day. At night, we fell asleep to the sound of his coughing.

So we had all this free time, my friend Sherab and I. Sherab was in my class but it wasn't at all inevitable that we would be best friends. After all, boys and girls weren't really friends back then, but we were. We spent all our time with each other. We were only eleven, we hadn't hit puberty yet, and so it wasn't weird then like it became later.

He was carefree and reckless, the kind of boy who always looked for a rule to break. He had an untameable cowlick on his forehead, which everyone said meant that he was going to grow up to be a troublemaker. The thing about Sherab was that he was very easygoing and eager to please once you were his friend. He had a natural kindness, and boarding school, which hardened many a softer person, never really stamped it out of him. For all his roughness, he could be surprisingly sensitive, which is why it was odd that he didn't hold back that day when we went to Momo Pasang's room.

I still remember the day clearly. We snuck out of the school to the bazaar. We made our way to the movie theater. Neither of us had any money, of course, but the theater in Patlikuhl had a strange custom where you could watch the trailers for free. In fact the trailers weren't really trailers of new movies but extended clips of older movies, movies that had been out for a year or longer, that the theater showed to entertain the audience till show time. Usually, they showed either the first half or the last half of a movie. There was one boy at school who had seen the first half of *Mr India* fourteen times without ever seeing the second half. Sherab preferred seeing the second half of films. He liked the last fights where the hero usually wears a leather jacket and rides a motorcycle and then dispatches any number of villains in gravity-defying maneuvers. I liked the first halves, though. I didn't need to know the ending, because I could always imagine it. But I needed to see the beginning to understand how it all happened. Beginnings, I thought, were most important. You couldn't begin to understand the end without knowing the beginning.

A beam of light moved up and down the aisle. The ticket man was signaling that the trailer was ending and the theater was getting ready for the feature film.

"Sherab," I said. "Show's ending. Time to go."

"Wait, wait," he said, eyes fixed to the screen. "Wait for her to die."

On screen, the hero wept as his widowed mother lay dying in his arms. She gasped out some last words. The heroine, also weeping off to the side, wore the hero's leather jacket hanging off her shoulders.

"What do you think she's telling him?" I said. "Farewell, my son, the movie is ending and I gotta go?"

"Farewell, my son, maybe I'll see you in my next life?"

"Maybe I'll be reborn as your child, so get on it and make some babies! But don't forget to get your leather jacket back from that girl. Looks much better on you!"

Sherab snorted, "Lhamo, you are ruining the end."

"I am saving the end," I said and stood up.

The three Indian men next to us shifted their legs but didn't get up, forcing us to squeeze past them, bumping their knees as we did so. We followed the few other trailer-watchers out. The moment that you came out of the dark theatre and stood blinking in the sudden harsh sunlight was always the most vulnerable moment. That was when you had the highest chance of getting caught by a teacher. I put my hands over my eyes, trying to blink into the light. My vision cleared. A bus idled on the other side of the street, but even as I watched, it rumbled and rolled crankily onto the road and took off. Now I could see an old Tibetan woman with her hand outstretched. My body reacted before my mind did, going hot with panic.

"Is that Momo Pasang?" I hissed to Sherab. When you were a child, you learned very quickly that sudden encounters with adults could be fraught with danger. Then I remembered that Momo was practically blind—that there was no way she could see us from across the distance. She looked so incongruous, an old Tibetan woman in a dirty raggedy *chupa* the color of a dishrag.

No one knew how old Momo Pasang was, or how she had come to be at Patlikuhl. Some of the older boys said that she was old already when Patlikuhl was founded. The other elders were former cooks and dorm mothers and tailors and seamstresses. They were staff at Patlikuhl or in one of the Tibetan schools. But what was Momo? She seemed to have always been an old woman. The other elders lived in the Old People's Home by the classroom buildings. Momo, the oldest of them all, lived by herself in a room below the school hall. The other elders were usually fond of students—they sat in the sun, sunning their backs, saying their prayers and chatting and they often had a smile or a sweet for you when they saw you. Momo never spent any time with the other elders. Whenever you ran into her walking around the school or on her way to the kitchen to pick up her food, she was always alone, muttering what seemed to be curses under her breath.

"What's she doing?" Sherab said.

She had her cane in one hand, and her other hand was held out for coins, with a small bucket dangling from the wrist, It took us a moment to understand what we were seeing. She was begging. If we had seen her hitch the skirt of her *chupa* up and start urinating there in the street, we could not have been more shocked.

Certainly I had seen beggars before, in Delhi, in Bangalore. Scores and scores of beggars, men, women, children, despairing and dying before one's eyes in the indifferent daylight. My parents, struggling as they were, helped them out when they could. My father always gave to beggars missing a body part, such as an arm or a leg. My mother gave to women carrying babies. But Patlikuhl was a very small town. There were only the local townspeople and no one was very well off, neither the Indians nor the Tibetans. But no one needed to beg either. And the thing was, I had never seen a Tibetan begging before. Later I would realize that there were many other things I had never seen a Tibetan do. I had never seen a Tibetan bus driver, or a honey-seller, or a milkman. Nor a Tibetan artist, a Tibetan actor, a Tibetan scientist. Tibetans were only certain things in this exile of ours.

We didn't stay to watch Momo Pasang. We fled and got back to school just in time for lunch.

After lunch, we were playing marbles behind the classroom buildings when the kulfiman came by. The teachers said the kulfiman made his kulfi with dirty water from the river but we didn't care about that. He kept it in a cane basket wrapped tightly with sackcloth. He carried the basket on his head resting atop a long rope of cloth that he fashioned into a sort of turban. Even in winter he came to the school to sell his kulfi although most of the children who remained for the holidays had no money.

"Kulfi! Kulfi!" said a voice above our heads.

An older boy was out on the ledge. He dropped down with an easy swing and held out one tattered rupee note to the Indian. The kulfiman sat his box on the ground and squatted. With one hand, he began unwinding the turban cloth from his head. He looked even sadder and thinner without it. He cut a large slice of the kulfi with his flat steel spatula, wrapped it in a newspaper page which featured a picture of Hema Malini, and passed it to the boy.

We watched the boy break the chunk of kulfi in two like a piece of burfi. He popped a piece into his mouth and ate it hastily, as if it were too hot and burning his mouth. Then carefully, making sure we were watching, he licked his fingers. He waited for us to say something.

"If you don't eat the rest quickly," Sherab said, "the ink will stain the kulfi."

"Oh, really? You know, maybe I got too much kulfi. I wouldn't want it to stain. Maybe I should share . . . hmm maybe not, maybe I'll just eat it after all." He grinned as if he had made a clever joke and we laughed. When an older boy thought he was being funny, you laughed along. He folded the newspaper sheet, held it between his teeth, and climbed out onto the windowsill of the first floor classroom. Rising carefully onto the balls of his feet, he grabbed the ledge and pulled himself up smoothly onto the second floor. He stood up gingerly, dusted his pants, popped the second piece of kulfi into his mouth and dropped the newspaper. A strip of red paper also fell along with it. We watched the boy climb back inside the classroom. The sheet drifted slowly to the ground and landed. Hema Malini's beautiful face was ruined. Sherab picked up the papers and stuffed them into his pants pocket.

After the boy went back inside the classroom, the kulfiman sat and waited for other students but there were no more buyers.

Sherab and I played marbles, watching the kulfiman out of the corner of our eyes. Finally the kulfiman tapped his wrist: the signal we had been waiting for. We went over, rolled up our sleeves, and held our wrists out to him. He cut two small slices of kulfi and placed one on Sherab's wrist and the other on mine.

"Ruko," he said. It was a word we knew. Wait.

Sherab and I began counting out loud: one, two, three . . . The slice of kulfi lay like a wedge of orange on the transparent skin of my inner wrist where thin blue lines crossed like railway tracks. Eight, nine, ten . . . First the kulfi felt like a sliver of ice on my skin, then of fire. Although the slice weighed nothing, it seemed to grow heavier against my wrist and I felt a dull pain. The outer edges of the kulfi began to sludge.

Fifteen, sixteen, seventeen . . . Sherab's face looked pinched. The kulfiman watched first Sherab, then me. A creamy drop rolled off my wrist. At Twenty-One, Sherab broke. "I'm done! I'm done!" he said and quickly gulped his kulfi down. I huffed, relieved. Sherab had lasted longer than usual. Angling my face, I brought my wrist carefully up to my mouth and swallowed the kulfi, feeling the sweet milky taste spread across my tongue. The kulfiman's face didn't change but I thought he was satisfied. He began to pack up. We watched him tie the rope-like cloth around his head like a Punjabi's pukri. Then he placed the basket on top. I held my wrist out to the sun. Although we knew the word "shukriya," we never said it. There was no need to thank the kulfiman. Whatever impulse it was that motivated him, we knew it was not kindness.

Sherab put his hand in his pocket and brought it out. Beside the crumpled newspaper lay a red strip of pataka. So that was what the older boy had dropped. Diwali, the Indian festival of lights, was around the corner and the stores in the bazaar sold all kinds of firecrackers.

"What should we do with it, Lhamo?" Sherab said.

I felt the pataka, the rough rounded nibs of the gunpowder which felt like pellets of sandpaper on my fingers. I remembered that Momo Pasang made a fire in the winter evenings. I had never gone to her room but some of the older boys in our dorm liked to go and sit by her fire. They said she was touched in the head and that she never knew who they were, but she let them stay anyway.

"I know," I said.

Sherab and I walked across the basketball ground, feeling as if everyone were looking at us. We tried to be nonchalant, as if we were just strolling in no particular direction. It felt as if everyone must know that we were headed to Momo's place and they would stop to ask us why. Momo's room was at the south end of campus, below the school hall and facing the outer perimeter of the school. There were a series of storerooms where knickknacks such as the school's dance costumes and instruments and old desks and chairs were kept. Momo lived in one of these storerooms.

Momo's door was unlocked. We knocked and then pushed the door open. She sat on her bed, hunched over, with dirty, straggly hair in a halo around her head.

"Who is it?" she said. Sherab and I looked at each other.

"Who is it?" she called out again. She peered at us and said, "Momo doesn't have eyes anymore."

"We are dorm kids. We just came to sit by the fire, Momo," I said to her.

"What?" she said. "Momo doesn't have ears anymore."

"We came to sit by the fire!" I said in a loud voice, which she finally heard. She nodded and waved for us to come in. A low cast iron barrel sat in the center of the room, inside which a scattering of orange coals glowed weakly under a film of ash. In place of chairs, there were upturned buckets. We went and sat by the fire.

Momo's room still held storage items. Great leaves of dusty blue tarp were draped over large, geometric shapes. They took up one half of the room. The shapes were strange, as if misshapen furniture had frozen under them. She lived in the other half of the room, which held her bed and a large aluminum trunk with a cloth over it. On the trunk, she had fixed a small altar. There was a picture of the Dalai Lama, the one with the Potala on a moonlit night and His Holiness's image in a sun on the left side of the picture. In the picture, the water in the pool in front of the Potala sat so still that a second Potala, falling where the other rose, hung perfectly upside down. Momo had placed a brass offering bowl in front of the picture. There was just the one instead of the usual seven and it was only half-filled with water. The white khata placed over the picture had yellowed and blackened. The single light bulb, strung along a string, cast a hazy yellow glow over the room. Momo and Sherab both looked jaundiced in its light. Grime had settled over everything, the sort of grime that's had years to settle on all surfaces and seep into all crevices.

Momo rose creakily. She chose two skeletal twigs from the pile on the floor by her bed and placed them into the fire. Then she poured some coals over them. The twigs hissed and spit, crackling into bright life that held steady for a blaze before weakening and dimming even as we watched.

"The fire needs some wood, some small logs," Sherab said. "The twigs burn up and out like that." He snapped his fingers. Momo ignored him. Maybe she didn't hear him. We waited. Sherab made a face at me and said, "I'll go and get some proper wood." He left with a pointed look at Momo's pile of twigs on the floor.

Momo and I sat there in silence by the dimming fire. In the reddish light of the fire, she looked huddled in a malevolent heap. Some of the older girls told stories of witches, of this coven of women who seemed harmless and ordinary enough in the daytime but who turned into flesh-eating demonesses at night. Silly stories, yes, but sometimes even the most fantastical stories can leave a mark on the listener. In all these stories, if someone said the wrong thing or did the wrong thing, the witch got them. You didn't want to give a witch any excuse. I wanted to break the silence, and abruptly, without quite intending to, the question that came out of my mouth was, "Momo, why were you begging in the bazaar today?"

"What?" Momo said in a quavering voice, "What did you say?"

"Momo, why were you begging in the bazaar? I saw you today," I said.

"What? I can't hear you," Momo said, and all of a sudden I felt perfectly certain that she could hear me just fine.

"Momo," I said again, loudly, insistent, "Why were you begging?"

Momo shook her head and said, "Momo doesn't have ears anymore."

Suddenly shivering, I pulled the bucket I was sitting on closer to the fire and held out my hands. A twig had fallen on the floor next to my foot. I threw it on the brazier. The brief, sudden blaze made my thin fingers look red, as if half my hands were on fire. How long was Sherab going to take?

Momo shook her head again and said, "Momo is old. Momo has no eyes, Momo has no ears. Momo has no work, Momo has no money. Momo is very very old. Momo is just waiting to die. There's nothing else to do now."

Momo had no one, no family, I knew that. As far as anyone at Patlikuhl knew, Momo had always been alone. It's only now that I realize she had already lived a life in Tibet. She had lived her youth in the old country, and who knows what she had then. A home, a hearth. A husband and children, parents and siblings. She was older than anyone else at Patlikuhl and if she had family before, now all she had were memories. Even then I could see that what she wanted more than anything at that moment was pity, and I mean pity, not sympathy. I could sense that she was bitter about her impending death, and that frightened me. But I had the pitiless conviction of the very young that death was the natural end to life—I had no sense of its loss, of why even an old woman with nothing to live for might yet want to live.

I might have asked her a question then. I might have said anything. How do you spend your days? Is this winter colder than the last? Do you want to come closer to the fire? Are you warm over there? I held my tongue and said nothing. I watched her and thought: "This is what adults become."

I was relieved when Sherab came back. He held a small bundle of branches in his arms. He dropped them by the twigs and then gave a vigorous shiver. "It's so cold outside, Momo," he rubbed his hands. He gave me a look and said, "I think we need a bigger fire." I wanted to say "no, no we don't" but Sherab started placing branches on the fire. He laid three in a triangle on the scattering of coals and then dropped some twigs over them. The twigs immediately caught fire but the branches sat dry at first. However, as we watched and waited, the wood slowly began to glow red. Momo had closed her eyes and was fingering her rosary. The clicking of the rosary and Momo's soft mumble were the only sounds in the room.

Sherab quietly tore the strip of the pataka in two and held one half out to me. The room was getting warmer; the branches were now haloed in flame and the fire burned steadily. Sherab called out to me in a whisper, "Lhamo!" I shook my head and gestured for him to keep both halves. But he continued to hold his hand out, insistent on sharing the pataka with me. We stared at each other. In the reflected firelight, the thin, coiled strip of brick-red paper gleamed like a living thing. When I reached out and took the pataka, it felt like a paper snake, with eyes dotted along its long, mean body. I felt a prickling in my neck and the skin of my back. In sync and in silence, Sherab and I held our halves of the firecracker strip over the fire and then dropped them. For a moment nothing happened.

Then the small rounds of gunpowder set off a series of small explosions in the barrel. PAK- PAK- PAK . . . PAK-PAK-PAK-PAK . . . PAK-PAK-PAK . . . .

Sparks flew out of the fire. It went on for what felt like a long time although in reality it was probably no more than ten seconds. I was startled at how loud the explosions were in the small room.

The effect on Momo was almost miraculous. She shot up from her seat. The rosary flew out of her hands and landed with a rattle by my feet. Then Momo started screaming. "The Chinese are coming! The Chinese are coming!" she screamed at the top of her voice.

Her eyes were unseeing under a film of white. With both hands grabbing the skirt of her *chupa*, she raised its hem, as if she were standing in ankle-deep water and she didn't want it to get wet. She looked so ridiculous, this old woman in a discolored and tattered *chupa* losing her mind over a firecracker.

Sherab and I dashed out of there and stood gasping and laughing outside her door. We were laughing so hard, holding our stomachs and doubling over. We clutched each other and said in unison, "The Chinese are coming! The Chinese are coming!" cackling all the while.

"Wicked kids, wicked wicked kids!" said Momo, raging. She raised her fist at us and started coming toward us. "Wait till I tell the headmaster! Wait till I tell on you!"

Sherab and I ran all the way back to my dorm. We told our success to the other students, stumbling over our words in haste, and everyone laughed and clapped as we got to the end. All that winter long, long after Diwali was over, until the shops in the bazaar finally sold out their supply of firecrackers, kids dropped pataka into Momo Pasang's fire and every single time, before she came to her senses and realized that it was just a bunch of children, Momo gave her eerie, ridiculous cry.

SNOW PILGRIMAGE

KYABCHEN DEDROL

TRANSLATED BY TENZIN DICKIE, CATHERINE TSUJI, AND DHONDUP TASHI REKJONG

She placed her walking stick between the rocks and the slate and looked at the horizon. The snow-covered mountain appeared in and out of her sight. Opening her eyes wide, she looked ahead intently. The blizzard blinded her momentarily. Just then, a stream of cold snowmelt wet her feet. She moved forward, taking another step. The blizzard cleared, but suddenly, a black frog jumped toward her, causing her to shriek and recoil. Her foot hit a rock and she fell over.

The day she left the house of red lights behind was the day she was able to leave behind not just the illicit, repulsive desires of men but also her own craving for money. As she walked away from the town, her bag felt empty, and with each step, she felt as if she were walking on air. Over the following days, she came across motorcyclists, shepherds, and cars along the way. When the passersby saw her, a lone woman on the road on a pilgrimage, they gave her spare change and food. She was able to completely forget the house of red lights. One night she stayed with a nomad family, and saw all the family gathered around a little girl, joking and laughing, and she was reminded of her own childhood. That night she even dreamed of Gota, her hometown, and Serchen field. The next day, she woke up with the sun on her pillow but she felt an uneasiness. As she was setting out, her hostess gave her some dried meat for the road. When the hostess said kindly, "Be careful on the road," she felt as if a cold wind had blown into her eyes and she teared up. That night she reached a town that traded in caterpillar fungus and she stayed at a very dirty hotel that was fifty yuan for a night.

After dusk fell she went to the courtyard to fetch some water. She saw a herd of people—Chinese, Hui Muslims, Tibetans, all in their different clothes—gathered like cattle around a building that housed prostitutes such as herself. Among the crowd, she saw that there were also prostitutes. As she was turning on the tap, two young men came toward her, and one said to the other, "Look, could be a beauty." Then he said, with a glance at the crowded building, "Compared to the Chinese women, this girl is only okay." The other man, undoing the rag wrapped around his head, said to her, "Hey, girl. How much for a go?" She glared at him and responded, "I don't understand what you are saying. Just let me fetch my water." The second guy said, "I guess she isn't one," and turned back. The first man followed him. As she was boiling her tea, several men came in succession to bang on her door but she just yelled, "You have come to the wrong place." If only so many men had banged on her door at the house of red lights. If she were to come back here next year at the same time with some girlfriends, she thought, they would do a lot of business. But it wasn't a good idea to think about business while on pilgrimage, so she took her rosary and began saying the mantra, "*Om benza siddi hum*." She went to the bathroom. As she was returning to her room, a man grabbed her sleeve and said, "Can I come inside with you?"

It was the man who had approached her earlier while she was fetching water. Without saying anything, she quickly went indoors and somehow he slipped in with her. She wanted to drive him out but she didn't have the courage to do so. Taking off his headrag, the man said, "I waited for you to come outside. I think I must have waited an hour."

He had longish hair, a dark face, a high-bridged nose, and even teeth that gleamed white. She wondered why a man like him would come to a place like this. Among all her customers she had never seen a man as handsome as this one.

"Why did you wait for me?" she asked.

Just then an old Chinese man banged on the door and called out, "Guniang, kaimen," asking her to open the door. The young man responded, "Ni xiang yao shenme" asking the man what he wanted. The man got frightened and quickly left. He laughed and said to her, "I am an AIDS prevention health worker. I pretend to be a customer and then do my research on the practices of the sex workers. I also try to educate them. Since it's caterpillar trading season right now, there are literally no hotels without prostitutes. They have even set themselves up in tents in the caterpillar markets."

"Why did you wait for me? I told you I wasn't a prostitute."

"To tell you the truth, I've been here some days. I am leaving tomorrow. I don't know anyone in this place and it's a bit lonely, so I thought we could chat."

"When we met by the tap, didn't you have a friend with you?"

"I didn't even know him. I saw him at another hotel, searching for prostitutes, and came after him. He's a local. He knew the hotels around here."

Washing a bottle she said to him, "I don't really know how to have a conversation." She smiled at him and poured him some tea. Holding the cup in his hand he said, "Thank you." Seeing her belongings on the bed, he said, "In another day you'll be at the foot of Machen Pomra."

As they talked, their bodies and their minds came closer and closer toward each other. She told him that she had been a nun but it was not her fate to be committed to the dharma wholeheartedly and so she had fallen back into the desires and chaos of samsara again. She wept in front of him, and pretended to be that woman she had been before she became a prostitute. He took great care with his words as he said, "I thank you for telling me your story without hiding anything. Even if your physical body were in a temple but if your mind kept wandering in samsara, that is suffering . . . that is sin and I don't think there can be much merit in that. Why is it completely okay for monks to disrobe but not for nuns? That is just a sign of the unequal place of women in our society. The fact that you were a nun once, that just means that you have accumulated so much merit. In foreign countries such as Thailand, there's even a practice where people go to the monastery for a few years. You shouldn't be uneasy about your past. If you can manage to make a living, then you'll be happy once again."

She wept as he consoled her. She cried because after she had disrobed and left her nun's life behind, she had not managed to earn a living and had been forced to become a prostitute, but how could she tell him that?

As she wiped her face with her right hand, her head bent, he brought his head close to hers, and pulled her into his lap. Her tears wet his face as he sucked and caressed her tongue. As was her habit, she wanted to remove her blessed chadud string from her neck to place it somewhere safe. But when she went to remove it, he kept kissing her neck and her face, touching her back, her hips and her buttocks and a state of intoxicated desire swept them both. He picked her up like a child and put her on the bed, whereupon he proceeded to undress her. Slowly, taking off her top and her pants and caressing her everywhere, he kissed her breasts and rubbed her sex. Her body opened like a flower-bud in ecstasy, without any shyness or hesitation, and wherever he touched her, that was where her mind went. With eyes closed, she moaned, bit her lip and nuzzled his neck. He felt a wave of tenderness toward the woman in front of him. Feeling as if they were two hunted animals, mother and child, that had escaped the hunter's bullet and reunited on an unfamiliar plain, he held her tightly. He felt the condom in his front pocket and wanted to put it on, but seeing her so lost in pleasure, the tresses of her hair falling in her face, all shame and shyness lost in ecstasy and the desire to be one with him, he wanted nothing in the way of their pleasure and their connection.

When she slept with her customers, she was always desperate for them to come quickly and she did whatever she could to finish them off. Whether they bit her lip or squashed the breath out of her, however they touched her, she felt as if there were only money between them, not real bodies, just cash that grew harder and more impenetrable until she couldn't feel anything. When some of the men became violent with her, she moaned and screamed to get them to climax quickly. Then as they rested heavily on her afterwards, she felt nauseous and often fought with the men afterwards. But this time, she could not restrain her emotions or control her feelings at all. Like the supreme steed of Indra, she followed where he led. That night in that hotel, all the senses and sensitivities that had lain dormant before, hidden underneath her skin, awakened. As he pushed inside her with his penis and rocked into her body, she felt an ecstasy that she had never experienced before and gave a long cry.

That night as the young man held her in his lap as if she were his beloved, she felt, for the first time since she had disrobed, that there was some kind of meaning to be found in this life. When she had slept with the man who had broken her nun's vows, her mind had been full of fear and terror. The man had inserted himself into her and moved but lacked the courage or the wherewithal to do anything else, and the terror in her mind had grown and grown until she pushed him away from her and ran out the door crying. Then she had roamed and wandered until finally ending up at the house of red lights.

She woke up the next day just before dawn. She couldn't decide if she should wake him from sleep to say something or just leave him be. She gently gave him a kiss on his cheek. Not fully awake he said, "Are you leaving?" He stretched out his hands, looped them around her neck and gave her his phone number. Then he said, "My name is Yeshi Tsering. Give me a call when you can." She replied, "My name is Lhamo. I hope you won't forget me." She kissed him again and then she left.

As she hurriedly left the town behind her, as if she had an appointment to keep with the dawn, she repeated his phone number again and again, carving the numbers into her memory. She felt a deep regret that at the moment of departure, she had not given him her real name but only the name that she used with her customers.

Far into the distance, the old snow mountain Machen Pomra rose majestically above the clouds into the sky. On the blackened dirt path leading to the mountain were pilgrims making this snow pilgrimage, all of them walking eastwards. As she saw these pilgrims, her faith rose up inside her and she said automatically, "Salutation to the Three Jewels," with her hands clasped in prayer and an image of Yeshi Tsering in her mind. If only he were with her now and they were making this pilgrimage together. Maybe she could call him after the pilgrimage. But would he answer, would he respond? Her bad karma from her previous lives had led her to some terrible actions but she would not go down that path again, she vowed, or there was no dharma, no three jewels. On the pilgrimage path, some of the old pilgrims raised their thumbs to her to convey their praise and appreciation. The younger pilgrims, close to her in age, chatted with her, as if they were friends. As they made their way around the mountain, she felt neither tired nor exhausted. Rather, she felt, strangely enough, as if she were going home. The snow mountain's cold air, dry wind, and fog and clouds slowly pushed the house of red lights away from her mind; slowly she forgot the heat, the sighs, the condoms, the disgusting emissions, the bad breath and the foul smells of the prostitutes, the noise and the ruckus and the crude jokes, the bad dreams and all the small sorrows of the house of red lights. As some of the pilgrims told their stories of their Mt. Kailash pilgrimage, she thought, if only she could go on a Kailash pilgrimage one day with Yeshi Tsering!

She spent nine days at Machen Pomra and completed three koras around the sacred mountain. Then one day, as she sat in one of the hermits' tents pitched at the base of the mountain, while drinking some tea and eating some *tsampa*, she saw a vision of her childhood home and felt as if a childhood playmate had tugged at her during their play. But her heart went cold as she remembered that in that faraway home there was now only her brother and his wife. An icy cold blast of wind swept through the playground and her vision vanished.

Her parents had passed away, too soon, some years ago. Her uncle had insisted that her brother now run the household and sent her to look after the cattle of a rich neighbor. Two years after that she ran away and joined a nunnery. She had been running for so long, running here and there and every which way. Where should she run now? Was there a place at the end of this road where she could live in peace? These thoughts passed through her mind. She wanted to buy a phone and get a SIM card to call Yeshi Tsering. Then she remembered that her ID was with the madam of the house of red lights, and a wave of sadness passed through her. She heard once again the hard, echoing sound of the door knock at that house, and old men close to their death creeping inside to get a taste of the young women. Without her

ID, she couldn't even open a bank account. She had to get her ID back somehow, then get a phone and a SIM card. She knew that her first phone call would be to Yeshi Tsering.

She slowly rapped on the door, a grayish head rag on her head and a white scarf over her mouth, breathing heavily. Her breath steamed through the scarf and wafted in the air in front of her. The madam's daughter opened the door. There were four or five men inside playing cards. She said to the daughter, "Can you call Sertso Kyi for me?" A fat woman with heavy makeup on her face and a gold tooth came to the door. One of the card-playing men beckoned to her and said, "*Aro*, Sister Sertso Kyi, bring her to me tonight." Another man said, "If you are going to sing, sing a love song." They all laughed and joked, carrying on with their game.

Sertso said, "Jangchup Dolma, I was worried you hadn't come back. I hope your family members are well? There's a new girl in your room. Tonight you can stay with Xiaohong and tomorrow I'll prepare a room for you." Usually when there were other girls around Sertso called her "Lhamo" but this time she called her by her legal name. Maybe Sertso didn't see her as a prostitute just then.

"Sister, please return my Resident ID card to me. I am very grateful to you but I can no longer stay in this place. I can no longer take money from your hands," she said.

Sertso forced out a laugh but said nothing. Since there were many prostitutes in the yard, Sertso grabbed her sleeve, pulled her inside and took her to a little room. There the madam proceeded to yell at her.

"When you first came here, what did you agree to do? Did you or did you not agree to stay for three years? Forget three years, it hasn't even been one year! Just because you have some beauty . . . No matter how beautiful you are, you are still a whore!

Do you really think all that will wash away when you leave? Ha ha!" said Sertso Kyi to her.

She spun around and started running, Sertso calling at her, "Ex-nun! Shameless ex-nun!" She ran out the door and into the street where a motorcycle almost ran her down. It was dark outside. A few men were hanging out here and there, some walking and leaning on each other for support. A man on a motorbike started to follow her. When she started yelling at this man, just as Sertso had yelled at her, the man shot off like an arrow. The roar of the motorbike reverberated through the cold and freezing street for a moment and then died away.

That night she stayed at another dirty hotel, paying yet another fifty yuan. She determined the next day to go to the next town and find a maid's job. What little money she had, she would spend on a rosary, a mirror, some Tibetan novels, and other good things.

She went to sleep with relief and joy in her heart at having left behind the house of red lights. She began to dream. She was climbing up the cliff behind their family tent, fearful of any snakes that she might encounter. She walked carefully and climbed up the face of a large rock. Clutching the branch of a salt cedar tree, she tried to grab at a cluster growing on the cliff when she heard her grandmother's voice calling her name.

"Metok, what are you doing here? You might fall down. Come here to Grandma . . . don't move, don't move." As her hands reached for the cluster to put in her mouth, she fell off the cliff. Terror engulfed her, but though she fell and fell, there was no bottom to her fall, no landing. There was nothing she could do to help herself.

She panted in her sleep but did not wake. Suddenly, as if she had been covered in a warm blanket, she fell deeper into her sleep. Her grandmother was bringing her some *tsampa* with butter in the small ceramic bowl that her father had brought her from Labrang. Her grandmother said, "You fell from the cliff but you are fine now. If you are hungry, knead some *tsampa* in here and eat." She replied, "Grandma, you knead it for me." Many guests came to the house. Their faces and her grandmother's face became blurry. She was filled with the same terror again, as if she was once again falling off the cliff.

Two months later, the snow was melting off the eaves of a certain Tibetan restaurant and steam was rising into the air. The traditional Tibetan door was kept open and it was quiet inside with only one or two patrons. A young woman stood by the counter. With a straight nose, fine eyebrows, and a bright gaze, she had a narrow, beautiful face with glowing cheeks and red lips. Her hair had red and blonde highlights and it was braided. Falling across her forehead, her hair was gathered in a bunch at the nape of her neck. She had a faint smile on her face and a mole on her left cheek. She looked up and down and around her, then quickly opened a random drawer and grabbed a phone. Into the phone she inserted a new SIM card that she had bought earlier. She then leisurely walked out of the restaurant.

Some of the water dripping from the eaves fell on the collar of her red shirt with black buttons. The droplets collected on her blessed chadud string, now faded in color, and dripped onto the skin of her neck. The coldness and the wetness didn't seem to bother her. She looked back at the restaurant, walked some more steps and then turned on the phone. She set it up. Finally, she entered the number that she had memorized and called Yeshi Tsering.

He picked up, "Hello."

"Hello, is this Yeshi Tsering?" she said. "This is Lhamo. I have come back from my pilgrimage now." She meant to give him her real name, Metok, and tell him where she was. It wasn't very cold but she was trembling.

"Lhamo," said Yeshi Tsering. "How can I tell you? We are finished! I don't mean to avenge myself, don't worry about that. May the three jewels save us!"

She froze and her mind went blank. She had no idea what to say. What did he mean? What had happened?

"What happened?" she asked.

"You have given me AIDS . . ." he said.

Her vision went blurry. A small bird landed on her shoulder, flapping its wings a few times, before it flew off.

She threw away the phone in her hand. She stood there, blankly, staring at nothing. Only one thought came to her mind. If only she could go on another snow pilgrimage!

ZUMKI'S SNOW LION

TENZIN TSUNDUE

Zumki stops her dad in the middle of the bustling New York street and insists that he tells her the snow lion story again. Her big pleading eyes narrow in anticipation. Her father looks to either side of the road and marches on, leading Zumki with his index finger.

Then Tashi, her father, makes a suggestion. "Can't we do this at home?"

"At home we have *Snow Lion* on TV!" Zumki yells amidst the din of traffic.

Tashi obliges, knowing how persistent his daughter can be. He begins: "Up in the highest mountains, among the white, white mountains of the Himalayas, live the snow lions. It is believed that only the kindest and purest of heart can see the snow lion. The only thing is, its head alone is the size of you!" Tashi pinches the cheeks of his little daughter who is now ecstatic with joy, her small hands clapping in excitement as she squeals with laughter.

"While its thick white coat keeps the snow lion warm in the snow mountains, a mane of bright green hair runs along its monstrous head, down its back and down its arms and legs," explains Tashi. "No one knows what snow lions eat but they have enormous mouths." Saying this, Tashi animatedly bares his teeth, opening his eyes wide. In a sudden swinging gesture he picks up his little girl, mounting her onto his shoulders. Then they sing and dance. "Tingti . . . tingti . . . ting, tingti . . . tingti . . . tingti, tiriti ti . . .

dance in the bustle of a street in the biggest city in the world.

Back at home, Zumki neatly seats herself on a square mattress on the floor right in front of the television set. Her father dutifully switches on the machine, showing a video recording of a snow lion dance performed by a Tibetan dance troupe in India. Zumki dances, waving her little hands and swinging her pony-tail.

When the father returns to check on Zumki, the little angel is fast asleep in front of the snow lion. Tashi lifts her up in his arms and lays her down in her bedroom. To the sleeping child he whispers, "When we go to India, we'll see real snow lion dances. Good night, my motherless baby." He switches off the lights and closes the door.

Zumki and her father are now in Dharamshala, India, to spend their summer break with Zumki's grandparents. Looking down from their street-side house on a first floor in McLeod Ganj, Zumki looks out for Lhasa apsos.

"Tomorrow we are going trekking to Triund mountain-top. Zumki, do you want to come? We will sleep in tents and make our own food among the trekkers," Tashi says.

Zumki thinks for a while and asks: "Are there snow lions up in the mountains?" Tashi looks at his parents and responds, "I don't know. We'll go and find out."

The next morning, straining with small steps up the steep slope, a line of trekkers follows its way up the ridge, huffing and puffing. As the sun rises in the golden light of dawn, Zumki is leading her father by a few steps. She crawls on her tiny hands and knees, climbing the large stone slabs that become the steps up the slope. Her father looks on.

After a curve in the road, Zumki's father finds her sitting on a rock feeding some of her Uncle Chips to a monkey. In a sudden reflex, Tashi rushes forward to chase the monkey away. Zumki is perplexed. “Zumki, what are you doing? These monkeys could bite you. Aren't you scared?” Tashi shouts at her, bending down on his knees and hugging his child.

“But, I am not scared of monkeys,” she says. “I love them.”

After walking for some distance, they all take a rest at a bend in the lone winding path of stone slabs. From there they can clearly see a green expanse at the nape of the Triund summit. The blood red blossoms of rhododendrons light up the hillsides among pines, spruce, and Himalayan oaks. The breeze that wafts up the valley mixes the fragrance of the blossoming flowers with a touch of humid air. The fog that surrounds them becomes clouds for the valley people, obscuring the snow peaks. Looking down over the spread of Kangra Valley, Tashi points to a small forested hill and says, “That's McLeod Ganj.”

“But I can't see,” Zumki protests, peering through over-sized binoculars.

The trekkers have now reached Triund. Tents are being raised, large rucksacks are being dug into. Clothes, bedding, and edibles are spread across the green cover of pristine meadows. Someone is already brewing tea on a hearth made of three rocks. Smoke from the wood-fire rises along with the vapor of the bubbling tea.

“After lunch we should climb up to the snow-line at Ilaka,” says Tashi's friend. “You should bring your snow lion girl with you. Who knows, we might get a rare glimpse of the mythical beast up there,” he teases.

Back in the tent, the tired little girl is taking a rest, lying down against her sleeping bag. Tashi leaves her in the care of an old man who is also staying behind. The rest of the group leaves for Ilaka.

As Zumki lies back in her tent, the sound of the snow lion dance, “Tingti . . . tingti . . . ting, tingti . . . tingti . . . ting,” alerts her. There's a hazy image moving outside her tent. As she slowly unzips the flap and gazes outside, she sees the tail of a large white hairy animal vanish behind her tent. She cringes and draws back inside. The familiar music of the snow lion dance continues to ring outside in the afternoon sun.

Summoning her courage, Zumki emerges from the safety of her shelter and stands rooted to the spot. A giant snow lion comes rushing toward her from the rocks and stops right before her. She doesn't move. The drum beats fall, everything has suddenly frozen in a moment of silence.

Zumki looks up at the giant animal and her jaw drops in amazement on seeing the humongous head of the lion. She slowly reaches out, to touch the white hair at the animal's chest. Her fingers, and then her little hand, feel the softness of the white coat. As she runs her hand down the length of the animal's arm, the beast shrugs a little. The eyes blink.

Suddenly the rhythmic music of the drum, flute, bells, and the cymbals comes alive and the lion jumps into action, dancing to the tune. Making a circle, it comes around to face Zumki who then dances with the lion. They prance around, to the right and to the left. Then the snow lion rises up, standing on its hind legs. Zumki claps loudly and repeatedly jumps up and down in jubilation.

Looking at the standing lion, Zumki raises her left hand and wiggles it in the air to tell him to follow her actions. Now her right hand wiggles, now she shakes her head vigorously and says, "Boo." Then she says, "Follow me." The lion raises both paws to his ears and jeers, extending his tongue. "Now shake your butt, like this," Zumki orders. "Now you do something," says Zumki as she runs out of antics. The lion winks twice with its left eye, then winks twice with the right one. Unable to follow this, Zumki breaks into giggles.

Then the lion lies down on its belly and touches its right

ear with its right foot. Zumki also lies down on the meadow, but again is unable to follow the lion's actions. She falls down flat on her back, breaking into laughter in front of the animal. Slowly touching the lion's right fore-arm, in a silent moment she feels the giant paw and measures it with her tiny palm. She then sits enclosed in the giant's embrace. Feeling the softness and the warmth of the white coat on her cheeks, she lies down and slowly falls asleep, breathing lightly in the arms of the mythical beast.

Just then, something moves in the belly of the lion; a heavily-sweating dancer emerges from the belly, disheveled and exhausted. And now the head of the lion descends to the ground, and out comes the other dancer. From behind rocks the musicians then emerge carrying a big round drum, a bell, a pair of cymbals, and the flute player. Someone picks up little Zumki and takes her to the tent. The head dancer says: "Come on, let's pack, the picnic is over. We've practiced enough, let's go back down. Else it'll be dark when we get home."

As the hikers return to the tents, the dance artists are seen leaving the spot in a single file, slowly descending the steep sides of the green hill, following the narrow and treacherous stony path.

Tashi wakes up his little girl sleeping in the tent and gives her stones that he picked up from the higher mountains. She rushes outside and looks around, turns back, and demands to know, "Where is the snow lion? He was here. I met him. We played together." Tashi isn't impressed. He says, "You were sleeping. You must have been dreaming."

"No!" protests the combative child. "He's real. He was here," she says, pointing to the green meadows that she rolled upon with the animal as they executed their dance.

Tashi follows his daughter to the patch in the ground where

she points. Zumki picks up something from among the blades of grass and hands it over in triumph as irrefutable evidence—long strands of white and green hair.

Holding the wisps of evidence clenched between his thumb and index finger, Tashi kneels down in front of his daughter and declares: "Yes, only the kindest and purest of heart can see the snow lion."

DOLMA

DHONDUP TASHI REKJONG

TRANSLATED BY
TENZIN DICKIE

1.

Dolma's full name was Tsering Dolma. Everyone at school called her Dolma. I also called her Dolma. We were friends from primary school. Our primary school was called Dornyin. From my hometown, the village where I was born, to Dornyin school was a walk of at least twenty minutes. First you walked down to the heel of a small valley, then you climbed up a rather steep hillside, after which you walked past several large fields. Finally, you came to Dornyin school.

Dolma and I were not just classmates, we were also friends. Her Tibetan was very good, my math was very good. I helped her with her math schoolwork and she helped me with my Tibetan schoolwork. Once, when we were in the fourth grade, after our afternoon Tibetan class was over, I had to remain in class because I hadn't finished my lessons. All the students left for home. Dolma had already finished her work but she remained behind and waited for me to finish.

"You don't have to wait for me," I said, a little embarrassed.

"We can walk together after you finish. I'll help you," she said.

"Okay, thanks," I said, nodding my head.

At first, I asked her a question if I didn't know the answer, and Dolma explained her answer to me. But soon enough I just started copying directly from Dolma's notebook. Dolma didn't say anything but just showed me her notebook. We had to make sentences with vocabulary words. If the sentence she made for the word "knowledge" was the following: "In our class, Bumkyab has a lot of knowledge," I wouldn't copy the sentence directly but I would alter it and write something like: "In our home my father has a lot of knowledge."

I finally finished the schoolwork, feeling very relieved and happy. Dolma had a smile on her face too. I wondered if she smiled because I had finished my homework, but I didn't have the guts to ask her such a question. I was fourteen at that time. Dolma was probably thirteen, but I'm not really sure.

When I missed class or when I was home sick, Dolma took careful notes in class and then went over the lessons with me. She continued to show me her homework. The fact that we weren't just friends but were also study partners meant that we started to care for each other. Our classmates saw that we studied together and helped each other with our school work, and some of them began to tease us, saying, "Dorjee and Dolma are a couple."

This phrase, "Dorjee and Dolma are a couple," became a news headline in Dornyin school for a time. This news even reached beyond the school gates to the grounds of my village. One day when I was on my way home after school, I ran into Pema, the village shepherd, who asked me, "So Dorjee, the news these days is that you and Dolma are a couple. Is that true?"

Not knowing what to say, I just gave him a smile. The truth is, I couldn't say whether Dolma and I were a couple or not. Were we dating or were we just friends? I didn't know.

Perhaps it was because I heard "Dorjee and Dolma are a couple" so many times. Anyway, my feelings for Dolma began to change from an affectionate friendship to love. But if someone had asked me—how do you love Dolma?—I couldn't have given them an answer.

During a math class, instead of keeping my eyes on the blackboard I couldn't help looking at Dolma again and again. The math teacher, Miss Kartso Kyi, noticed that I was looking at Dolma and to recall my attention to the blackboard, she threw a piece of chalk at me which hit me squarely in the forehead. My classmates laughed. I felt my face burn in humiliation. I couldn't look at Miss Kartso Kyi and I definitely couldn't look at Dolma anymore. I kept my head down. My classmates laughed but Dolma did not. Why didn't Dolma laugh along with the rest of the class? Was it to support me silently or was she also embarrassed? Ever since I had fallen for Dolma, all my thoughts were drawn to her. She was in my mind constantly. Sometimes before it became dark, I went up on the terrace at home and stood looking in the direction of Dolma's village. I hoped that perhaps in her village too, Dolma sat looking in the direction of my village.

"Son, what are you doing just standing there? Come down here," said my mother several times, after seeing this strange behavior from me.

I wouldn't reply. My poor mother was puzzled. I used to sit by the hearth and write my lessons for the next day or just talk about anything and everything with my grandmother as she sat on the hearth. But as Dolma began to appear in my thoughts more and more, I began going up to the terrace more and more.

Dolma was shorter than me. She had a small mole on the right side of her mouth. Her hair was neither long nor short. She kept it in two braids that she tied with rubber bands that had a yellow flower. She wore coral earrings . . . sometimes when we had gym class and we played on the lower school playground and ran around, her earrings swung from side to side. She usually wore red pants and colorful red socks with her canvas shoes. There were three buttons on the sides of her red pants. Sometimes in class when I was bored, I bowed my head and out of the corner of my eyes looked at Dolma's canvas shoes, her socks, and the buttons on her pants.

2.

School started again after our summer vacation on the eighth of August. I was going to be in the fifth grade. The morning of the first day of classes, I was so excited. I was up early in the morning waiting for breakfast. I wanted to eat as soon as possible so that I could go to school. I only drank half of the tea that my mother poured in my teacup before getting my backpack and setting out from home. My mother was astonished at my eagerness.

"Son, why are you so excited for school?" my mother asked.

"I am off!" was the only answer I gave her.

I didn't tell my mother why I was so excited. I wasn't excited for school but to see Dolma again, and to once again be in the same class with her.

Our first class that day was math class with Miss Kartso Kyi. We were now in the fifth grade but we were still in the same classroom. Before Miss Kartso Kyi arrived, everyone sat down in their seats. But Dolma still hadn't arrived. I waited for her . . . as I sat there thinking about Dolma, Miss Kartso Kyi came in. She handed out the fifth grade math textbooks to all the students.

"Now you guys are in the fifth grade. You are no longer young kids. In two years, you'll have to take the middle school examinations. So, the fifth and sixth grades are very important for you all," said Miss Kartso Kyi, looking down at us from the platform under the blackboard.

We watched Miss Kartso Kyi respectfully and waited for her to continue. Glancing at a few students who were making a ruckus outside our classroom, she said, "My hope is that all of you will pass the middle school examinations. It's very important for all of us to work hard together." She stopped.

I heard Miss Kartso Kyi's words, but I was thinking about Dolma. Was Dolma sick today? Was she just late for classes? I couldn't focus on the class, all my thoughts were focused on Dolma. Before class was over, Miss Kartso Kyi took a roll call but strangely enough, she didn't call out Dolma's name. I wanted to raise my right hand to remind her of Dolma but I knew that my classmates would tease me about it, so I kept my hand down.

During the break, I went to the school office. By the door there was Mr. Kathup, the third grade Tibetan teacher, holding a cigarette between his index and middle fingers.

"Who are you looking for?" Mr. Kathup asked, inhaling from his cigarette.

"I . . . our math teacher, Miss Kartso Kyi," I said, flustered.

"Wait a second." He threw his cigarette on the floor and went into the office.

On my tiptoes I quietly looked into the office window. Miss Kartso Kyi sat at a table stacked with many books and she was leafing through one. The school had only one office building, and there was a shared office for all the teachers to do their work together. One or two teachers shared a desk and that was their workspace for their teaching and administrative work. Soon Miss Kartso Kyi came outside. In her right hand she held the book she had been looking at earlier.

"Dorjee, were you looking for me?" she said. "What is it?"

"Yes, I . . . Dolma—"

Before I had finished, she interrupted, "What about Dolma?"

"I came to get the math textbook and notebook for Dolma," I forced myself to say.

"Dolma isn't coming to school. Her mother is sick, and she wants to keep Dolma at home," said Miss Kartso Kyi.

"Oh, then, will she come to school next term?" I asked.

"That I don't know. Now you should get back to classes," said Miss Kartso Kyi and went back inside the office.

Dolma wasn't coming to school. I felt as if someone had thrown a bucket of cold water over me. Lost and confused, I wasn't sure what to do next. I barely knew how the next class started or ended. Later that day when I got home I told my mother that I wasn't going to school the next day.

"What is the boy talking about now? This morning he was so excited about going to school. Now he isn't going anymore, he says," said my mother, looking at me in surprise.

"After today, I am not going to school anymore," I said, with a sad look on my face.

"Don't let your father hear that you won't go to school," my mother warned me and then went into the kitchen.

"I really won't go anymore. If I must go, I'll go to Hainan but I won't go to Dornyin." I followed her and kept insisting, but she just ignored me.

I had absolutely no desire to continue at Dornyin now that Dolma was gone. I wanted to go away, far away. I wasn't going to see her again and I had a constricted feeling in my heart. I felt that I must get away.

I continued to hound my mother about sending me to another school. During classes I couldn't concentrate on what the teachers said and often fell into my own reveries. Often, instead of looking at the blackboard I just looked at the lines carved into my desk. The teachers must have noticed my behavior in class. The school director sent two notices to the house saying that I had stopped paying attention to my studies. Finally my mother gave up and called my father and told him to bring me with him to Hainan because I wasn't doing well at Dornyin.

Not long after that, I left Dornyin and started school at Drakmar Primary in Hainan Mongolian Prefecture. My father was teaching there. I still couldn't forget Dolma. I came back home for the summer and winter holidays and each time, I wanted to see Dolma so badly. I wanted to just see her. But I was too chicken to ask anyone in the village if they knew what Dolma was doing. And I didn't have the guts to go and see her. The truth is, although I knew where Dolma's village was, I had no idea where her house was. Her village was Nyinglo village, further divided into Upper Nyinglo and Lower Nyinglo.

Then one winter there was a wedding in our village, and I heard that Dolma was among a group of girls and young women coming from the other villages. It was my friend Namkha Jhida who gave me the news. He knew that I had a crush on Dolma. I had talked to him once about her. When I heard Dolma was there, I immediately went over to the wedding venue. I was filled with a nervous delight. If she asked me how I was doing, how would I answer? And what if she ignored me? What would I do then? From a distance I saw that Dolma and a group of girls were outside the house. Dolma was wearing a red patterned scarf over her head. I walked in front, as if I were passing them, and Dolma saw me. Before I had a chance to say anything, she spoke.

"How are you?" she said.

"Hey, how are you?" I said to her.

"You are here for winter vacation?" she asked.

"Yes, yes," I said. I couldn't think of anything else to say. I was so nervous. Dolma waited for me to say something else. I was frantically thinking of what else to say when one of the girls with Dolma started calling her.

"Okay, then. Take care," said Dolma and she left.

I couldn't even reply to say, you take care too. I just watched her as she walked away. That was the first time I had seen her since the fourth grade.

3.

When I moved to Henan Mongol Autonomous County, I went back home less and less and I began to hear less and less about Dolma. My high school was in Henan, too. After finishing my high school examinations, in 2003 I received the opportunity to study at Northwest University for Nationalities at Lanzhou. At Northwest University, my studies were focused on literature and writing. At university, I dated a lot. I couldn't even tell you how many Tibetan or Chinese girls I dated, but I still couldn't put Dolma out of my mind. I even wrote and published a poem called "Dolma" in the campus poetry journal. But there was no way that she saw the poem. In fact, had she heard the news, she might not even have believed that I had written such a poem. After all, it had been seven or eight years since I had last seen her.

After I graduated from Northwest, I was luckily hired at the Qinghai Television Station as contract staff. That was thanks to my uncle. My uncle was the head of the Tibetan section. I couldn't have told you what relation there was between the literature I studied at university and the work I was now doing at the TV station. But I was very proud to be at the TV station, even as a contract staff. Moreover, my uncle told me that if I worked hard for three or four years, then I could even become full time staff at the station. At first, I stayed at my uncle's place. He had three children, though, two daughters and a son, so I moved out quite soon. Next, I shared an apartment with a friend in the

Chinese area of Yangzhate, near the TV station. A number of the newer Tibetan staff at the station lived there as well. The area was relatively cheap. My friend and I paid a rent of three hundred yuan each per month—the local Xining Tibetans even had a Tibetan name for the area, Yanglung Village.

I think it was around August, but I don't remember for sure, when I went back to Dornyin village. I arrived in Malho city and then set off on the walk home. Compared to how it used to be, there were very few people walking on the path. Ever since they built the roads, people rode their motorcycles and their cars. As the price of caterpillar fungus rose, the number of people who bought cars and motorcycles also rose steadily. A friend of mine who worked in Xining told me that whenever he arrived in Malho, he just asked people to come and pick him up. There were very few other government staff walking this path.

But I wanted to walk. From Malho to Dornyin was only just over an hour's walk. First you walked past several houses in Sakyil village and then you climbed up to Tamakhe pass. There you followed a long trail that led to a valley. Walking through this valley, you came to a place called Ludonnang, where there used to be a spring that has since dried up. On the other side of Ludonnang was the village of Adong. If you kept walking straight, then you came to a place called Dolma's Image where there used to be an image of the divine Dolma, the goddess Tara, on a big boulder—an image that the village people believed was holy, since it had been naturally manifested. I had no idea how science might have explained the image. Anyway, the Dolma image had disappeared after the highway was built. If you kept going, the juncture of Gyamoshong divided the valley into two sides. On the right side was Nyin village and Arol village. On the left were the villages of Nyinglo, Seyza and Gyamo. Here at Gyamoshong was the rest spot where the villagers rested on their way back from the city. I also sat down there to rest. Opening my water bottle, I sipped some water. As my mind wandered, a woman appeared in the distance. She was carrying a blue-green bag on her right shoulder, and a plastic bag in her left hand. It was only when the woman came closer that I recognized her. It was Dolma.

"Hello, how are you? I haven't seen you in so long," I said.

Without so much as a hi, how are you, Dolma said, "We village folk always see each other, we just don't see the city folk so much." She was smiling.

"Haha," I said with a laugh. She laughed too.

"I was just joking," Dolma said and she sat down.

I was flustered, not sure what to say to her.

"Did you go to the city?" I said.

"Yes, my husband has been sick for several days. So I went to buy some medicine. There's only my husband and my mother at home. My mother's old now, so these days it's been me running the household," she said politely, looking at me.

"Oh, I didn't even know that you had married. I am sorry. I must congratulate you," I looked at her.

"Yes, I am kind of married now. After my brother got married and left the house to live separately with his wife, we brought in a bridegroom for me. My marriage was arranged by my parents," she added, giving me these details and making our conversation more serious and intimate.

"I see, I see. Well the important thing is to love each other. If you get along, then it's all good. Tibetans have always had arranged marriages, it's long been part of our tradition," I said, trying to sound smart and educated.

Dolma did not respond. Instead she grabbed a small stick and hit the grass with it, repeating this over and over. I took out a bottle of water and gave it to her.

"No, I brought some water," she said and took water out of her plastic bag.

"And you? Are you married?" she asked.

"No. I only moved to Xining recently. Marriage is not really on my mind right now. My family also hasn't really mentioned it yet . . . even if I wanted to get married, it's hard to find a good woman," I joked. We both laughed.

"You are an educated government worker. If you can't find a good woman, I don't believe it," she said.

I was about to answer when she continued, "I have also been to Xining a few times. My mother was sick last year so we brought her to a hospital there. The little reading and writing I know came in very handy that time. My husband can't read or write; he just herds the sheep."

I had all these questions for her, questions about her mother and why she hadn't come to school after the fourth grade but I didn't have the courage to ask them just then.

"Well if you come to Xining again, you must contact me. I can help you. Do you have a phone?" I said politely.

"Yes, yes, I have a phone." She took out an iPhone 5. Thanks to the caterpillar fungus, I thought, even the ordinary people have iPhone 5s in their hands. I took her phone number and rang her phone.

Her phone started to ring. Her ringtone was a song from the singer Tsering Samdrup called "An Arrow of a Glance Shot at You from Dechen Town."

"That's my phone number," I told her. We were both silent for some time. I didn't know where to restart the conversation, now that we had exchanged phone numbers. Perhaps she was waiting for me to say something. We could see a monk and an old man coming in our direction.

"Shall we go now?" I said.

"Yes, let's go. Let's keep in touch by phone," she said and stood up.

We said goodbye. I entered the valley to the right of Gyamoshong. Dolma went to the left. I heard Dolma's words again in my mind, "My husband can't read or write, he just herds the sheep."

After dinner, everyone went to sleep. But my sister and I stayed up. She was preparing the yeast for the next day's bread. We chatted for a bit, but soon I went up to bed as well. The night was silent, except for a dog barking in the distance. I lay in bed, thinking over my conversation with Dolma. As I was recalling my meeting with her, my phone began to blink. When I looked, it was Dolma's number.

"Hey, do you have WeChat?" said her message.

"Yes. If you put in my phone number, you'll find me. My name is Wild Yak."

"My name is Shepherd Girl."

I opened my WeChat. I saw that Shepherd Girl had just sent me a friend request, which I immediately accepted.

"What are you doing?" she wrote.

"I am hugging my knees," I couldn't help typing.

"Poor guy. How sad that a government official has to do that . . ." she wrote.

"If you feel sad for me, why don't you come sit in my lap," I wrote.

"Why, do you want me to pull your dick?" she replied.

"Be careful what you say, or I'll be horny and then I'm in trouble," I said, going all in.

"If it wakes up, then come to me. I'll wait for you with my legs open," she continued the dirty talk.

"I am just kidding," I wrote. "We better stop. If your husband finds out, he'll come and kill me tomorrow." I did feel anxious and uneasy.

"He already went to bed. I am in the kitchen." It seemed she wanted to continue the conversation.

"If I'm not afraid, why are you? I open my legs for you but you can't even come to me. Ha ha."

"If you can make the time, maybe we can meet soon and catch up? I'll be here for a few days. But now you should sleep . . . good night." I felt uncomfortable continuing with the dirty talk on WeChat.

How would Dolma respond? I waited, but there was no response. I kept looking at my phone. A minute went by, then two. After ten minutes or so, she sent a message.

"Good night." There was nothing else.

I didn't write back. I didn't dare. I felt joyful but also uneasy. Dolma had not forgotten me. Not only did she still remember me, but she was willing to flirt and sext with me. But what would happen if anyone found out about this?

I kept thinking about her. Sure, she had gotten married but she must not love her husband. She had said, "My husband can't read or write, he just herds the sheep." Wasn't she insulting her husband when she said this? If she cared for her husband, would she say such a thing to me? When marriages were arranged in the villages, did they care whether the couple loved each other? If people were to find out about this WeChat conversation between Dolma and me, didn't that open the door to a whole new problem? I had best keep quiet. These thoughts went around and around in my head.

Two days later, Dolma again messaged me on WeChat. "Are you still here? Why haven't you sent me a message?"

"I'm so sorry, I am no longer there," I lied as I wrote back. "A thing came up at work and I had to come back to Xining. I am at the office right now."

"You are lying to me," Dolma wrote.

"I swear on Rongwo monastery," I swore. "I am not lying."

"Well, I won't disturb your work then. Good bye."

"Good bye." That was that.

I hadn't left for Xining, I was just too nervous to see Dolma again. If I wasn't careful and I got involved with Dolma, I foresaw that it would create a big problem for the both of us. So I restrained myself.

4.

I came back to Xining and quickly became caught up in my own busy routine. For the next two weeks, I didn't even get a chance to see any of my friends. One day, as I was leaving work on a Saturday afternoon, my friend Dortse called to ask if I had time for dinner with him at Mingdu Restaurant. I told him I would meet him there. I loved this restaurant which had some Tibetan elements. Dortse was a friend of mine from college. He came from Chabcha and worked at Gangdanang studio. I went straight to the restaurant where Dortse was waiting for me. He couldn't keep his smile off his face.

"Wow, you seem very happy today," I said as I sat down.

"Let's order first. Then I'll tell you my news," he smiled.

"What news? Do you really have some news? Are you going to become a journalist like me?" I laughed at him.

"Who doesn't have news these days?" he said, browsing his new iPhone. "Just kidding, I don't have any special news. But I am seeing a girl tonight. She's from Rebkong." He checked his phone again.

"What part of Rebkong?" I wondered who this girl was.

"I don't know her village. Her name is Dolma though. We met through WeChat. It's been about six months now since we met."

Her name was Dolma. I started to feel a slight uneasiness.

"Do you have a photo?" I asked. I really wanted to figure out who this girl was.

"I've only one photo of her," he said, searching his phone. "This is her, isn't she beautiful?" He showed me her photo.

I just looked at the photo, speechless and shocked. It was my Dolma, Dornyin Dolma. She was even wearing the same red headscarf. I still couldn't believe my eyes.

"Why are you so quiet? You don't like her, do you?" Dortse said, noticing my reaction.

"Ha ha, she's very beautiful," I said, trying to hide what I felt.

"She's staying at the Tibetan hospital. She's been in town for a few days. I invited her to the Everest Hotel tonight." The smile was back on his face.

"I see, I see," I didn't know what else to say. I didn't say one word to Dortse about Dolma. He didn't ask me whether I knew her and I just pretended that she was a total stranger to me.

After dinner, we went our own way. He took a cab to the hotel and I walked home. Questions rose like a summer flood in my mind. If Dolma was in Xining, why hadn't she called me? How many men like Dortse did she meet through WeChat? Why was she staying at the Tibetan hospital? Did her husband know that she met these men? The more I thought about Dolma, the worse my headache got.

About a month or so after I had dinner with Dortse, my phone beeped at the corner of my desk. When I checked, there was a message from Dolma.

"Are you in Xining? I am at the Xining railway station. If you can, please come. I would like to see you. At 3:30 pm this afternoon, I'm leaving for Lhasa."

"Yes, I'm in Xining," I wrote back. "Why are you going to Lhasa? Are you taking your mother and husband on a pilgrimage?"

"No. I am alone. I am going to Lhasa alone, and maybe on to India . . ."

I turned off my computer and left the office without even telling my boss. I took a cab to the railway station. As I watched the people on the streets, I started seeing all the different Dolmas in my mind. She was various in her manifestations—the Dolma of my primary school, the Dolma at the wedding ceremony, the married Dolma, the Dolma on WeChat, the Dolma who met men like Dortse in hotel rooms and the Dolma who was just now at the railway station waiting for me.

TIPS

PEMA BHUM TRANSLATED BY TENZIN DICKIE

He woke up feeling as if his bladder were about to burst. He immediately ran to the bathroom but the bathroom door was locked from the inside. He tensed his thighs.

"Open the door. I really have to pee!" he said to his wife who enjoyed taking her time putting on her makeup in the bathroom.

"Wait a second, I am almost done," she said.

"Please, I can't wait. Open the door quickly," he pleaded, tensing his muscles some more.

"Why can't . . . you hold . . . for just a few seconds . . . is your bladder . . . made of paper?" Her words came choppily through the door. She was probably putting on her lipstick.

Kunchoksum. Here he was in America, the land of the free, and he didn't even have the freedom to take a piss in the morning! He became upset.

"What's this?" he said. "You are just going off to serve people, not do a performance!" He needed to piss so badly that he felt a sudden chill throughout his body.

"Don't be such a loudmouth," his wife said. "Even if I am not going to do a performance—"

She opened the door and made way for him. He rushed into the bathroom. A sweet scent filled his nose. He didn't even hear the end of what his wife was saying. As the stream of his urine hit the toilet bowl, his whole body relaxed and a deep relief spread through his bones. He could stand straighter now.

He wanted his wife to finish her sentence, the one he had cut off earlier. He said, "What were you saying? Even if you are not going to perform—"

His wife interrupted, "Just finish your piss. You almost broke down the bathroom door just now and yet you keep yacking away . . ." Saying so, she pushed the bathroom door closed. He realized that he hadn't even closed the door.

He finished peeing. Then he washed his face. His wife was now in the bedroom getting all dressed up. He was off that day and planned to hang out in the city with two of his friends.

Was there anything he needed to buy for the house today, he wondered as he drank his tea. He made a note to ask his wife when she came out of the bedroom. He finished the tea, but she still hadn't come out of the bedroom. He thought again about what she had been saying earlier when he cut her off.

"Even though you are not going to do a performance . . . what was it you were saying before?" he asked.

"What was I saying?" said his wife, coming out of the bedroom. She searched for something in her purse. "Even if I am not going to do a performance, if I don't get all dressed up, how can I make three or four hundred dollars in tips in one day?"

He felt a shock of surprise. It wasn't the money that surprised him so much as his wife's appearance. Her hair fell shining and loose on her shoulders and she looked stunning, like a weeping willow that had been caught out in the rain. Her pupils sparkled under her dark eyebrows. Her lips, painted with lipstick, looked like a red two-petaled flower that had just bloomed, except that it lacked dew-drops. Her breasts stuck out, high and rounded, under a skin-tight turquoise top and her black skirt hugged her thighs and hips. He gazed at her with new eyes and suddenly didn't want her to leave.

"Those poor restaurant patrons . . . they haven't got a chance. If I was your patron, I wouldn't be able to help leaving you a ten or twenty dollar tip," he said, going toward his wife and pulling her.

Knowing what he wanted, she grabbed his hands and stopped him. She glanced at the altar behind him. A statue of the Buddha sat on the altar, his eyes directed downwards at the tip of his nose, as if he were trying to avoid looking at the couple's behavior.

"We can go to bed early tonight. But right now I don't have time to get dressed again," she said as she let go of his hands.

She stroked his face, and then left the room. Her turquoise top was soaked where the wet ends of her hair had dripped water on it. As her hips had caught his eye before, so now the round curve of her ass in that black skirt caught, and held, his attention.

The three friends started their day in the city by going to their regular café in Chinatown. The first friend, the one who knew New York City and its streets and subways like the palm of his hand, said this as he placed their teas in front of them: "There's a Japanese girl at my barbershop. She speaks pretty good English."

"She was lying," said the second friend, lighting a cigarette. "Last year I went to this brothel, and this Chinese girl there said she was from Shanghai. Later I saw her at a massage parlor. She didn't recognize me but I knew it was her. That time she said she was from Korea." The friend inhaled deeply on his cigarette.

He was still thinking about his wife, how beautiful she had looked that morning, and not really paying attention to his friends' conversation. He said carelessly, "Do you two really care about the girl, what country she's from? If she's pretty, who cares what country she's from?"

His smoker friend put down the newspaper he had just started reading. He took another drag of the cigarette and said, "Looks like you came here and you have become American.

Americans don't care what country you're from, where you're from—they just want the best and the brightest." The friend inhaled and then, slowly blowing out the smoke that hung in his mouth, said, "We lost our country to the Chinese. Even here, even in America, we work our asses off for the Chinese. And the wages that we get for that, we spend on Chinese ass. We just can't get away from the Chinese, can we?" Saying that, he put out his unfinished cigarette in the ashtray.

His statement hit home for them. Neither of his other friends affirmed what the smoker friend said, nor did they contradict it. They were all quiet for a while.

"Alright, alright, today's our day off," said the first friend. He had had enough of the quiet. "It's supposed to be a fun day. Even His Holiness has said again and again that he doesn't seek Rangzen! Why are we talking about such big things, we who bust our asses off for the Chinese?"

"I'm not talking about big things. All I am saying is, why are we spending our hard-earned money on Chinese ass?" said the smoker friend, lighting up another cigarette.

"Okay, okay. Come on, let's lighten up and have some fun. We won't do anything to harm the Tibetan cause," said the first friend, worried that the whole day would be spent on such serious topics. "What do you say?" He looked at his friends. He had an idea. His friends looked at each other. He saw the expectant look on their faces, the look that said they were ready to be diverted. "Guess what, I ran into that madam again. And she told me that they now have some beautiful girls from India!" he said and watched his friends' faces. The two friends looked at each other again.

The day wasn't too hot. But by the time they arrived at the building after a walk of several blocks, small beads of sweat had formed on their nose and foreheads. The building was a four-storied building with a Chinese fish market on the ground floor. He wanted to buy a drink to quench his thirst but unfortunately, the first thing in his line of sight was a row of dead fish. Next to the pile of dead fish was a big glass case, with water bubbling inside it, full of live fish, their mouths opening and closing and their tails twitching in sync.

Next to this case was a doorway. It looked like the main entrance into the building. As soon as they reached the doorway, before they had even pressed the buzzer, the door was buzzed open for them. The flight of stairs in front of them looked extremely narrow. There was just enough light to see the stairs. As they climbed up the second flight of stairs, two Chinese men were on their way down and they had to pass each other on the narrow stairs with their bodies sliding sideways against the wall.

"*Kunchoksum*, you really think there are Indian girls in there? The shop downstairs is Chinese, those men were Chinese," said the smoker friend uneasily. No one answered him. Silently they kept walking up the stairs.

As they were about to go up to the fourth floor, a door on the third floor landing opened. A woman leaned halfway out the door and said, "It's a private family residence on the fourth floor. What do you want?" She looked Chinese and was probably in her fifties. Her broken English was just barely understandable.

"Didn't you use to be on the fourth floor?" said the first friend, the one who knew New York like the palm of his hand. He seemed to know the woman.

"It's been a long time," the woman said. She recognized him now. "We were getting so many patrons that we had to get new girls—a lot more girls. The fourth floor space was too small. We moved here when we got a bigger space on the third floor."

She let them inside.

"We came to take a look at the Indian girl. Is she here today?" said the first friend to the madam.

"Oh, that was you asking about the Indian girl?" replied the madam, putting her hand on his shoulder. "Yes, yes, we have several Indian girls working here. They don't work here all the time, they just come from time to time."

When they reached the waiting room, she said, "You came at a good time. We do have an Indian girl today." They went inside.

"She might be with a patron right now. Just wait a moment, she'll come out," the madam said and left.

The waiting room was artificially lit. There were no windows for natural light to come in. In the middle of the room was a large table, quite low, set with long sofas on three sides. Some girls sat at the table, playing cards. They were likely waiting for patrons. Aside from the front entrance to the waiting room, there was another door to the right. As soon as they sat down, three girls came over to talk to them.

The Chinese girl in front of him had just enough English to say hello. She touched his shoulders and his arms. Although she didn't rouse his interest, he wanted to show off his English to her by asking where she was from. As soon as he started to say, "Where are—" the door to their right opened. A girl came out. He could hear the sound of a toilet flushing. The extra light from the bathroom briefly brightened the waiting room. Without a glance at the waiting room she disappeared through the main door. It seemed that was where they took care of the patrons.

"Where are you from?" he said to the Chinese girl in his best American accent.

She gave him an answer but his mind was suddenly arrested by an image. Although he hadn't paid any attention to the face of the girl who just came out of the door on the right and went out through the front, the image of her back in a turquoise top flashed in his mind. Wasn't his wife also wearing a top just like that? He thought of the way his wife had looked that morning before she left for work.

He looked around to see what his friends were doing. One of them had a Chinese girl on his lap, her right hand draped around his neck and her left combing his hair. The other friend was busy gesturing at another Chinese girl. They seemed to be having some difficulty making themselves understood.

"Are you Japanese?" the girl said to him, caressing his upper arm. Usually it pleased him very much when strangers asked him if he was Japanese but his mind was occupied with the girl in the turquoise top and he didn't even hear the question. Absently he thanked the Chinese girl, stood up and walked out.

Out on the street, he once again saw the fish in the glass case, their mouths opening and closing and their tails twitching. If only he had saved the phone number, he thought, flipping through the pages of his little phone book. His wife had given him a number saying it was her work number but he remembered that he hadn't saved it. Still, maybe he would find it written down somewhere. He looked through the phonebook for the number, in vain.

He thought he had bumped into someone and said, "I am sorry." But he had not bumped into a person but a doorway. When he looked up, he saw that he was in front of a green doorway. The door opened and a blonde woman came out. She was saying to someone, "The movie is most likely at 5:30." He got a quick glimpse of the bar inside. He could see it was stocked with all kinds of alcohol. He suddenly really wanted a drink. He bumped into someone, for real this time, and said again, "I am sorry." It was the woman's companion, shoving his arm into a jacket as he came out the door.

He had never been to such a bar before. It was very dim inside. Candles flickered on small low tables with two or three chairs. A soft, gentle music filled the whole room.

He was wondering if he had to go to the bar to get a drink or if a server would come and serve him where he was seated when he heard someone exclaim: “How did you come here!” His wife stood there in front of him with a jug of water and a glass. Her hair didn’t fall loosely on her shoulders anymore but was up in a bun on her head. Her top was no longer the same skintight top that she was wearing that morning. Instead she had on a collared white shirt that hid her curves instead of hugging them like a second skin. A bowtie in the shape of a butterfly tied her collar at the base of her throat.

Unable to look directly into her astonished eyes, he dropped his gaze. She was wearing a server’s apron that covered her hip-hugging skirt. The apron had two pockets. One of the pockets held an order booklet and two pens and from the other, which bulged a little, he could see some notes peeking out—her tips.

Ring, ring, ring.

The phone rang and his wife went to pick it up. He woke up. He was lying on the sofa at home. The Hindi film he had been watching before he dozed off was still playing on the screen. As he lowered the volume, his phone rang. It was his wife. She said one of the servers at the restaurant had taken the day off, and so she wouldn’t be able to come home early. As his wife was talking, he cleared up the empty beer bottles around the sofa. When she hung up, he felt as if his bladder were about to burst. He ran to the bathroom.

THE VALLEY OF THE BLACK FOXES

TSERING DONDRUP

TRANSLATED BY TENZIN DICKIE
AND PEMA TSEWANG SHASTRI

1.

About sixty kilometers north of Tsezhung county was a mountain pass with a stone cairn and some prayer flags. If you looked northward from that pass, you saw a green valley thick with vibrant vegetation. In the middle of the valley, there was a swamp as large as a cattle ranch with many streams merging together to form a clear river that ran through the valley.

In July and August, the valley was filled with flowers of all kinds. High up in the valley, there grew flowering shrubs such as meadowsweet, cinquefoil, silverweed, and rhododendron bushes. The middle ranges of the valley were covered in heaps of edelweiss and stellara, with gentian blooming all over in the autumn. Along the river running through the valley, there grew yellow aconite, also known as monkshood or wolf's bane, many kinds of louseworts including louseworts with yellow-golden flowers, and snow lotuses. Meanwhile the valley floor was filled with blooming sheathing groundsels and meadow bistort, rotating Jerusalem sage and white snow lotuses, Himalayan asters, dandelion, and wormwood. There were many other flowers and plants that even botanists would have had a hard time identifying. Every few days the meadows changed color and new fragrances filled the air; the valley might well have been the famous Tsara Pema Tongden of the Gesar epic, the Meadow of a Thousand Lotuses.

Now a nomad family lived in this valley with some five hundred horses, yaks, and sheep. Hearing their neighing, lowing, and baaing or seeing the animals at their quiet and peaceful rest immediately brought to one's mind the phrase "Beautiful and Prosperous Pasture!" This valley had an unusual name. It was called the Valley of the Black Foxes.

This was because all the foxes of the valley were black. In fact, it was not just the foxes but also the marmots of this valley that were black.

Even though the people of Tsezhung county hadn't paid any attention to this fact, when the pasture lands were divided and this valley became the lot of Sangye's family, Sangye had plucked at his beard and said, "Ah, it's a bad omen. Everywhere else the foxes are red, so why are all the foxes of this valley black?" When Tsezhung county's Alak Drong came to visit the house, Sangye kneeled in front of the lama and said, "Rinpoche, everywhere else the foxes are red but the foxes in our family pastures are black. Now people are even calling this place the Valley of the Black Foxes. Are there any rituals and mantras to dispel this bad luck?" Sangye said "our family pastures" because when the county officials were marking their measurements on the map, they had given Sangye a document titled "The Proof of Pastureland." Here written in both Tibetan and Chinese were the dimensions of the land, the number of acres it contained, and a notation that said that Sangye's family had the use of this land for fifty years. Alak Drong gave Sangye a piece of paper on which was written two lines of text. Sangye went to Tsezhung Monastery, found a monk he knew and handed him the piece of paper along with a hundred-yuan note.

2.

Sangye, thin and dark, was fifty years old. His jaw was entirely covered by an uneven beard. Some years ago, when he owned a pair of scissors embossed with the figure of a bat, his beard wasn't quite as extensive. But at one point, either he or his wife Ludron or one of their kids had stepped on this pair of scissors or perhaps used it for some other purpose until it stopped trimming his beard so well. Then, one day when they were moving camp, the pair of scissors went missing. Since then, Sangye's beard had grown thicker and longer. Whenever Sangye had any free time, he thumbed his rosary with his right hand, while with his left hand he helplessly plucked out hairs from his beard. Whenever he was lost in thought, whenever he was in a hurry, he plucked so fast that it was difficult to see the plucking. Yet unfortunately, compared to the teeth of his missing scissors, his fingers could only trim a negligible amount of his beard.

Sangye was usually a man of few words and he had a very gentle nature. But he could also be an eloquent and aggressive speaker. Before Sangye took the lease for the pasture land, he hung out with the town's young men, telling tall tales and jokes and teasing each other.

Gonpo Tashi, who was very dark-skinned and very fat, said to Sangye, "Oh, Bridegroom Sangye, Aku Jamyang has tanned your groom's hide and he won't even let you eat your food. How will you pass this spring? Poor man!" Everyone laughed.

Sangye replied, "Oh Gonlug, you defeat both yourself and your friend. I find it hard to bear your yak's belly. If only you were a thin yak, then if your belly were cut open with a knife I am sure some yellow fat would come out but even so it would be such foul smelling fat that other people wouldn't be able to eat it!" Everyone laughed again.

Gonpo Tashi tried to interrupt but Sangye didn't give him the chance. "Ah Gonlug, are you still singing love songs to your sister these days?" The men laughed even harder than before. Gonpo Tashi realized that he would not get the better of Sangye today and he gave a small laugh. "Alright, alright, today I'll bow down to you."

The joke of "singing love songs to your sister" came from an incident involving Gonpo Tashi. Sometime soon after Gonpo Tashi had taken a wife, he was coming back from the county seat when he saw a woman riding a yak ahead of him. He immediately began singing a love song about how he was a single man and did the woman have a lover and did she want to be with him. The woman, who was very frightened, kicked at her yak to make it go faster but how could a yak outpace a horse? When Gonpo Tashi easily caught up to the yak, the woman turned out be a sister of his who had gone as a bride to another town. He was so embarrassed that he lost his wits, turned his horse around, and ran away.

Sangye's wife Ludron loved to talk until she fell asleep. She said that the son of the Tipu chief family had become a monk, that the chief had bought a small car, that the money the Ruyong family received for fifty sheep turned out to be counterfeit money, that Ama must have some new clothes this year, that they should give an answer to the Kasho family about whether they were giving them their daughter for a bride. As she kept talking, Sangye finally snapped at her, "Hey, do you think you can shut up for a bit? Even if your mouth is fine, my ear is in pain."

"I have a mouth and I should have the freedom to speak. If your ears are hurting, then you don't have to listen."

Not wanting to fight with her, Sangye just plucked his beard and stayed silent. Ludron continued, "When we took the lease for the land, didn't they say that there would be no changes for fifty years? What is this 'removing animals to grow grass'? How can we get meat, butter, and chura from an empty animal pen? Aku Sonam's family said—"

Sangye grew even more irritated. He said, "Oh, what's the use of saying such things? We have already sold off a lot of animals, and paid up our contribution. We took the government housing. Most of the families have already moved to the county center. They did say that pastures need to lie fallow for a few years but that nomad families still own these pastures as before. If we really cannot make a living, we can always come back. When Aba and Ama return, we'll move down to the center."

"What, aren't we moving after the new year?"

"Most of the families have already moved to the center, no one will even come for the new year. Besides, I have heard that the houses are very nice. It will be nice to spend the new year in the new place, won't it?"

"..."

Ludron's Aba Jamyang was seventy-two years old and her Ama Yangzom was now seventy years old. Even though both of them were still in good health, they had turned over the reins of the household to Sangye and now most of the village called the family Sangye's family instead of Jamyang's family. Sangye's son Lhagon Kyab had been sent to school, but after middle school, he had left school to become a monk at Labrang Monastery. He was now called Gedun Gyatso. Some days before, he had gone on a pilgrimage to Lhasa with his grandparents and his sister Lhatso Kyi.

Sangye had nothing to worry about, nothing to do. Restless and uneasy, he started plucking out the hairs of his beard more quickly than ever.

3.

On a very cold morning Sangye went and borrowed two trucks. In one truck, he put sacks of dung and piled containers of dried meat with a skinful of butter on top, in addition to neatly folded squares of sheepskin robes, animal rugs, pots, pans, bowls, and other household stuff. In the other truck, on top of sacks of pellets, went the family altar, followed by the family members and the family mastiff. Amidst the din of engines and the black dust raised up by the trucks, they travelled through the valley. Everyone in the family raised their heads, as if heeding some unheard call, and looked back for one last long look at their home in the Valley of the Black Foxes. When they reached the bend in the mountain, Sangye suddenly took out a sheaf of lungta from his *chupa* and flung them to the wind, sending the paper wind horses into the sky for merit and fortune. As he did so, he shouted "*Kyi kyi so so lha gya lo*! Victory to the gods!" with all his might, but just then the truck accelerated and Sangye's victory shout was hardly discernible over the din of the engine.

It was only around 3 p.m. in the afternoon that they reached the Tsezhung county seat. Here they had to memorize the phrase "Xingfu Shengtai Yimin Cun," which was the name of the place they were searching for. They asked a man where they should go, and told him they were coming down from the pasturelands to resettle in the town.

The man said to them, "Then you have to go to 'Shengtai Yimin Cun' but there are a number of these. Which valley are you from?"

"We are from Tsezhung valley."

"Tsezhung valley, Tsezhung valley—I believe most of the yimin of Tsezhung valley are to the north of the county seat. If you ask for 'Shengtai Yimin Cun,' you'll get there."

"What was that—" Sangye pulled his beard and said, "Ximpo Trin.."

"Xingfu Shengtai Yimin Cun."

At that point, the driver of the truck said they must get off. If they wanted to go and look for the house, they had to pay extra.

"How much extra?"

"Ten more yuan for each tractor. I can drop you off at Xingfu Shengtai Yimin Cun."

"Ok, let's go then."

As soon as they turned the trucks around, a police officer signaled for them to stop. The truck drivers' faces instantly turned pale. They braked immediately and the trucks ground to a halt. But the policeman ignored the two drivers and peered hungrily into the back and said, "Do you have anything old to sell? Pots and pans, lima and thangkas, old rugs and old tinderboxes? The older, the better."

"The saddle—" Ludron said when Sangye interrupted her to ask where the Xingfu Shengtai Yimin Cun area was.

The policemen paid no attention to Sangye and said to Ludron, "Do you have a saddle to sell? Is it silver-plated? Is it old?"

"Kan—hmm," Ludron pointed to Sangye's saddle resting on one of the wheels and continued, "What are you going to do with a saddle without a horse? Someone wants to buy, we should sell, don't you think? It's of no use to us."

The policeman looked closely at the saddle and said, "Five thousand."

"We're not selling the saddle," said Sangye.

Now the policeman's gaze fell on the mastiff and said, "How much for the old dog?"

"We're not selling the dog!" the whole family answered as one. Again, Sangye said. "Xingfu Shengtai . . ." The policeman ignored him, paid no attention to the two drivers, got back on his motorcycle and rode off. After two or three miles, the drivers stopped the truck and said, "This is Xingfu Shengtai Yimin Cun. Give us the money."

4.

Seen from far away, the rows of houses looked like rows of bricks drying in the sun at a brick factory. The houses were each the exact same size and color. Around each house was an identical fence with a large banner hanging over each gate on which were written the words "Xingfu Shengtai Yimin Cun." If you were looking for a house here, you couldn't use the traditionally backward and ignorant way of wandering around and asking, "Hey, where is the house of Sangye from Tsezhung village?" You had to know Sangye's house number. For instance, if Sangye lived at House Number 04, Row Number 17, Fence Number 21, then you had to look for the numbers "211704." Of course this was not easy for an illiterate nomad. But luckily that day they had their monk son Gedun Gyatso with them. They also met with a friend from their own camp who had moved there some ten days before.

The friend took them to see a female staff member with hair as red as blood, a face as cold as winter, and hands as slow as a tortoise. Without too much hassle, they received a bunch of keys along with a sheet of paper on which their house number was written. Each family was to have a three-room house with a small yard, called a flower garden, surrounded by a fence. Each house had an iron-plated gate with iron pipes and a five-starred red flag hoisted on top. The walls were made with hollow cement bricks, then plastered over and white-washed. Maroon pentoks with white borders decorated the walls. Sangye's family members were moved to see that the house design and decoration incorporated national characteristics. As they surveyed each room, Jamyang was so moved that he said with tears rolling down his face, "How can we repay the kindness of our leaders? Even Drong Rinpoche's bungalow is not better than this. Can our karma handle such affluence?"

The house was partitioned by walls into two rooms, one room for the kitchen and another for what must be the bathroom. There was a big white ceramic basin in the corner of that room. Both Sangye and Ludron exclaimed that it must be the wash basin, causing Gedun Gyatso to laugh and say, "That is the toilet."

"What! If we use such a beautiful basin for peeing and pooping, our merits will diminish and our anuses will block up, won't they?" Jamyang said.

His wife Yangzom agreed and said, "Just leave it there, if we don't know what it is for. But if you tell me that this is for pee and poop, it's a joke for this old woman."

"*Azi! Kunchoksum*, this is a toilet," swore Gedun Gyatso. "These days, such toilets are found everywhere and I have used them many times."

Just then he felt the need to relieve himself and so pulled up his robe and sat down on the toilet seat. He felt much more comfortable after relieving himself. But unbelievably, when he flushed the toilet afterwards, there was not even one drop of water. He found after a careful investigation that there were no water-pipes whatsoever attached to the toilet. So his sister Lhatso Kyi had to clean the stool with her right hand while covering her nose and mouth with the other hand.

Though there was a toilet bowl in the house, there was no stove or oven. So Sangye went to the county seat to buy an iron stove. He also bought a bottle of milk and returned in a small three wheeler cab that he had hired.

When Ludron went to the door to make a tea offering to the gods, it was almost dark. The old dog, tied at the corner of the yard, barked unhappily as she came out. Only then did she realize that the poor dog hadn't eaten anything for the whole day. Feeling very sorry, she went inside the house and without a second thought brought out a whole kilogram of sausages and fed the dog. For the last six or seven years, the dog had been like a member of the family, the only difference being that it couldn't speak and mostly lived outdoors. Alas, this was to be the dog's last supper. The next morning, the dog was nowhere to be found, as if it had disappeared into the earth, along with its chains. All the family were distraught over the missing dog. Their only consolation was that at least the dog had a good supper the night before.

5.

The nomads called a dog that stole food a "dog thief." Likewise, a shameless thief was also called a "dog thief." But a shameless thief who stole dogs really deserved the name.

So Sangye plucked his beard and wondered, "Who could be this dog thief?" while thinking about all the items they needed to buy such as a TV, beds, thermoses, door curtains, etc. The Gregorian New Year had come and gone but the Tibetan New Year was soon approaching. The county and village authorities made their visits to extend their greetings for the "Two New Years" or "Two Festivals" and distribute such items as rice, flour, sugar, tea, and calendars. The authorities also brought compensation money to the nomads for leaving nomadic life and adopting city life. If there were any problems or requests, the leaders promised to handle these in a timely manner. Sangye's family was profoundly touched by these gestures. Jamyang and his wife couldn't hold back their tears of gratitude. They nearly prostrated themselves as they said, "Our leaders are so kind, our government is so kind. Getting so much money and necessities without any work at all, isn't this like a dream? Thank you, how kind of you, how kind of you. Now we have no problems. We have absolutely nothing to request."

When the leaders went away, Jamyang told his family, speaking in particular to Sangye and Gedun Gyatso, that they must never forget the kindness of the Communist party and that they must abide by the rules and regulations of the camp. He also said they should go to the market to buy a photo of their leader. Jamyang meant Chairman Mao's photo but Sangye went to Xinhua Bookshop and bought photos of not just Chairman Mao, but the other leaders as well. He went so far as to buy a faded photo of Stalin that had lost its color from remaining in the bookshop all these years. When Sangye put these photos up above the altar, which was filled with photos of Alak Drong and other lamas, the whole household seemed to acquire a new air of majesty and brilliance. Thereafter, whether Jamyang was spinning his prayer wheel or Sangye was plucking his beard, their glances went respectfully and automatically toward these photos of the leaders.

Even in their wildest dreams, they never thought of making a living without work. And so this Dekyi Keykham Pobang Village or Happy Resettlement Village indeed appeared to be a happy place to live. However, one day, soon after they had moved in, Jamyang wanted to make a visit to town, to the county seat. He thought he would also see whether he could get any information on his missing mastiff. Many years ago, Jamyang had been an ordinary official and even attended a Level 3 meeting at county headquarters. At that time he knew the county seat like the palm of his hand, but now the place had changed completely, developing as rapidly as a horse trot. It had turned upside down. He didn't even know whether he would be able to find his way home. And if he were able to find his way back, would he be able to remember those all-powerful house numbers? He was crestfallen.

Unable to go out into town, Jamyang began to feel as if he were imprisoned in that settlement. He began to spend his days sitting by the door, his view blocked by the rows upon rows of other houses. One day, as he stared at the corner where they had tied the dog, the Valley of the Black Foxes appeared before his eyes. Then he heard the sound of his dog barking. After that Jamyang began to speak less and less.

Sangye purchased a color TV, a refrigerator, and a sofa set for the house. Watching the Tibetan programs on the TV brought a new joy to their lives. They found the New Year's Concert on Losar eve especially entertaining and exciting. It was their first time seeing Menla Kyab on TV. They talked about Menla Kyab as if he were a member of the family.

During Losar, Sangye's family fulfilled two big missions. One was giving their daughter, Lhatso Kyi, as a bride to Kasho the bachelor. The other was keeping Lhatso Kyi's daughter at home, as per Yangzom's wish, instead of sending her with her mother. Lhatso's daughter was born out of wedlock. The family decision was that, instead, they would enroll her in school when the fall session began.

6.

Spring came. Caterpillar fungus harvesters, construction workers, and road builders all descended upon the county seat and the peaceful grass plains changed into a chaotic scene. The stores of meat, cheese, yak dung, and sheep droppings that the family had brought with them from the Valley of the Black Foxes were now being depleted. Ludron and Sangye found themselves visiting the market, turn by turn, at least once a day, to buy some necessity or another. The price of groceries began to rise daily. Sangye now looked around for a job in town, three or four kilometers from his settlement. This meant he had to buy a motorcycle to get around. If they didn't want to offer their motorbikes to thieves, they had to keep their motorbikes in the house day and night. That three-room house, which they had previously found so large and spacious, now felt small and cramped. Fed up with the lack of space, Sangye pulled up the useless toilet bowl and left it out by the door.

"*Ah ma ma!*" It was the red-haired woman who had given them the house number and keys on their arrival. "What are you doing, pulling out the toilet bowl like that?" she cried. "Tomorrow the shicha will be here for inspection! Oh no, this is terrible, this is terrible. These people are barbarians!" She began walking up and down in agitation. When he heard about the inspection tour, Sangye became so frightened that he just stood there with his mouth open.

It was Ludron who said, "This thing is useless and it just takes up the space . . ."

"Even though it's useless, we need it to show the shicha when they come for inspection. Ah ma ma, this is awful, now it is finished!"

Ludron was about to say something when Sangye blurted out, "*Ah zi, ah zi!* Now what's the best thing to do?" He looked at the red-haired woman as if asking for her protection.

"The best thing to do . . . my foot! Go look for a plumber immediately and fix it. If the shicha finds out, then we are finished."

"A plumber."

"Yes, go get a plumber quickly."

Sangye immediately went into town on his motorcycle and without any haggling gave a hundred yuan to a plumber and brought him home. The plumber mixed a handful of cement and two handfuls of sand and attached the toilet bowl back where it came from. When Sangye remembered the facial expression of the red-haired woman, he felt that the shicha who was to come tomorrow must be a terrifying person. Restless and uneasy, he went in and out of the house plucking his beard.

Jamyang found it difficult to keep his eyes open in the sandstorms but he continued to sit outside the door, spinning his prayer wheel and staring at the spot where they used to tie the dog. He hardly spoke anymore. When Yangzom sat beside her husband and tried talking to him, he gave a one-word answer. But he wouldn't talk any further. Not knowing what to do, Yangzom sat beside him for a while and then went back inside the house to watch TV. Whether the programs were in Chinese or Tibetan didn't matter to her. She just watched the images. She didn't even seem to understand the highly formal Tibetan language that was spoken on the screen. She enjoyed watching the pictures, and so found it easier to spend her days than her husband.

The "shicha" that Sangye had been so concerned about arrived at last, surrounded by a number of county and village leaders, followed by journalists and photographers. But the man was not at all as frightening as Sangye had imagined. On the contrary, fat and jolly, he seemed like a compassionate man and reminded Sangye of a Chinese Laughing Buddha. Whatever people told him, he responded by saying, "Ha ha ha! Ho ho ho! Good, good." Even when he saw the useless toilet bowl from afar he just said, "Ho ho," which was a big relief to Sangye. After the friendly and loving inspection tour went away, each family, one after another, threw away their toilet bowls. The red-haired woman didn't say anything. So after a few days, Sangye too confidently threw away his toilet bowl once again.

7.

After two months of continuous sand storms, a mixture of rain and snow came at last. Then it rained without stopping. All the settlement houses started leaking and became quite unlivable. The most serious thing was that the bricks had been cemented not with cement but with mud. With rainwater seeping through the four walls of the house, from outside as well as from within, the black mud began to sludge, the whitewash washed away, and the houses were stripped naked so that one could even see through the crevices in the foundation bricks. Even the photos of the leaders, pasted on the walls of Sangye's family, were in danger of getting damaged. Sangye was compelled to take them down.

"After paying so much money, what kind of house did we get? The government says it even spent so much extra money on this project," Ludron said angrily. She continued, "Even though our house in the Valley of the Black Foxes looked ugly, at least it never leaked and it was warm. Now Aba and Ama are going to freeze." She was suddenly struck with a thought, "Hey, wouldn't it be better to just pitch a tent in the yard, bring the stove out there and live in the tent?"

"We might just have to do that . . . but what would the red-haired woman say?" Sangye said plucking some hair from his beard.

"That is right. It looks like the red-haired woman is responsible for our welfare. If we called her and let her see the condition of the house, she would have something to say. I can't imagine the house is in such condition after we paid such a huge amount of money for it."

"Oh dear, I am nervous of that red-haired lady," said Sangye.

"There is nothing to be afraid of. If you're afraid, then I will go!" said Ludron as she stood up and walked out the door.

Truthfully it was doubtful whether Ludron really had enough confidence to talk to the red-haired woman. But since she had made this boast to her husband, she had no choice but to follow through. Luckily, when she arrived at the red-haired woman's office, the Secretary of Tsezhung settlement, along with other officials and many nomads, were already there. According to a Tibetan-speaking official, "The issue has already been taken up before the county committee and the county government, and the county committee and county government are treating this issue very seriously. All the houses will be repaired within two or three days soon as this ugly rain stops. Until then we ask the public to have patience for the time being," he said.

"If that is the case then we have nothing to complain about. We are very thankful to the Party and the government," a young man with a very loud voice told the officials on behalf of all those present. One after another, they left the office. Ludron returned home with a smile and said, "The leaders told us to have patience for a few days and said they would do the house repairs very soon."

Jamyang broke his long silence. With a joyful expression on his face, he said, "The Party and the government are just like our parents." Sangye stopped plucking his beard and said, "I'll go to the town to purchase some meat. The town is really very strange. You can get fresh fatty meat even in March."

The rains stopped at last. Every house facing the sun had about four inches of weeds growing at the edges of its walls. The repair work finally began in the settlement. This repair was very simple. First they removed the slates from the roof and laid down a sheet of plastic. Then they applied a half-inch thick mud paste on the plastic, after which the slates were put back again. They also plastered a thin layer of cement on the walls. After white-washing the walls, they drew the Pentoks and Dungtreng with maroon and white paint and voilà, the work was finished. A prefectural level delegation came to inspect the repair work, pronounced it "great" and left.

The house didn't leak again that year, even when it rained torrentially. But unbelievably, when the spring rains came the following year, the leaks began all over again. The nomads again assembled at the office of the red-haired woman. Some of them wanted their money back and wanted to return to the grassland. Again the county government and the county committee regarded the issue with the utmost importance and repaired the houses free of cost. But the irony was that they repaired the houses in exactly the same way as last time. The nomads said they were just "throwing mud on shit."

8.

Now there were fewer and fewer yak-dung sellers in Tsezhung county. But people began to see another fuel called coal. Previously, only the high officials of the county and the rich offices could afford coal. Now there were more and more coal sellers, and it wasn't as unaffordable as before. But the coal was still expensive enough that the nomads called it "expensive black stone." The coal was not only expensive, but also dangerous. In the Happy Resettlement Village alone, nine people from three families died of carbon monoxide poisoning. Four government workers drank too much at the county seat and went to bed drunk. One man woke up thirsty at midnight, and went over to the stove to pick up the pot. He forgot to close the stove. In the morning, they were all found dead. The news scared a lot of people in the settlement.

Due to the grace of the Triple Gems, Sangye's family did not suffer such tragedies and obstacles. But they had their difficulties.

Their money was running out. On top of that, one third of their recently purchased coal turned out to be ordinary beach stones and rocks. So while Sangye was thinking about all these issues, with his hand on his beard, Ludron said, "The butter you bought is very, very old. Yesterday Aba ate some *tsampa* pudding and he had stomach pains for the whole day. This morning he only ate *tsampa* without any butter. You didn't even check whether the butter was fresh or not."

Sangye interrupted her, "I did check, but the price of fresh butter is sky high." Upset, he kept pulling at his beard.

"I think it is time to sell the saddle," Ludron said. "What's the use of a saddle without a horse?"

"Haven't you heard the proverb, 'A horse is easy, but a saddle is difficult'?"

"Don't they also say, 'If one has a horse, getting a saddle is easy'?" replied Ludron.

"Maybe it's easy to get an ordinary saddle but my saddle is not an ordinary one."

"Whatever it may be, if we don't get fresh butter, it's a big problem not just for Aba and Ama but for us as well."

"However big the problem may be, unless they give us the compensation money for the grassland, we have no other means," said Sangye.

Ludron sighed, "The tea is black, and the butter is old. Poor Aba and Ama."

"I'll go and get some milk." It was hard to say whether Sangye felt sorry for the old folks or was simply irritated by Ludron's nagging but he stood up to go shopping. When he opened the door, their son Gedun Gyatso had arrived in the yard.

As if Gedun Gyatso could read his parents' faces, he asked his grandparents what was going on as he kissed them. Then he took out two thousand yuan notes, crisp and new, and put them in his father's hand.

Many monks disrobed these days. Young boys were beginning to gamble and steal. Young girls were selling their bodies. In just their settlement alone, five or six young boys had been arrested and three or four girls had disappeared. Five monks had left the monastery and disrobed. One of the ex-monks even returned to the monastery and attempted to steal a sacred Thangka painting of Palden Lhamo, a Thangka that had a history older than the monastery itself. The thief was arrested while trying to make his getaway and remained in police custody. Such things were happening all around them. But happily, Gedun Gyatso remained busy and engaged in his spiritual practice. Unlike the other monks, he did not spend his money extravagantly but saved all the offerings he received from the public and helped his family instead. As these thoughts passed through Sangye's mind, he felt a great desire to embrace and kiss his son. But he had not done either since Gedun Gyatso had grown up and he didn't know how to start now. Deeply moved by his son's gesture, Sangye said, "I'll go buy some meat" and he left the house.

Ludron came to the door and said, "Don't forget to buy a bottle of milk. Don't buy it from the Industrial and Commercial Bureau store. They sell fake milk."

There were many kinds of this fake milk. Some of the milk was adulterated with water. There was also cow milk being sold as yak milk. Worst of all, chemicals were added to the milk in summertime to keep it from spoiling at all. Even a demon wouldn't have thought of that. Sangye's motorcycle roared to life. He probably didn't hear his wife's words.

"He's going to come back again with fake milk," Ludron said to herself. Her father Jamyang was sitting outside, staring at the spot where they kept the dog. She grabbed his *chupa* sleeve and pulled him saying, "Aba, let's go inside."

9.

As soon as Jamyang came inside the house, Gedun Gyatso stood up. Jamyang glanced at his grandson's face and asked, "Who is this monk?" Gedun Gyatso was dumbfounded. He just looked helplessly at his mother. "Grandfather's lost his mind," Ludron said in a low voice. At that time Yangzom said, "*Ah zi*, what happened to this old man? Isn't he our grandson? Didn't he greet you just this morning?" But Jamyang just became upset and asked angrily, "*Ah zi*, grandson, when did you arrive? Why didn't you tell me that you had come?" Gedun Gyatso didn't know whether to laugh or cry. He embraced his grandfather and kissed him, and Jamyang sat down mollified.

"Your grandfather's fine now," Ludron said in a low voice to her son. "Every evening he comes to the door and says, 'Have you fed the old dog? Has that old Gyatho been returned to the corral? Tie the horses Kyalo and Nagur together.' I don't even remember these animals. But according to your grandmother, Gyatho, Kyalo, and Nagur were animals they kept when they were young a long time ago."

Suddenly Lhari Kyi yanked opened the door and, breathing heavily, asked, "Has uncle arrived?" Before Gedun Gyatso could say anything, Ludron asked, "*Ah zi*, has your school closed this early today?" After putting down her satchel, Lhari Kyi gave them some bad news. She spoke in a mixture of Tibetan and Chinese. Lhari Kyi's first news was that the roof of their school had collapsed, killing two students and injuring four. The second was that the day before, after a student had stolen some money from a teacher's house, the teacher had beaten the student and badly injured him. Today the elder brother of the student had brought some friends to take revenge. The teacher was now bed-ridden.

"So the Xiaozhang said no shang ke today," said Lhari Kyi, explaining the events that led to the school closing early. Yangzom embraced Lhari Kyi and said in a decisive manner, "*Ah ho*, what would we do if my girl were to get crushed under the debris of the fallen roof? We can't send her to school anymore. From tomorrow, no more school!" Lhari Kyi was Yangzom's favorite. She had not allowed Lhatso Kyi to take her daughter along to her new husband and her new household, and had even been reluctant to let her go to school. Now she had a pretext to keep the girl with her twenty-four hours a day.

They heard a motorcycle outside. This was followed by Sangye's arrival. With him was his sister Youdon, a young woman, carrying a heavy load on her left shoulder. Youdon's household had not been resettled yet. They had no need to buy their dairy products and in fact they produced a surplus for sale. Every time she visited, she brought meat, cheese, butter, cream and other things for her brother's family. Being of a generous nature, she shared as much as she could. This time Youdon's load consisted of a whole sheep carcass, two kilos of preserved sausages, five kilos of butter, three kilos of cheese wrapped in a black plastic bag, a can of yoghurt, and a bottle of milk. She asked after Jamyang and Yangzom's health, and then gave them a ten-yuan note each. She also gave one to Lhari Kyi. Sangye's purchase turned out to be three kilos of dried meat and some bottles of juice. Ludron immediately minced the meat and kneaded some dough to make momos for their dinner. They heaped the coal on the fire, excessively, so that the stove turned red.

The house was warm and filled with chatter. Every now and then, there was a burst of laughter, a sound that had been missing in this house for a while now. The worries that Sangye and Ludron had been discussing just a few hours ago, and the fearful tragedy that Lhari Kyi had told them, were temporarily forgotten. Jamyang went to bed early and soon after Yangzom and Lhari Kyi also went to sleep. The others prepared to go to bed about two hours later than usual. Finally as the night was ending, they went outside to relieve themselves. This was when Sangye burst out crying, "Oh no! Oh no! My motorcycle, my motorcycle! Those bloody dog thieves . . . those bloody dog thieves." Devastated, he walked back and forth, back and forth.

10.

The female staff, whom everyone in Happy Resettlement Village called "the red-haired woman" behind her back, came to visit the house. She told them that if they didn't pay their electric and water bills immediately, then she was going to cut off their electricity and water. Sangye, who had grown braver and also more temperamental, said to her, "As soon as you give me my grassland compensation money, I will pay the electricity and water bill. Otherwise, if you cut off my electricity I am just going to install solar energy. As for water, well, we'll go and fetch water from the Tsechu."

"Ha ha ha," the red-haired woman laughed and said, "Don't you know that Tsechu has now become contaminated and not even pigs drink that water?" When Sangye was about to say something Ludron took three or four steps further and then suddenly gave an ear-piercing shriek. She turned and stood there with her mouth open as though she had lost her soul. Sangye immediately turned back and saw that Jamyang had fallen on his stomach. He ran to Jamyang and tried to pull Jamyang's head but the body was stiff, almost frozen.

According to Ludron, he had been sitting up straight. She wanted to take him inside and when she pulled him by the sleeve, he fell down on his stomach. When she touched his head, it was as cold as stone.

"I was near him and I couldn't even support his head when he breathed his last. How unfortunate am I . . ." Ludron said, weeping.

"Now don't cry . . . Say some mani, say some mani," Sangye said trying to console her.

"I couldn't give him even a cup of milk tea. I couldn't even give him a bowl of *tsampa* with fresh butter, this morning also he just had plain *tsampa*. Poor Aba, what a pity . . ." Ludron cried louder than before.

Sangye couldn't control himself: tears rolled down his face as well. He deeply regretted that he wasn't able to give Jamyang a cup of tea and fresh butter before the old man died. He felt a deep pity for him and was embarrassed by not being able to fulfill the duty of a son-in-law. Nevertheless, the past was gone and there was no benefit to regretting the past. They could at least do a proper prayer ceremony for the old man. So instead of continuing to console his wife, he unwrapped his studded saddle, put it on his back and readied to go into town. At the last moment, he thought that it would be unconventional to leave two women near the body, so he put the saddle down and went to the door.

Their neighbor heard the crying. Both the husband and wife came to check on what was happening. "The old man has suddenly died," Sangye told the neighbor. "My kind friend, please stay here for a while with mother and daughter, while I go into town to inform our relatives and to see whether Drong Rinpoche is available." After that, he picked up the saddle again and went out. But remembering something else, he came back to the house and pulled off the sheep-skin *chupa* from the dead. The old man had a rosary in his left hand and a prayer wheel in his right. When Sangye tried to take them out, the neighbor, who was older than Sangye, said, "*Ah zi, ah zi*, he is a lucky man, he is an extraordinary man. I think we shouldn't take them out right now. Even if we do that, I think it is better if a lama were to take them out." Sangye left the rosary and prayer wheel as they were, and also put back the sheep-skin *chupa* on the body.

The owner of the shop with its "Hih Pris for Old Antigs" sign board, written in a very ugly Tibetan handwriting with atrocious spelling, meticulously evaluated all the parts of Sangye's saddle, and then held up his finger. Sangye shook his head no. Then the shop owner said in broken Tibetan, "Then you tell me, how much is the price."

"Eight thousand," said Sangye.

"Eight thousand," repeated the shop owner.

"Eight thousand."

"Eight thousand, eight thousand."

The owner didn't laugh or cry. He shook his head but then immediately counted out the money and gave it to him. Sangye was somewhat satisfied as he left the store. At that very moment, he saw Alak Drong Rinpoche getting out of a car. He quickly approached Alak Drong and invited him to his house for a prayer ceremony as his father-in-law had just passed away suddenly. Unbelievably, Alak Drong got into the car again and said, "Let's go, let's go now." That response made Sangye nervous. "Excuse me . . . ah . . . we haven't made any arrangement as of yet. Can you come tomorrow?" he said.

"Tomorrow I need to go to Xining. Do you have a vehicle? If not, come in the car," Alak Drong said. Sangye did as he was told.

Fortunately, when Sangye arrived home, many people from Tsezhung living in the Happy Resettlement Village had already called each other and were assembled at Sangye's house. The old folks of the camp figured everything out for Sangye. Consulting with Alak Drong, they even decided the day of the funeral. Alak Drong said the necessary prayers and transferred the old man's consciousness to the desired realm and prepared to leave. At that moment, the neighbor lifted the sheep-skin *chupa* from the body and said, "Rinpoche, please check this out." He showed the rosary and the prayer wheel still in the hands of old man. But the disappointing thing was that Alak Drong only said, "Why are these things still in his hand? Take them out." Other than that, he made no comments on this auspicious sign.

11.

After Jamyang's death, Yangzom began to get up from her bed very late in the morning. She no longer watched TV anymore but just went out and sat in the spot where her husband used to sit. Staring at the gate, she waited for Lhari Kyi to return from school. When Lhari Kyi came back, she often had more news than the news anchors but most of her news was bad news. Just the other day she had brought home two pieces of news. One was that all of the boarding students at school were sick with food poisoning and had to be hospitalized. The hospital couldn't save five of them, who died. The other one was that one of the endless coal delivery trucks, which were as big as mountains, had run over a car with four people in it and flattened the car like a plate. When Yangzom heard such news, she closed her eyes, clasped her hands together and murmured, "I pray to the Buddha, the Dharma, and the Sangha that such tragedies do not befall sentient beings." But who could have predicted that such a tragedy was approaching their own family.

One very cold and windy morning, Lhari Kyi went to school early. Yangzom was still in bed. Sangye and his wife were outside cutting up an old cloth belt and filling up the holes in the walls with it. Sangye wasn't concentrating on the task in front of him, he was instead thinking about the security guard recruitment office in town. All of a sudden both of them felt that they couldn't keep their feet on the ground. At the same time, all the houses started collapsing one after another. All they could see was a cloud of black dust rising into the sky. The two of them were stunned and petrified. Suddenly a man nearby ran past crying, "Earthquake, earthquake!"

Now both of them, as if awakened from sleep, cried out in one voice, "Ama!" They began to remove the bricks and slates as quickly as possible, as if they were crazed. When they removed the wooden beams lying on the rectangular folded tent, the couple was very happy to find Yangzom without even a minor injury. In order to make sure that she was fine, they helped the old woman stand up and asked again and again whether she felt any pain. When they realized that she really was alright, they couldn't stop saying their prayers and expressing their gratitude to the Three Jewels. Then another man came running and shouting, "Oh no! Oh no, the students have been crushed!" Sangye and Ludron both cried "Lhari Kyi" and started running toward the school.

It felt to Yangzom as if a year passed, when in reality it was just an hour. Then they came back. Sangye carried the small and blood-smeared body of Lhari Kyi in his arms. He kept saying, "The gods have no eyes. The gods have no eyes." Ludron didn't cry and wail as she had done when her father died. She breathed deeply and her eyes glimmered with tears that did not fall. Later they learned that it was only a 4.0 magnitude earthquake on the Richter scale. Except for the Happy Resettlement Village and some schools, the buildings held up and there wasn't much damage. The government immediately provided the earthquake victims with tents and food and compensated the families of the dead and injured. The government also promised to build stronger and better houses, as soon as possible, free of cost. The nomads were again moved to the point of tears by this kind gesture.

But Sangye's family no longer wanted to live in the new settlement. They had lived there patiently so that Lhari Kyi could go to school. Now that Lhari Kyi was no more, they didn't want to continue their lives in that place. So, one morning they hired a truck, packed all their belongings, and embarked on the journey back to the Valley of the Black Foxes. Along the road, the endless coal delivery trucks were so busy running to and fro that they nearly ran them off the road. Ludron, suffering from a heart problem, took long breaths and continuously rubbed her chest. Sangye didn't look too well either. He kept plucking hairs from his beard and did not speak a single word. They were compelled to go very slowly because of all the traffic on the road. As it had been a slow journey, the sun was now nearing the western horizon.

When they finally reached the pass leading into the Valley of the Black Foxes, the sight that met their eyes shocked them even more than the untimely death of Lhari Kyi. The whole of the Valley of the Black Foxes had been excavated. The entire valley was dug out. There were cranes, conveyer belts, tractors, and machines everywhere. The place was crawling like an ant's nest. The sound of machines and motors and the chaos of laborers filled the valley. There were so many new roads built from the pass to the valley that the truck driver had to brake and ask Sangye for directions. But Sangye just sat there stunned. He had even stopped plucking his beard. When he slowly came back to himself, he looked around to confirm what had happened. Was it possible that they had come to the wrong valley? But the cairn and the blackened prayer flags on the pass showed him that they were on the right path. "Now I understand why the foxes of this valley are all black," Sangye said. Ludron, who had been silent the whole day, finally spoke. "All that expensive coal came from here, from the Valley of the Black Foxes."

CONTRIBUTORS

Pema Bhum, writer and scholar, is the author of two Tibetan memoirs of the Cultural Revolution. His first memoir, *Six Stars with a Crooked Neck,* was published by *Tibet Times.* His second memoir, *Remembering Dorje Tsering,* was published by Amnye Machen Institute in Dharamsala, India, of which Bhum is a founding director. He has taught as associate professor of Tibetan Literature at the Northwest Minority Institute, PRC, and visiting assistant professor of Tibetan Language at Indiana University. He is the director of Latse Contemporary Tibetan Cultural Library and Lecturer in Tibetan at Columbia University.

Kyabchen Dedrol is a leading figure of the "Third Generation of Tibetan Poets," a literary movement composed of a group of young Tibetan writers centered around the border town of Ziling, Tsongon (Xining, Qinghai). A major poet and an essayist, Dedrol is also a fiction writer and novelist with works translated into English, Chinese, French, Spanish, Japanese, and German. He is also the founder of *Butter Lamp,* one of the most important online Tibetan literary journals.

Tsering Wangmo Dhompa is the author of three collections of poetry: *My Rice Tastes like the Lake*, *In the Absent Everyday* and *Rules of the House* (all from Apogee Press, Berkeley). *My Rice Tastes Like the Lake* was a finalist for the Northern California Independent Bookseller's Book of the Year Award for 2012.

Dhompa's first non-fiction book, *A Home in Tibet*, was published by Penguin India in 2013 and republished as *Coming Home to Tibet: A Memoir of Love, Loss, and Belonging* by Shambhala Publications in 2016. She teaches creative writing and is pursuing a PhD degree in literature at the University of California Santa Cruz.

Tenzin Dickie is a writer and literary translator in New York City. Her writings and translations have appeared in *Tibetan Review*, *Indian Literature*, *Cultural Anthropology*, *The Washington Post* online, *Himal SouthAsian*, *Words Without Borders, and Modern Poetry in Translation*. She is editor of *The Treasury of Lives*, a biographical encyclopedia of Tibet, Inner Asia and the Himalayan Region. A 2014–15 fellow of the American Literary Translators' Association, she holds an MFA from Columbia and a BA in English literature from Harvard.

Tsering Dondrup was born in 1961 in Malho (Ch. Henan) Mongol Autonomous County in Qinghai, China. As a child he tended the family livestock before going to school at the age of thirteen to study Tibetan and Chinese. He has worked in the fields of education, law, and historical research, among others, and in 2013 he retired to focus on his writing. Since 1982, Tsering Dondrup has published a number of short stories and novels. His work has been translated into Mongolian, English, French, German, Japanese, Swedish, Hungarian, and other languages, and is now included in textbooks used in Mongolian and Tibetan areas. Tsering Dondrup is the recipient of a number of Tibetan, Mongolian, and national literary prizes in China.

Tenzin Dorjee is a writer, activist, and a researcher at Tibet Action Institute. His monograph *The Tibetan Nonviolent*

Struggle: A Strategic and Historical Analysis was published by the International Center on Nonviolent Conflict. His writings have been published in various forums including *Global Post*, *Courrier International*, *Tibetan Review*, *Tibet Times* and the CNN blog. A Huffington Post blogger and political cartoonist as well as a musician, his second album *Madro* is forthcoming in 2017. He has a BA from Brown University and a Master's degree from Columbia University.

Takbum Gyal is a leading novelist and short story writer. His work has been extensively published in the leading Tibetan language journals like *Light Rain* and *Tibetan Art and Literature*. His short story collection *The Song of Life* received the 2011 Minority Literary Award in Beijing and was translated into Chinese by filmmaker and writer Pema Tseden.

Lauran Hartley is Tibetan Studies Librarian for the C.V. Starr East Asian Library at Columbia University, and also serves as an affiliated lecturer in Tibetan Literature for the Department of East Asian Languages and Cultures. She received her PhD in Tibetan Studies from Indiana University in 2003, and is co-editor of the book *Modern Tibetan Literature and Social Change* (Duke University Press, 2008). Her current research focuses on Tibetan literary production and intellectual discourse from the eighteenth century to the present.

Jampa is a translator and a researcher for a nonprofit in Dharamsala, India. He now lives in the United States.

Born in India, Tsering Namgyal Khortsa attended universities in Taiwan and the United States. His previous books have included a collection of essays on the Tibetan diaspora and a spiritual travelogue-cum-biography of His Holiness the 17th Karmapa, published by Hay House India in 2013. His novel *The Tibetan Suitcase* is forthcoming from Sampark Publishers India. He is currently based in Hong Kong, where he has a day job as a business journalist.

Tsering Lama is a New York-based writer who was born in Kathmandu. Her writing has been supported by grants from the Canada Council for the Arts and the Barbara Deming Memorial Fund, and she has been an artist-in-residence at the Lillian E. Smith Center, Omi Writers International, Catwalk Institute, WildAcres, and Playa Summerlake. Tsering's work has appeared in journals and magazines such as *The Malahat Review*, *Grain*, *Vela*, *LaLit*, and *Himal SouthAsian*, as well as the anthologies *House of Snow* and *Brave New Play Rites*. She is also a co-founder of Lhakar Diaries.

Jamyang Norbu is a novelist, historian, playwright and polemicist. He is known as one of the best, and certainly the most controversial, Tibetan writers at work today, principally on account of his numerous essays on Tibetan politics, history and culture. His novel *The Mandala of Sherlock Holmes* won the Crossword Book Award, India's equivalent of the Booker Prize, and has been published in a half dozen languages. Norbu was a member of the Tibetan resistance force in Mustang on the Nepal-Tibet border. He currently lives in Tennessee with his wife and two daughters.

Christopher Peacock is a graduate of the School of Oriental and African Studies, University of London, and a doctoral candidate at Columbia University, where he specializes in modern Chinese literature. His current research focuses on the place of Tibetan literature in the People's Republic of China and issues of ethnicity and nationalism in contemporary Tibetan fiction, poetry, and intellectual writing. In addition to his research, he works on literary translation from Chinese and Tibetan.

Jane Perkins is a journalist, editor, and author. She has extensive work experience in Hong Kong and Singapore.

Dhondup Tashi Rekjong is editor of *Tibet Web Digest*, a project of Columbia University's Modern Tibetan Studies program. He is also editor of *Karkhung*, a site that publishes translations of English and Chinese language articles into Tibetan, and former editor of the popular Tibetan blog *Khabdha*. He has published his short stories in *Butter Lamp* and *Tsenpo* under the pen name Jigmey Nubpa.

Pema Tsewang Shastri's first novel, *Cold West, Warm East* published by Tibet Times in 2000, was the first Tibetan language novel in exile. His books include two novels, a historical fiction, a collection of short stories, and a collection of Tibetan sayings titled *Like a Yeti Catching Marmots* published by Wisdom Publications. A former Fulbright Scholar at Harvard University, he has translated works by Dr. Gene Sharp and Charles Dickens. He is a foreign rights manager at Wisdom Publications.

Bhuchung D. Sonam was born in Tibet. In exile he studied at the Tibetan Children's Village School. He has published five books, including *Yak Horns: Notes on Contemporary Tibetan writing, Music, Film & Politics* and *Songs of the Arrow*. He is co-publisher of BlackNeck Books and lives in Dharamshala, a small town in northern India.

Pema Tseden was born in Trika, Amdo (Qinghai Province) to a nomadic family. He has published two collections of short stories, *Man and Dog* and *Deception*. The leading Tibetan filmmaker, he has also written and directed five internationally acclaimed films: *The Silent Holy Stones*, *The Search*, *Old Dog*, *The Sacred Arrow*, and *Tharlo*. He is a graduate of the Tsolho (Hainan) Nationalities' Normal College in Chabcha and the Northwest Nationalities University in Lanzhou.

Catherine Tsuji is an editor at *The Treasury of Lives* biographical encyclopedia of Tibet, Inner Asia and the Himalayan Region. She received a BA in Russian from Middlebury College and an MA in Religious Studies from the University of California, Santa Barbara. A native New Yorker, Catherine lives in Brooklyn with her husband and two children.

Tenzin Tsundue's first book of poetry, *Crossing the Border*, was published while he was a Master's student at Mumbai University. His second, *Kora: Stories and Poems*, is the bestselling book of the Tibetan diaspora, having sold out its eighth edition. His third book, *Semshook*, is a collection of essays, and his fourth is *Tsengol: Stories and Poems of Resistance*. He won the Picador-Outlook Prize for Nonfiction in 2011.

Woeser is a poet, writer, and journalist. Her first book, a collection of poetry titled *Tibet Above*, was published in 1999. Her second book, *Notes on Tibet*, published in 2003, became a bestseller and was subsequently banned in China. Her second poetry collection, *Tibet's True Heart: Selected Poems*, was published by Ragged Banner Press in the United States. Woeser is a recipient of the Freedom of Expression Prize from the Norwegian Authors Union and the International Women of Courage Award.

ACKNOWLEDGMENTS

My deepest thanks are due my parents Pema Tsewang Shastri and Chodon Tenzin for their love and their sacrifices. I thank my beloved brother Tenzin Dorjee and sister-in-law Tsering Choden for their support and their example. This book is as much their accomplishment as mine. I thank my dearest friend Tenzin Palkyi, my lifetime partner in crime, for her love and friendship; my cousin sister Tshering Shrestha for her encouragement and her company; my mentor and professor Susan Bernofsky for her guidance and her generosity.

I am grateful to my NYC writing circle for friendship and solidarity: Eleanor Levinson, Saramanda Swigart, Joanne Yao, Suzie Hanrahan and Franny Zhang. And my Queens friends for their art and activism: Sonam Wangdue, Tenzin Tsetan Choklay, Lobsang Tara, Tenzin Dhesal, Diki Dolkar, Tenzin Choeying and Tenzin Khyentse, Tenzing Rigdol and Chungpo Tsering.

Thank you to my dear co-conspirator Catherine Tsuji for her book smarts and her street smarts. Tsewang Phuntsho for his integrity and his support. Lobsang Nyandak for his kindness. Tsering Shakya and Robbie Barnett for their encouragement. Praveen K. Chaudhry and Souzeina Mushtaq for their fellowship. Alexander Gardner, Donald Rubin and Shelley Rubin for their support. Didier Augur and his family in France, thank you for inviting me into your family. Peter Richards, Dorla McIntosh, Emily Raboteau, Alice Guthrie, thank you for your guidance.

Pema Bhum and Dhondup Tashi Rekjong have been instrumental in helping me put this book together. I am greatly indebted to them, and also to Bhuchung D Sonam, Tsering Wangmo Dhompa, and Lauran Hartley for their help and support. Special thanks to Tenzing Tekan, Tenzin Tsundue, Kunsang Kelden, Tsering Lama, Tsering Gyatso, and Tenzin Dhondup (Anto) for their encouragement and friendship. My friends Khewang, Kelsang Choden, and Dechen Dolma, thank you.

My love to the following folks from college years: Theresa Chan, Elena Sorokin, Cathy Cohn, Becky Hammer, Emily Riehl, Katie Giblin, Jackie O'Brien, Tim Shwuchow, and Ryan Cortazar, as well as my dear Kuenga Wangmo and Anita Raghuwanshi. My Boston friends Tashi Tsarong, Tsephel Thangpey, and Tenzin Youdon: thanks for all the good times and I look forward to many more.

Joseph Shay and Laura Zimmerman watched over me like guardian angels. All the writers in this book trusted me with their stories. John Oakes and OR Books believed in this project. I am deeply grateful to them, and to my teachers: James Wood, for teaching me how to read. Donald Antrim and Stacey D'Erasmo, for teaching me how to write. Susan Bernofsky (again), for teaching me how to translate. And my brother, for teaching me how to live.